SPEAK
WITH
SUN

ALLEN & UNWIN
F I C T I O N

SPEAKING WITH THE SUN

NEW STORIES FROM AUSTRALIAN AND NEW ZEALAND WRITERS

Edited by
STEPHANIE DOWRICK & JANE PARKIN

ALLEN & UNWIN

First published in 1991
Allen & Unwin Pty Ltd
8 Napier Street, North Sydney, NSW 2059

National Library of Australia
Cataloguing-in-Publication entry:

Speaking with the sun.
ISBN 0 04 442296 2.
1. Short stories, Australian — 20th century. I. Dowrick,
Stephanie, 1947– . II. Parkin, Jane.
A823.010803

Set in 10.5/12 pt Goudy old style by SRM Production Services, Malaysia
Printed by Australian Print Group, Maryborough

Creative writing program assisted by the Australia Council, the Australian Government's
arts funding and advisory body.

Australia Council
for the Arts

CONTENTS

INTRODUCTION

Is it well enough known that writers of fiction rarely do what they are told? And why should they? Their professional frustrations are many, but among these is seldom the need or even the desire to toe the line as others define it.

The brief to each writer whose work appears in this collection was, more or less, to express something that seemed to that writer significant about living, as a woman, in the South Pacific in the last decade of the twentieth century. But that brief has been creatively disrupted by some of the contributors. Perhaps forgotten by others.

Yet a pattern does emerge: one that is not a grand statement about women's lives in the South Pacific, but one that reflects a heightened version of those similarities and differences between people which make short story reading, like chance conversations, so intensely rewarding.

The South Pacific is not culturally unified; shortish physical distances can loom large with distinctions sometimes scrupulously observed. The writers speaking here — with the sun — do not often speak to each other or to each other's readers. Some of the writers will be better known to European or North American audiences than they will be to the citizens of the country nearest their own. Australian readers are not interested in New Zealand writing, or so we hear. And New Zealand readers are not interested in Australian writing, comes the echo across the Tasman.

But these stories suggest a different outcome. The freshness of the writing mixes powerfully with familiarity. There will be favourites, different for each reader, but they are unlikely to occur along national lines. Sometimes the stories do express an intense, self-conscious awareness of the cultural climate which hatched them.

(Could a sentence be any more Australian than Jan Hutchinson's laconic line, 'We were down the coast and I was on his back.'?) Sometimes the outer world fades almost entirely, usually in the face of the kind of inner dramas which fuel good writing everywhere.

Speaking with the Sun is the first of a series of short story anthologies which will insist on the optimistic (common sense?) claim that readers within our region deserve to hear from the most interesting writers drawn from the entire region — whether Australian, or New Zealand or from one of the smaller South Pacific countries.

And for readers outside our own region, who have anyway traditionally had difficulty telling us apart, there will be discoveries of a different kind, some of them absolutely specific to place as well as to time, and some of them intensely personal, coming out of the one single tradition to which these stories belong: that of excellent writing by women.

It has been a pleasure working with these writers and reading and re-reading their stories. I believe it will be a pleasure — and perhaps an eye-opener — to read them.

Stephanie Dowrick
Summer, 1991

MY NEW LIFE

Susan Johnson

Susan Johnson was born in Brisbane in 1956. She grew up in Sydney and, after leaving school, joined the *Courier Mail* as a cadet journalist and completed an arts degree in journalism and English. She has since worked on the *Australian Women's Weekly*, the *Sun Herald*, the *Sydney Morning Herald* and the *National Times*. In 1984 she began writing full time. She co-edited *Latitudes: New Writings from the North*, and has written two novels, *Messages from Chaos* and *Flying Lessons*.

MY NEW LIFE

The summer I turned fifteen we started our new life. I sat in my usual place behind Dad, who was driving, so that I could look at myself in the rear-vision mirror. I liked my eyes, which looked beautiful to me: I looked at them, imagining a new life not yet begun. I saw whole moons and constellations: I sensed the shiver of skin at triumph.

My father once went to Russia. When he came home reporters were at the airport to meet him. He sat in a chair with the sleep machine on his head, explaining to the men how it worked. Photographs show him with his eyes obscured; two round metal discs cover them like glasses, his head is encased in what looks like an old-fashioned diving helmet. He told the reporters that the Russians were leading the world in sleep research. Dad was still a Communist then: it was the year that Yuri Gagarin became the first man in space and when my brother was born Dad talked Mum into calling him Gagarin. Dad said he was a child of the future with a name which also marked history. My Nana Glynne said he was a child with a father who was off his rocker, with a name he would come to curse.

By the time I was turning fifteen and starting a new life, Gagarin was calling himself Desmond. Dad had been expelled from the Communist Party by then: at night he looked at maps, studying the colours of countries. He was reading a lot of books about those Australians who set up a farming community in Paraguay.

I remember it was hot in the car. Alexandra and I made Desmond sit in the middle because he was the smallest and the rule was *no touching*. Alexandra was named for Alexandra Kollantai, that unsung heroine of the Revolution, but my sister liked the name so she kept it.

1

I was called Nancy. As far as I know there has never been a heroine called Nancy but my mother wanted it, so I was named Nancy Elizabeth, the Elizabeth for my Nana Glynne. My mother was a famous beauty who was once a Miss Eureka: she met my father at a socialist youth rally and quite soon they imagined a future.

My father was always imagining a future. Nana Glynne said one day he would wake up to find it arrived, no different from the present after all.

It was the first time we had travelled north. Before, we had always gone south, to new schools and new friends, protected by the glamour of Sydney. Once Dad came to our school, to see the headmaster about this marvellous new teaching method of which he had just heard: we stood around the headmaster's office waiting for him to come out. He was quite famous even in Melbourne, having recently been in the papers over some ballot scandal in his union. Alexandra and I stood proudly amongst a small group of friends waiting to prove he was our father. But when he came out he looked distracted and patted me absentmindedly on the head before leaving. 'He's a Commo,' offered Debbie Bates. 'Of course,' said Alexandra, pulling me to the gate to wave goodbye.

We stopped at the Big Banana. 'It's only a toilet,' said Desmond, who certainly had imagined more. We looked at banana products and were allowed a banana milkshake, which we drank with three straws. I walked to the edge of the road where the banana farm started to rise up the hill. 'Why are the bananas covered in plastic bags?' asked Desmond and Dad said, 'For ripening.'

He was possibly already imagining himself a farmer. Mum sat in the car complaining of the heat but Dad told her it was only going to get hotter.

Further north, the air grew stiller. Our room had an air-conditioner but Alexandra said she was freezing so we turned it off and switched on the overhead fan. 'This is our home now so I expect you to treat it as such,' said Mum, unpacking clothes from our bag. 'When are we moving to our farm?' asked Desmond and Mum looked at Dad. 'Directly,' he said before moving across to Mum and stilling her hand. 'Margaret McDonald,' he said, 'would you care to join me for a swim?' She began to say no but he grabbed her and said surely she would like a swim in the nuddy? 'In the nuddy!' shouted Desmond, 'in the nuddy in the dark!'

We all went down to the beach then. I waited till everybody had stripped off before I went in, holding the towel around me till the last. The sea was black and rolling: there was nothing between it and our skins.

Every day Dad came home from looking at farms without buying one. He and Mum would sit on the verandah drinking beer before dinner: it was mosquito time, so a mosquito coil smoked between their chairs, sweet. If they were frightened it did not show.

Alexandra and I spent every day at the beach, browning our faces with baby oil. Our mother gave us both hats, which we only put on as we came into sight. 'Queensland has the highest incidence of skin cancer in the world,' she warned but we did not care. Desmond and his new friend dug for pippies with their feet, standing in the water where the waves broke, twisting their heels in the sand. The pippy shells rose to the surface to be claimed for the bucket. Mum tried to cook some as a favour to Desmond but could not get rid of the sand.

I liked this hot limbo, where our new life was endlessly about to begin. I hovered on the crest of possibility: all potential, all scope. I remember the night Dad came home to tell us he had bought a pineapple farm, how Desmond shouted, how beer was drunk, and how I mourned, having grown fond of anticipation.

Our new house stood on the crest of a hill. Pineapples fell in rows down the slope; sugar cane grew on the farm at the bottom. It was burning time: all night the cane crackled; the sound carried. The man who was going to help Dad advised us to watch for snakes fleeing the flames; Desmond hoped to catch one. 'No,' said our mother, 'and I mean it.'

We watched Dad put on his new boots and his farmer's hat. 'Farmer Joe,' said Mum, at the door. At any time she could watch him from the window working in the pineapples below. Also, he came home for lunch. 'Don't worry,' he said, 'you'll get used to it.'

In the town people stared. 'It's rude,' I said to Mum but she did not reply. At school they stared too as if coming from Sydney was like coming from beneath the sea. 'We were allowed to smoke at our old school,' Alexandra told a girl on the bus. She was lying but I did not mind.

It was new but it was not wonderful.

I remember it was a Friday when the cyclone came. All morning the sky had moved oddly; writhing clouds passed too swiftly; by lunch-time they hunched down one end of the sky. 'The sky's green,' said Desmond, raising his head to the unnatural colour. We walked quickly, sensing danger, the breaking of rules. School was closed; the air ready; we walked when we had been told to catch the bus.

At home we listened to the cyclone warning on the radio, turning it up loud as a siren. 'Off!' said our mother, 'now give me a hand with these windows.'

When the wind started we watched: loose objects rolled, our fence clattered. Rain broke against glass; the earth rocked. Each of us felt the tremor of exultation; a wild joy that the world was so fierce.

It was then that I turned to look at my father. I recognised that the wind had grown louder, and felt the house shake. Desmond began to cry: my father moved us all into the bedroom.

Afterwards we woke becalmed, as if in the aftermath of terrible pain. There was Mum and Alexandra and Desmond and me, all in Mum and Dad's bed: it was quietly raining.

I went to the window to look at the sky but looked down instead, to see that the pineapple rows had been ripped out as if by a fist, to see the hills of our farm now empty.

Then I saw Dad walking in the mud. I could see that he had forgotten his hat, and that his feet on the ground were bare. I could tell that he was crying.

We moved several times after that, but never again with such ardour. As I grew older I came to know that my father was often in debt and understood what Nana Glynne meant when she talked of his hare-brained schemes. I saw too that she had stayed in the same house for most of her life, journeying only in dreams.

It is only now that I am as old as my father was when he took us to start a new life that I find my heart travelling. At night I imagine beginnings, a new life not yet begun. My new life seems imminent and glorious, in a country unfamiliar to rain. Often I think of my father, and always with the sleep machine on his head. His eyes are blind but his head is dreaming: he is thinking of the ceaseless movement of geography, of the infinite wonders of history. He is certainly planning for victory.

IT TOOK UNCLE ALBERT TO DIE

Judy Duffy

Judy Duffy has worked in a variety of occupa-
tions, including singing in a pub and school
teaching. At the age of thirty-seven she
completed a BA Hons degree, and she is
currently writing fiction and teaching fiction
writing at the Royal Melbourne Institute of
Technology. Her first book, the short story
collection *Bad Mothers*, was written with the
aid of a Literature Board grant, and was
published in 1988. In 1989 *Bad Mothers* was
commended in the Victorian Premier's
Awards.

IT TOOK UNCLE ALBERT TO DIE

My wife links luck with life in a way which infuriates me. Her mind is a tangled mesh of superstitions and omens. However bleak a misfortune, Edith will find in it, somehow, a glimmer of light, a streak of good-fortune.

And so, when news of Uncle Albert's death crackled through the phone wires from Queensland, I waited for Edith's personal interpretation of the tragedy.

It came, two and a half hours later, while we were driving fast up the Princes Highway, packed and ready to travel day and night for two days to arrive in time for the funeral. Edith squeezed my knee while I was overtaking a semi-trailer. Back on the left of the road, I risked a glimpse. She was excited, happy, wriggling about in her seat, fussing over the lunch she had packed, rearranging the thermos, positioning a huge box of tissues on the dashboard, settling a cushion behind her back.

'Uncle Albert hasn't died for nothing.' She lifted her skirt, positioned the vent for air to flow up her plump white legs.

'Our stars are right for travel and harmony,' she explained.

'It took a death to jolt us into a holiday. Now maybe we'll rediscover each other.'

She laughed, fiddled with the radio dials, sang at the top of her voice, 'On the road again . . .'

It wasn't until I saw her packing that I realised she intended to come with me. I had wanted to take this trip on my own. I needed time away from everything, even Edith, time away to rest and think, to think about the rest of my life.

She's a big woman Edith, big-hearted, big-spirited, big-bodied. Big but easily bruised. I'd assumed she'd be too busy with her domestic chores and her womens' groups to even contemplate coming.

And I didn't have the heart to say what I was thinking. No heart to be heartless. That's me.

'He may be small,' Edith is fond of saying, 'but his heart's too big for his own good.'

I'd told her that after the funeral in Bowen, I would travel into the outback of Northern Queensland, beyond Mt Surprise, where my parents eked out a living prospecting for tin and gemstones. It would be an adventure. I'd be there on Melbourne Cup Day.

Edith disappeared into her room. The silence said she was meditating or consulting her charts. Searching for omens or signs of significance. When she emerged she said, 'Now it may seem silly but this year, 1984, the Melbourne Cup will be a highly significant omen for our future.'

It was then that she began to pack.

We arrived at 3 am on the morning of the funeral but they were waiting up for us. My cousin Ann, her husband Bob, and Aunty Jane. Aunty Jane, tiny and fragile and stunned. The house was full of flowers. The old woman explained. 'If you live to be ninety you get to know a lot of people even though most of your friends are dead.'

'Ninety!' Edith blew her nose loudly into a wad of tissues. Ann moved anxiously towards the kettle. Bob foraged in the fridge for a beer.

'Well almost ninety.' The old lady smiled. 'It would have been his birthday Melbourne Cup day. Tuesday next.'

I cringed under Edith's private glance. Since Townsville she'd been meditating on the Cup, waiting for the winner's name to flash into her mind, waiting for the significance of the Cup to reveal itself.

Aunty Jane continued.

'Sixty-four years we'd been together, Albert and me.'

'Sixty-four years!' Edith lunged her head into my shoulder.

'Did you hear that Harold? Sixty-four years! Together!'

My family had met Edith on only two occasions. At our wedding and at Ann and Bob's wedding. Edith had blubbered loudly at both events. She'd covered the front of her own wedding dress with great drifts of black mascara and she'd done the same to the shoulder of Ann's gown. It was a family joke. A topic treated often in the letters. Edith didn't wear mascara any more but I could have told them, even before it happened, that she was on the brink of a scene that would almost certainly outdo both the others.

I was right.

Turning from my shoulder and sobbing uncontrollably, she scooped my tiny aunt into her arms. It looked a bit like an elephant swinging an ant. Then they were sobbing, both of them, and Ann was shouting, 'Go on Mum cry! Cry your bloody heart out! It will do you good.' Ann started sobbing too and Edith scooped her up into the huddle. They howled, the three of them, for over half an hour. Bob and I pretended this was normal. We sat opposite each other in soft grey arm chairs, sipped stubbies and talked about weather, job success, house prices and how Aunty would manage financially now Uncle Albert had gone. When it was over I tried to say something. It was 'The Something' I'd come to say.

'Australia is a very big country...' I tried again. 'Time gets away...'

Edith could see I was floundering, that everyone was waiting for me to get my words out but she did nothing to help, she just stood there with the others watching. An eternity passed before she rescued me.

'We wish we'd come sooner. In time...'

'There was no time.' Aunty's voice was fragile with the memory.

'He'd just had his breakfast.'

'Eggs and bacon with two rounds,' Ann sobbed.

'He was putting on his socks.'

'He always put his socks on first.'

'Mum dressed him.' Ann's eyes held mine. She wanted me to understand something. 'He was such a big man but somehow she managed to dress him. Dress him in his dinner suit, before the ambulance arrived.'

I gave Edith my handkerchief. It was a hint for her to control herself.

Aunty shrugged. 'I had no choice. Imagine his embarrassment at being seen naked.'

Edith said she understood. She told them that I would have been the same. They stared at me. The three women. Stared and nodded. Yes. Nodded. All three of them. Aunty broke the silence.

'I told him. "It's an occasion Albert. I'm not sending you off looking like a scrag".'

'Mum's White Knight. Eh Mum?'

It was time, I decided, for a good stiff whisky. A night cap. I'd bought a bottle of the best. One each. I poured. Edith drank three and turned amorous.

'It's the first time in years we've been able to be together.' She slobbered, whisky-breathed, into my cheek.

'He's been so wonderful. Imagine putting up with me all these years.'

'I don't deserve him.' She almost choked on her cigarette. Her words embarrassed everyone into silence.

Later, in bed, I told her I was too tired. Too upset.

She wrapped her great white legs around me.

She understood, she said. Within seconds she was snoring.

We are alone, Edith and I. No other car, no other person occupies this great barren plain. Before us the land stretches deceptively flat and orange; the mountains, far in the distance are misshapen and grey. The heat is visible. It hovers on the road before us shimmering like a wall of water. Orange dust puffs cloud behind our vehicle alerting the huge canopy of sky to our movement. The sky would see us in miniature. The sky, I decide, would be indifferent. Because it is necessary to keep the windows up, the heat of the day is locked in the cabin with us. Heat and Edith and me locked into a small space in the universe.

Marriage. For thirty years.

We drive for miles in silence. Edith is sweating. Her red hair, wound high on her head, is wet. The armpits of her green dress have drenched into half-moon patches. She sighs constantly, wipes, with folded wads of tissues, her forehead, her neck, her inner thighs. The used tissues she crams into a plastic bag. She has her feet resting on pillows because her legs, from toes to knees, are grotesquely swollen. I watch her press a finger into her calf muscle, see the white dent it leaves turn yellow then fade to normal. She doesn't look after herself, Edith. She eats too much, drinks too much and smokes too much. Just as she worries, talks and thinks too much. She'll make herself ill one of these days and then others will have to care for her. I should speak to her of her excesses, her selfishness. But I don't have the heart. I know she would shatter with the shame of it.

Edith's hands are large, her fingers long and graceful. She has them clasped in her lap, finger through finger, clutching. Watching her I think, 'You are a strong woman Edith. No matter what happens I will always respect you . . .'

No matter what happens? The thought terrifies me. I surely can't be contemplating a life apart — a life without Edith?

It is a long time before I dare risk another glance at her.

She smiles.

'Retaining fluid.' She laughs. 'At least you don't have to stop every half hour for me to wee.'

I'd warned her, before we left Bowen, that I wouldn't be stopping here there and everywhere. A to B. That's me. Make the miles disappear. But I did stop once. I needed a wee myself. Edith was out of the cabin like a flash. She'd seen a blackboy plant standing solitary in a landscape of grey and brown rocks and decided the plant was dancing. A tuft of green spiked leaves sprouted like a pineapple top from its head and its two branches were angled like ecstatically spread arms. Next thing Edith was scaling the smooth rock surface until she was small in the distance, her green dress merging her into a grey-gummed landscape. Then she was dancing, holding the outstretched branch of the plant like it was an arm and imitating its crazy stance. I laughed. Laughed again when Edith yelled, 'He's my Black Knight in landscape armour.' Laughed until Edith called out, 'Get a photo Harold. It will give them a laugh. Back home.' Her last words echoed through the gully. 'Back Home'. I shuddered. It was as if I'd received a prison sentence. Needless to say Edith grazed her legs on rocks on the way down and for mile on mile blood soaked tissues were stuffed with the others into the plastic bag at her feet.

Innisfail is the last big town before Mt Surprise. For miles Edith has sat with the Cup Page of the *Melbourne Age* folded in her lap. Asking me to stop without saying a word. If Edith had her way we'd stop every hour while she wasted time taking her endless photographs, or exploring, as she put it, touching the earth, the plants, squinting into the horizon and gushing on about the perfection of everything. She discovered the universe was perfect years ago and has raved ever since. Plants are perfection. So too are trees, birds, babies, you name it. Love too is perfection. If it's not, she maintains, it's not love. Typical of Edith to have it both ways. The print on the newspaper is running with her sweat. I give in, stop at a TAB, give her forty dollars. 'Ten on the nose of four of them,' I tell her. 'One each for Mum and Dad and one for each of us.' Edith will never bet on a horse if its name spells out a bad omen. She'll go for horses like Affable, or Affinity, or Enchanteur, or Mapperly Heights. Positive sounding romantic names. As soon as she's gone I realise that I've wasted my money.

Back in the truck Edith writes a name on the back of each ticket. Mum. Dad. Harold. Edith. I brace myself for a rave about omens but she says nothing. Just fiddles constantly with the radio dials. For miles static screeches through the cabin until she finds a station. God knows where it's transmitting from but it's opera. Opera in the outback and Edith in her own world, her head rolling around the headrest consumed with thoughts of the passion and pain of love.

I take it for as long as I can and then I say turn the damn thing off and let's have some peace. Instantly Edith snaps into a sulk. Edith is the Mistress of the Sulk. She turns her head to look out the window and cries without a single give away movement or sound. Tears drip down the side of her face, over her jutted chin and into the wrinkles of her neck.

I estimate two hundred miles for this sulk. Two hundred miles of peace.

Moving inland, the landscape changes constantly. In places the track is narrow, humped and twisted. I need all my concentration to keep the wheels on the ridges, avoid the cracks, the chasms. In other places, dark grey river sands, deposited from floods in the wet season, threaten to bog, even swallow the car. Once the car spins out on me. Forty yards it takes before I can stop safely. Another time I lose the track completely and have difficulty finding it again. During all of this, Edith sits in silence. I look at her. 'A great suffering monument,' I decide, 'consumed by your sulk.'

We pass the Mt Surprise Post Office and take the bush track towards the river. Within ten miles the landscape begins to soften and green but the earth itself—beside the car—is parched and black, littered with rocks and dried twigs. Edith has been silent for so long that her sudden scream, 'Stop the car! Stop!' causes me to brake dangerously to a halt. A heart attack! The fluid gone to her brain! I grab for her but she's half out the door pointing to two grey and black speckled eggs. The size of footballs they perch on a mound of twigs and branches only yards from the wheels of the utility. Their colours match perfectly the colours of the nest. I grab for Edith's arm, try to prevent her leaving, point to the pluvers, their grey and brown stripes making them difficult to distinguish from the burnt out tree stump about which they flap and circle.

'I'll drive around them,' I tell Edith but she's out there, lifting the nest and placing it carefully away from the track. The pluvers run for her squawking their outrage. I roar the engine, blast the horn and Edith, puffing and sweating, clamours back into the cabin.

There she beams expecting my approval.

'They'll have nothing to do with the eggs now,' I tell her. I'm not sure that this is right but I need to get that 'heroine' look off her face, and fast.

I succeed.

'You mean I've killed them,' she says, 'but I thought . . .'

'You don't think Edith,' I say. 'That's half the trouble.'

They have the radio on a tree stump beyond the caravan, an aerial running up a gum tree. They've been hoping we'd arrive in time for the Cup. We kiss, hold each other, say how strange it is to be together, here. Who would have thought? Took Uncle Albert to die.

'Well! A Melbourne Cup at Mt Surprise!' I'm trying to get Edith out of her gloom. 'No fancy hats, green lawns and champagne in car parks for us eh? How about a "tinnie" cold from the river sand?'

The sun is blazing.

Edith points to rocks beyond the river. 'Think of all the time, all the changes, they have seen. While for us change is terrifying isn't it? Major change, I mean . . .'

We accuse her of melancholy, of 'launching poetic'.

We clank tins. Wish each other luck.

'Are we lucky? Do you think?' Edith is directing the question at me. In front of everyone.

'What is luck . . .' I begin but she interrupts. 'In love, I mean?'

There is a strange look on her face. She is staring again . . .

'You and your omens Edith,' I laugh, embarrassed.

Edith hands out the tickets.

'Maybe we should let the Cup decide our future. If a good omen wins we'll be fine. If not . . .'

I've had enough.

'That's fine by me,' I say.

The radio crackles and shrieks. Most of the race is inaudible. Except for the name of the winner. Black Knight. Edith weeps. She's won over four hundred dollars and she's howling. My parents laugh. Mum insists Edith put her swollen legs up on a cushion.

'You'll piss half the night.' She laughs. 'But it will eventually run out of you. The fluid and the miseries.'

Early in the evening Dad takes us deep into the bush. He will show us, he says, what love really is. A small, squat man he lifts his legs high on the track, stopping every now and again, a finger to his lips. We stand on the top of a clearing and look down on a huge, exposed nest. A bower bird's nest. The twigs are loosely woven but the centre is remarkably smooth. The male, Dad says, flattens it in anticipation, with his feet, with his dance. In front of the nest a collection of colours glint in the sun. Blues and reds and silver and yellow. Edith is delighted. She is laughing like a young girl.

'What an outrageous little Romeo,' she says and we see what she means. His offerings are the red lids of cream bottles, the yellow of plastic bags, the blue of broken china, stubby lids turned gold side up, the amber of glass, and the silver—a pair of nail scissors and a teaspoon.

Watching Edith's face I realise how completely she would respond to love bower bird fashion. I realise also, that whoever released such passion in her would have to be strong enough not to drown in what he released. I see Edith as she used to be. Loved and slender. I feel suddenly very protective of her. She would be far too vulnerable and naive to survive in a world without me. The surge of affection I feel for her is so strong I reach for her hand. I hold it. Edith's eyes brim with tears. She squeezes my hand, squeezes my hand so tightly, so damned tightly, that I have no choice but to pull away from her.

The evening is casting shadows over the day, over the years.

'Please don't worry Harold,' Edith says. 'It has to be.' She laughs. 'Besides, it's time I learned to dance again.'

WE COULD CELEBRATE

Barbara Anderson

Barbara Anderson was born in Hawkes Bay
in 1926 and began writing in her late fifties.
Her first collection of short stories, *I think we
should go into the jungle*, was published by
Victoria University Press, Wellington, in
1989. Her first novel, *Girls' High*, was published by Victoria University Press in 1990
and in the UK by Secker & Warburg in
1991. Barbara Anderson lives in Wellington.

WE COULD CELEBRATE

Sooze who is my friend, and Bryce who is Sooze's friend have lent Cliff and me their bach at Paraparaumu for the weekend. They have gone to the wedding of their friend Hester in Te Atatu. Cliff and I watched them as they loaded the car. It made me feel quite faint. All that mountain of stuff in the back for a one-year old, their son Jared; reuseables, disposables, restrainers, containers, you couldn't see out the back window.

I was pretty thoughtful as they left and Jared waved a bear in a red jacket. So was Cliff. We didn't say anything as we walked back inside.

—Let's go for a swim, I said, leaping to my feet. I like swimming in the sea. I always start off in my bikini so as not to startle the natives but take off the top and usually the bottom because I like swimming like that, and the part where we swim there aren't many people. In the surf you have to hook the straps round your arm then put the same arm through a leg of the bikini so you don't lose them. I did lose a top once but it's worth it for the feel of the sea. I don't like sunbathing unless I have a book, especially now with melanomas.

Once when I was in the Coromandel with a previous friend of mine called Barry who ditched me, we walked miles and miles up a deserted beach. Right at the end there were three small bachs nestling (there is no other word) beneath gnarled old pohutukawa in full bloom, it was lovely. But the thing I remember most was an old couple without a stitch on who sat reading in canvas chairs so low their behinds were almost on the paspalum. They were pakeha but they were tanned mahogany and they just sat there after a quick glance up from their paperbacks and continued reading like a couple of wrinkled old literary kippers. I thought that was great and I'd like to have told them so but Barry was getting embarrassed so we walked on. Sometimes I think I'd like to try it but I suppose it only works when you're old, and only then if you've got the sense to play it your way and not fuss about other people.

The shape of her, Christ the shape of her when she swims naked in the sea, leaping over each wave, her nipples hard with the cold, she nearly finishes me. And she has no idea, no vanity, when she's swimming, that's what she's there for. She grew up near a good surf beach and still flings herself in front of an unbroken wave like a twelve-year old, arms clamped to her sides for a good run.

Now I know Carmen I can believe everything I've ever read or seen about 'the expense of spirit', the fever in the blood; Anthony, the poor wimp with the terrier who abdicated, Othello, the head-mistress who killed the diet doctor, any of them. I tell you I could join them, count the world well lost for love and lust and it drives her insane. We have rows about it, flaming dirty gut-wrenching rows because I watch her, want her too much. She calls it eating her. — Don't eat me Cliff, she says, but what can I do. I'm a painter, I look at things, I watch her legs, the angle of the knees as she folds onto the floor, the way she springs upright in one sinuous movement shall we say. I can't stop watching her. I sketch her and she's not mad about that so I have to be quick to catch the angle of her moving arm, the curve of her bum. Hokusai said any artist should be able to sketch a man as he fell from a high window to the ground and I'm getting better. Her arms are the most beautiful I have ever seen. I watch her plait her hair each morning. She does it without a mirror, she bends over to brush it forward, then swings upright, her hands scoop the pale hair upwards to plait, her fingers move swish swish and it's done. I've got dozens of her plaiting her hair because she's concentrating then and doesn't notice me so much. And of her sleeping. She can sleep on her back, one hand under her head, her elbow in the air. Try it sometime. Every movement she makes is graceful. Her toes are prehensile. When she leans her rounded arms over the back of a chair I am hypnotised and that's just her arms for God's sake.

So what I do, to try and cool things so that I don't explode and wreck everything, is I clear off quite often. I get out into the Tararuas with my brother who used to be a deer culler and still hunts. I don't shoot but I like the tracking and Gavin doesn't mind my help in humping 100-kilogram stags back through the bush to the car.

And I'm working towards an exhibition, aren't I. Last week on the hottest day for three years I had two free periods from Girls High where I teach and I went round the galleries to show my stuff. I could feel my feet sweating in their canvas containers which didn't help as I ran up the narrow stairs to the first gallery. The guy was small with a pink and white face and baby hair and he was wearing one of those suits that dogs and bears wear in kids' picture books; crumpled and sort of hairy, the colour of Scotch mist. I burst into sweat all over in sympathy but he was cool, very cool and sharp. He didn't say anything as he looked through the portfolio and very little afterwards except that he'd let me know, and we talked about the art scene in New York and how would I know about that except in magazines and I don't see many of those. I left feeling sick, sick in the gut.

The next owner was a woman. She wore a black beret and it suited her, perched on the back of her head surrounded by curls. I wanted to ask her to take if off so I could see if she looked as good without it but I didn't. I didn't feel I was in a position where I could make that sort of request. She was a nice woman and the gallery had a good light. She said she'd let me know. And it went on like that until my feet and I were really stinking and I went home to Carmen's where I live and fell into her bath which has claws for feet and damn near wept. Then Carmen came home from school and got in too, though I told her I stank, and things got better.

That's the trouble I suppose. Nothing else matters though I'm painting better than I've ever painted because of her. I always wonder about poor buggers like Van Gogh who never sold anything or only one while he lived. How did he keep knowing he was good? I don't see much point in posterity. Did he know he was great or did he just slog on, obsessed with nothing but the next stroke of paint? OK he had vision but that doesn't answer the question. I'd really like to know the answer but there is no one to ask. I could ask the man in the suit maybe. He would say something but we'll never know. Not really.

I touch his bare foot with mine. — Let's go for a swim, I say once more.

He looks up blinking.

— Swim! I demonstrate, clawing the air with my arms.

He swings his legs up on the sofa. He has good legs like Edna Everage and my brother Stephen who says he has the best legs in Hawkes Bay.

Cliff drags up one foot to pick the big toenail. Toenail checked out, he sits up. — I think I'll go to the store first, he says.

— What the hell, we've just arrived.

— Yeah, but that guy, the dealer guy, he said he'd drop me a card, c/o the store. I said we were going to be here and he said . . .

— He won't.

Cliff looks at me, not pleased. His mouth tightens. — He said he would.

— Yes but people say, people say, people *say*! My hands are all over the place trying to disperse my previous negative comment.

— It's not important to him see, I explain to my lover who is not in fact handicapped. — It's only important, rush-wise, to you. The sands of non-support move beneath me. I bog deeper in the mire of not understanding a thing about it.

— I'm going. Cliff leaps to his feet and goes. I read the *Kapiti Observer*. I like the For Sales best. You could pick up anything.

He is back in five minutes flat. He leaps in the french doors and seizes me. He flings cushions in the air. If he could do a backward somersault of delight like the decathalon man at the Commonwealth Games he would. He can't contain himself. He is beside himself with pleasure.

— Let's have a look, I say taking the card. The man in the furry bear suit wishes to mount an exhibition of my lover's work.

I share Cliff's joy and all is harmony and fairies on the lawn and at the bottom of the garden I shouldn't wonder.

He stops in the middle of a strong clutch and pulls back. — It'll be a ton of work, he says. — This guy's good. He stares through my head. — I'll need three nudes, he mutters. — Three at least, I'd say.

His gaze refocuses on my face. He looks at me. — Oils. Of you.

I smile. The muscles clench. — Three? I say.

— At least, he says.

— Let's go for a swim, I say yet again.

And we go, leaping down the track, up the track, down the track through the marram grass; sand flying, wind tugging, tumbleweed on the scoot. We are yelling as we fall into the sea which can solve everything. All frustration, all longing, all despair the sea can cure but only when you're in it. When I am old I will live by the sea and potter about poking at things with a stick and watching the young. When I am dead I will live in it.

We swim naked.

We make love afterwards on Sooze and Bryce's bed. The room smells musty like the bach bedrooms of childhood when you brushed sand from the soles of your feet with flattened palms before climbing into your bunk.

Nothing wrong with the action though. Cliff is even more charged with creative imagination than usual. I love him dearly.

— We could celebrate, he says afterwards. He picks up my hand and inspects it closely. — Celebrate, he tells it. — Make a booking at that restaurant in the village.

I roll over to bite his ear. — What's it called?

— I can't remember, he says.

But we remember later. We make a booking and we go clutching our BYO. The restaurant has a theme and the theme is sport. The wall by the entrance shows cricket memorabilia. An Edwardian child in knickerbockers presents a straight bat, there are framed and auto-graphed photographs of other straight batters and strong bowlers. Several of them have moustaches. There is an old etching of the Hambledon cricket ground.

The other wall is Rugby. More moustaches, photographs; deathless tries. I like sport, I'm not knocking it. I like playing it. It is just that here the images are trapped like beetles in kauri gum.

There is a mural in the main room. Pale mauves, lilacs and greens define shadowy figures, most of which are static. Men in white stand near the crease, sit in the pavilion with hats on, converse. Up the Rugby end they tackle and fall on their faces. The heads of the figures are transparent, defined by outlines, you can see the dark or light green bushes through them. Cliff is interested in the murals which he finds effective — as murals. He whips out his sketch pad and begins drawing.

I read the menu. I read that our hosts are called Trevor and Fay and that the restaurant is on the corner of Wairoa and Glenfield Streets which we already know.

There is a slice of lemon in the water carafe beside our bottle of Te Mata Estate White which the waitress has opened. It is not full, the restaurant. One table has a lone male diner with fluffy white hair curling over the back of his collar. He eats slowly, entertaining himself.

Cliff has his pad beneath the table as he sketches a party, if you can call it that, of five. There are two middle-aged men, one handsome, one had it, who sits squeezed and bosomy inside a souvenir shirt labelled Fiji with a hibiscus surround. One woman's lilac spectacle frames match the blotched flowers on her frock. She tries to keep up with the men who are laughing and having fun. The two women opposite have given up. One wears her hair screwed on top in American Gothic style. Flamenco dancers flaunt on her cream jersey silk. She is sick of being here. Gran tells me this happens when you are old. You get sick of it and wonder why you came though this can happen when you are young and often does.

The rain is hosing down outside, water slams against the windows. The blades of one of the overhead fans on the ceiling moves faster than the other. They must be on different settings.

—Well, I say, lifting my glass to Cliff. —Here's to the exhibition.

Cliff has a beautiful smile. It happens comparatively rarely and it pleases me to watch the lips part, the dent in one cheek deepen, the eyes gleam. Rarity has value. People used to get excited when the young Baxter turned up sober for a reading.

—Well, replies Cliff, lifting his glass to clink mine. He reads the menu — Do you want your oysters *en crepe* or looking at you?

—Looking at me.

The door opens. Thundering past the memorabilia, damp with rain and slapping each other, come a gang of eight. They are drunk, these young men. Their faces are red, their clothes are a mess, their feet stumble as they weave around the table laughing and groping for chairs. They are very happy. The eyes of the other diners concentrate on their plates except for the lone male diner who has not yet noticed their behaviour. The waitress, smiling strongly, ushers them to a table alongside ours. One of the young men focuses on me. — Shit, he informs. — Get a load of that lot.

Eight pairs of glazed eyes turn in my direction. Eight drunken hoons gape, their mouth slightly open. They are not a pretty sight.

I order oysters *au naturel* and venison that something time-consuming has happened to. The waitress is very pleasant. I think she must be Fay because she cares so much. She wears the type of long apron worn by French waiters which is not a good idea because her stomach sticks out and is clamped and bound by the stiff fabric. Periodically she glances at the hoons and gives a quick smile as though she meant them to happen.

She takes Cliff's order and moves on to more dangerous territory. She is patient, amiable, she smiles into their stunned mullet eyes in her attempt to pretend that all is well; that they are civilised welcome guests at mine hosts' (Fay and Trevor's) table. It is uphill work. She moves around explaining, smiling as they order, shout, hit each other, belch, drag bottles of wine from a chilly bin and slam them on the table. They make gestures behind her back to indicate that though she is old enough for kissing she is too fat to tango.

I am getting angry.

—Cliff, I say.

He is sketching again, his hand moves with authority, he glances with swift stealthy up and downs of his head at the table of five. Even upside down I can see that he has got the spare dignity and resignation of the American Gothic woman to perfection.

—Nnn? he says.

—Cliff!

His hand is still moving. — Yes?

I wriggle my shoulders and indicate the table next door with a sideways jerk of the head. — Drunk, I hiss.

—Certainly looks like it, he says, and carries on sketching.

My eyes meet those of the lone male diner. He picks up his lilac napkin and presses it against one corner of his mouth then the other. He returns the napkin to his lap, places his hands on the table and stares at them. He reminds me of something.

I remember. Barry who ditched me and I were staying in a motel in Tauranga where the dining room invited us to enjoy our smorgasbord in a family atmosphere. The salads were inventive: kumara and bacon, tamarillo and red cabbage, brown rice. There was a lot of kiwifruit. There was kiwifruit in every salad, slices of kiwifruit decorated plates of cold meat, the pavlovas, the fruit salads and the trifle. It was the ultimate kiwifruit experience. At a table beneath a Martin firehose decorated with a frizzled tinsel wreath left over from Christmas sat two men, one older than the other. The older man's sparse hair was swept across his scalp. He had a tip-tilted nose and gold chains. He was ashamed of smoking. He took furtive puffs behind one curved hand. He spilt ash and swept it from the table with quick brushing movements of the same hand. The young man's fingers fanned between their faces dispersing smoke. The older man pressed food. The younger man ate. There was no conversation. The young man had a good haircut, his Docksides were splayed at ten to three. When he was not eating his hands were clasped together or hung down in despair. He was offered treats, sweets for the sweet. He ate two helpings of trifle decorated with kiwifruit and they departed in silence. It was infinitely sad.

I smile at the silver-haired man. He dips his head but does not smile back. He raises his eyebrows in agreement. He does not enjoy the hoons either.

The noise is increasing at the table next to ours. One man all red hair and ears is telling us in song that there is a bridle hanging on the wall, there's the shoes that his old pony wore. If we ask him why those teardrops fall, it's that bridle hanging on the wall. A man with a mean Hadlee moustache is telling a story with a lot of fucks and ducks in it. All the men are drinking like fishes except that fishes are breathing when they gulp. Someone throws a roll. There is uproar at the table.

The good-looking man at the table of five summons the waitress who is looking distracted. She spreads her hands wide in answer to his complaint. Her body language tells me what she is saying. What can she and Trevor do? They didn't know when they took the booking they would be like this did they.

His outrage informs her that someone ought to do something and smartly. — The proprietor, he mouths. She looks even more miserable but moves quickly to the kitchen presumably in search of Trevor.

Trevor does not appear.

I am fidgeting about on the seat of my chair in rage and shame for them all. Cliff is totally oblivious. He is now sketching the particular way the silver curls fall on the collar of the lone diner's jacket who sits very still staring straight in front of him.

—Good one! The table roars at the punch line of the fuck and duck story.

—Down trou! someone screams. The red head staggers to his feet. Pale and sweating, his head down, he fumbles with his belt. His trousers and underpants fold about his ankles. His hairy white buttocks are presented for inspection two yards from my face. The table roars with approval.

I am on my feet. So is the lone diner.

I haven't been watching. I sense that Carmen is getting a bit toey but the sketch is going so well and I want just a few more minutes and then I'll stop sketching and then we'll celebrate and rejoice in each other which is what we have come for, I do realise that.

I glance up from my pad. The camp man with the silver hair has disappeared from his chair. The table of five is in shock, their knives and forks suspended in mid air. Carmen has disappeared. There is a lot of noise. I see some guy's white bum for a second before he pulls up his trousers amid thundering applause from the rest of them. Carmen and the old gay are standing side by side in front of the table. Carmen is flaming. Someone has lit her fire.

— Get out, she hisses. — Now!

Their obscene comments on her beauty melt on wet lips. They stare. Their mouths are slack. The old man puts one hand on her arm. — I think perhaps the young lady is upset, he says gently. He stacks their half-empty bottles upright in the chilly bin with care. He smiles at them all. — Why don't you leave now, he suggests. — The kitchen will give you corks for the open bottles. There's a good takeaway just round the corner on Highway One. And please, he begs with clasped hands, *please* take taxis home. He slips a twenty-dollar bill into the chilly bin beside the bottles. He looks at them with love. — You are too young to die, he tells them.

Now they will kill him. There will be a gay bashing. I leap up ten minutes too late.

Not so. The table crawl to their feet and stumble out clutching their grog. They do not say anything. They do not look at the old man or Carmen. I am still standing, one hand on the chair, the edge of the seat digging the back of my knees as they go out the door.

Carmen and the old man turn to each other. They shake hands. He waves one hand towards his table, he asks the jittery waitress for another glass. He holds the chair back for Carmen to sink into. He pours her some wine, showing her the label as he does so. They lean towards each other with their arms on the linen cloth. They talk together, nodding occasionally. They smile at each other.

SLOW RAIN

Rosie Scott

Born in Wellington, New Zealand, in 1948,
Rosie Scott's books include *Glory Days* and
Queen for Love. *Glory Days* was shortlisted for
the New Zealand Book Awards and has been
published in America, England and Germany
and is to be made into a feature film.

She has also written an award-winning
play, *Say Thank You to the Lady*, and a book
of poetry, *Flesh and Blood*. Her latest novel,
Nights with Grace, was published in 1990.
She lives in Brisbane with her husband and
two daughters.

SLOW RAIN

I didn't even notice the state of the city when I first came home after many years away. My parents had just died, leaving the family business to my sister and me. I'd led a quiet life in front of my typewriter for so long that it was all too much to cope with at once. I was completely preoccupied with my sadness at their death and delight at seeing my sister again. It was only later that the full impact of the place hit me.

They were still my childhood streets but, as the days went by, I saw more and more clearly that everything had changed, the slant of light, a feeling in the air as if they had been disconnected from life. They looked grey, remote, as disturbing as a half-remembered nightmare. At night the homeless people lit huge bonfires in rusty petrol drums and I could see the shadow of the flames flickering on the storeroom ceiling as I lay on a mattress on the floor trying to sleep. I kept hearing their harsh voices, sudden, jolting snarls of rage, the clink of bottles, a snatch of ragged singing. They were like voices from the dead, remote, an undercurrent of menace, a strange and ghostly community. In the daytime there were no signs, just newspapers blowing in the wind and young guys walking past like cowboys, stiff-legged, eyes ahead, past the derelict shops.

'They're the ragged army,' my sister Violet told me. 'There's thousands of them now. Families camped out in the streets, in old cars, under the freeway flyovers, in shopping malls, in cardboard boxes on the side of the road. There's nowhere for them to go.'

Dark puddles of some unknown liquid spilled out onto the pavement, soaking the nests of wadded newspapers, syringes, rags lying everywhere. A lot of the shops around us in Kingsland were boarded up or had been turned into cut-rate flea markets, sex shops, strip joints, and the people selling cheap jewelry on the pavements had the tough knockabout faces of the truly desperate. Big semi-porno hoardings were tacked over the facades of the buildings. Women outlined in neon with huge breasts and idiot faces leered and winked down onto the streets.

Queen Street was like another country. The streets around there were almost deserted. Mounds of rubbish lay in the Post Office square and weeds grew in the cracks, creating an air of desolation and unease. The buildings were all strangely corroded as if some toxic process was occurring continuously, slowly breaking up the surfaces, wrenching them apart like an earthquake in slow motion that stirred and cracked the walls before your eyes. The mirror glass on the office blocks was splintered and bleared over. The offices themselves looked like unloved plastic toys left out in the rain. I thought of the old Mid-City Centre, softened by giant indoor trees with shining green leaves, alive with children parading every Saturday night in their bright clothes. It was all gone, as if the streets had been emptied by a plague. But it was the main Auckland library which really hit me like a blow to the heart when I saw it. The windows were boarded over, there was a broken padlock on the door, impenetrable darkness inside.

'I couldn't believe it,' I said to Violet later. 'It was somehow the worst of all, even more than the homeless people. It was like the end of the world.'

'Round here there's no one left but street people and the only thing they want books for is kindling.'

'Kindling?'

'Fires to keep them warm,' she said. We sat at the table in the backroom of the shop, drinking cask wine, our elbows on the table, watching the rain and waiting for customers.

'I'm going there to see if I can save some of the books,' I said. 'We can store them here. Or lend them to customers. There's plenty of other kindling they can use.'

'It's too dangerous to go out,' Violet said. 'The kids prowl round the streets like zombies. They're all wired up on stuff like crack and ice.'

There was silence in the room except for the sound of the rain.

I spoke at last. 'We could make this into a small lending library. Maybe a bookshop.'

'Sure, why not?' Violet spoke heavily, drunk from the wine. 'We could call it "The Bookshop at the end of the Road".'

But all the same she came with me the next morning. We had fallen asleep at the table and woken at dawn with rain still falling and the sound of sirens in the distance. We put our overcoats on and got into the car without speaking, both of us sick from drinking. We drove to the Grafton Library because that was the one we both knew. Standing by the old stone steps I felt a terrible ache as I looked up. The building had been like a sanctuary for us with its huge wooden doors, its silence, the librarians sitting like deities on their thrones. It had been a way out of the narrow world of our childhood, a polished, orderly place where horizons stretched, comfortingly timeless. Now it stood forlornly, shamefully filthy, glass in a winking trail through the smashed front door, a smell like the sour breath of a beast wafting out from the darkness inside.

'We'll knock out the walls then,' I said, half crying. 'Make our own library.'

'Where?' asked Violet as we walked through the littered hallway.

'The empty shop next door.'

'Oh hush,' Violet said, amused. 'Hush your mouth.'

'Look at this.'

We stood in the Adult Fiction section, a sea of wreckage, broken glass, the desolation I would never be used to. The dark wooden panelling of the shelves still looked polished and intact, but littered all along the ledges were plastic coke bottles, idiot jumble, rats' nests: a display that reminded me of a Warhol painting, vacant offerings of the undead. The gracious room stood above the rubble, the morning light coming softly through its crafted, lovely transoms.

'Faith,' Violet called me, trying to comfort. 'There's a shelf left back here.'

I went over to look. The shelf was a little alcove at the back of the room, slightly hidden, and the books were stacked there in neat lines, waiting for deliverance. I picked one up and put it in the carton.

'Let's just take all of them and then we can weed out the trash after,' I said, starting to load more into the carton feverishly. 'We can come back if we want to.'

We worked for a while in nervous silence before my eye was caught by a shocking burst of colour exploding into the room, a froufrou of lace and sequins, scarlet chiffon, husky voices, menace. I stood up startled, dropping a book, and there they were, crowding in at the door on the other side of the room. Impossibly tall drag queens, their faces made-up eerily in swirls of colour, dyed dancing feathers in their hair, perfume drifting in hot waves, each of them holding a shining knife.

'What you doing, man?' one asked in a sleepy voice.

'Rescuing the books,' I said.

'Looting?' one of them suggested kindly. 'Taking what does not belong to you?'

Violet whispered to me very softly, 'Get the cartons and go out the back way.'

'What's that you say honey?' Their voices were languorous and silky, violence was trembling in the air.

'Books,' one of them said at the doorway. 'You poor little girls. You only want them for firewood. But we hafta teach you.'

Looking at them in terror, I saw that their eyes had no pupils at all, they were huge and milky and blank, terrifyingly blind. The queens were wafting together in some deadly sea of chemicals, they rocked back and forth in the currents, calling to each other, their voices drifting in an uneasy siren song. They were lost in a dream of violence and death and we were the victims floating in the undertow towards their swaying predatory dance.

'Save me,' I muttered at the sight, and in our panic we took off down the back alleys of the library and out into the light before they could even make a move towards us. We leaned against the fence briefly to get our breath back, shifting the cartons from one arm to another, but too frightened to put them down even for a minute. I imagined the queens inside, swaying, smiling at nothing, already in wait for another plaything.

We drove home fast, badly shaken. In the back seat the books had a musty unloved smell about them that overwhelmed me.

It was the first of many trips into the city. At first we worried about seeing the queens again, but as we became addicted to our dawn raids we were more daring, breaking into derelict schools, galleries, even private houses in our search. Afterwards we waited all day for customers, drinking, talking dreamily, staring out the window. The rescued books gradually spilled over into every corner, piling up everywhere, filling the room with voices, the musky ancient smell of generations of grace, until the shop reminded me of an archaic ship so laden with treasure it could barely stay afloat.

Spring came, the rain fell every day, and the baby peach trees in the backyard sent out buds like paper flowers. The city seemed to be holding its breath, waiting for something. In the mornings the air was smoky with night fires and the streets had the same terrible calm as a deserted battlefield after the dead have been spirited away under cover of night. Every day when I went outside to take down the shutters the place seemed stranger to me. Once when we were going into the city before dawn I even thought I saw animals like horses in the Domain, great white beasts galloping away into the darkness, but Violet said I must have been dreaming.

THE BLACK GARBANZO

Annamarie Jagose

Annamarie Jagose is currently living in
Wellington, New Zealand, where she is writ-
ing her PhD thesis on lesbian textuality at
Victoria University. She has published short
stories in *New Women's Fiction 3* and *The
Exploding Frangipani: Lesbian Writing from
Australia and New Zealand*, both published by
the New Women's Press.

THE BLACK GARBANZO

One night after dinner, Freyni's mother says to Freyni's father, 'Don't they speak fast?' Two weeks in the new country and the world has been unevenly cleaved in two: them and us. The larger group is constantly swirling past, confidently calling to each other over low fences and hedges in strangely inflected tongues, driving down their wide streets, proprietary pudding faces gleaming a little behind the glass, the husbands clumping self-consciously on each other's back lawns, charring unidentifiable cuts of meat on outdoor grills while the wives ferry the contents of their kitchens into the garden. The smaller group has never felt so small. They are two specks on an inhospitable rockface, roped together and inching upward, away from everything known and familiar that sprawls its dangerous invitation on the plains below.

One night after dinner Freyni's mother says to Freyni's father, 'Don't they speak fast?' Freyni's father thinks about the people at work. He calls them his 'colleagues', a label that is not reciprocal since to them he is always 'the Indian manager'. News of his appointment was retold in dozens of homes with the same frisson of respectable illicitness that accompanies the arrival of the Ringling Brothers Circus in the city. 'They're bringing in an Indian at our place.' They speak fast although not to him. He hears them in the corridor speaking an English unrelated to his own, which proceeds correctly, fastidiously even, in deference to the language's idiosyncrasies (too capricious to be called rules). As if they know a single word or phrase will never suffice, they speak furiously, like someone pitchforking hay, each bale being bound up interrogatively with a rising inflexion before being flung aside.

When they step into his office, however, something changes. The worn carpet at his threshold conceals a forcefield as elemental as magnetism, more insistent than gravity. Their step, their breathing and heartbeat, even the hands on their watches are affected. Their speech is slow. And loud. It is as if they think that the brown skin which encases Freyni's father also grows impermeably across his aural canals. A word is offered to Freyni's father on the end of a long-handled spoon and, after an awkward hesitation, scraped off his chin and offered again.

One night after dinner Freyni's mother says to Freyni's father, 'Don't they speak fast?' Freyni's father clears the table, scraping the leftover *kharoo bhejoo* into a blue-ringed bowl and rinsing the plates in the sink. He has heard but does not answer. Just below the surface of the tabletop a blunt head rears up. Freyni's ears are bubbles turning inward from the skin on both sides to the rear of her brain, skin folds and bulges of mucous membrane. Freyni hears but does not answer. As yet, her silent mouth opening gapes uselessly over her heart.

More shocking than the news of the Indian manager's appointment was the realisation that his wife was Irish. Coached along by Dave Burns' anthropological lectures of ex-Merchant Navy authority—'And if he's married, she'll be a little black lady in a bedsheet'—everyone had been quite prepared to endure, if not actually encourage, this exotic addition to the town's population. More than half of the town, however, could trace their ancestry back to Ireland and hackles rose and hearts hardened with the implications of this new information. No man invited Freyni's father to the pub for a quick drink and a bitch about their respective wives' shortcomings; no woman popped in on Freyni's mother with a plate of scones and a shrewd eye as to the value of the household furnishings.

'She's made her bed,' said Eileen Gradey, to a meeting of the Catholic Women's League. 'Now she can lie in it.'

The women blushed savagely and hurried their fevered imaginations home.

My father's people have a saying which accounts for every event in history: future, present, past. My mother's people have a similar saying. I have no such saying. My tongue lies curled up at the bottom of my mouth, a piece of schnitzel beaten too thin. Am I not my people's people? Here I stand on land damp from being fished out of the sea, on land whose truths are not mine, with no brave words to place between myself and lack.

Some years ago Freyni asked her father to translate his saying for her. The silence lengthened and lengthened until Freyni's father was a serpent's fang, a dark speck on a far horizon. Freyni refocused her eyes and waited. In a newly small voice, whittled away by distance, she heard her father say:

'Do you know the pipal tree?'

The people tree, the people tree. And there *is* something leafy, impossible to make out at this distance, growing behind her father's shoulder. Do you know the pipal tree? The trees Freyni knows are kauri, totara and matai; Maius dasyphylla, Taxus baccata and Larix russica; those monstrous iron-hearted myrtles and the cherry hung with snow. Freyni knows the date palm, the dwarf palm and the fan palm. She knows the red, the purple, the golden, the blue-green, the white, the violet willow; the hairy, the weeping, the shrubby birch. The pipal tree she does not know. She can only imagine the shade it offers, its roots dipping down to the centre of the earth, its trunk something solid to lean against while she stares further back to that place where her father's saying lies, innocent as an egg.

Freyni knows that her life is an advanced form of organic arithmetic. She sees the interconnectedness of things. Every new discovery or detection she makes is part of the calculative calisthenics that leads her inexorably to her destination. At some inestimably golden moment she will have solved every unknown variable, the double-barred gate of the equals sign will fly open and the entire equation will be in her possession. Then she too will have something small and valuable through which to explain the world. Or perhaps it is not that the equation is small (*Do I contradict myself? It is large, it contains multitudes*) but that like a reversed telescope it can shrink the present, past and future into a manageable, explicable figure. At times she thinks she has caught a peripheral glimpse of this equation of which her life — her daily movements, her decisions, her destiny — is only the diagrammatic representation.

Freyni is a university graduate, a fact her parents will squeeze into any conversation you care to have with them. A degree is something to be embarrassed about? they demand of her when she rolls her eyes in exasperation. Pray God this is the most embarrassing thing that ever happens to you. Freyni's degree is in English but her real interest lies in her extracurricular research into the politics of space. Postgraduate work in this area interests her but she can never decide what department to approach. Sociology? Anthropology? Physics?

If anyone asks what Freyni is doing these days Freyni's father says, 'She's working for a big company, big. Foreign paper products firm.' Freyni's father left India in the late 1950s when big and foreign were high-status adjectives. Freyni's mother adds, 'The creative side of things. She's her own boss.' Freyni's mother struck out on her own when she was eighteen, leaving Ireland and her small fishing community. In the company of Freyni's (not yet) father, she headed for the other side of the world. She values independence. Freyni's parents must have heard each other say these things a hundred times although neither of them is sure exactly what they mean. The only thing they've got to go on is what Freyni has told them. Freyni has told them what she tells everyone: 'I'm in research.'

Freyni is not always so lacking in specificity. At work she calculates the number of people in each room, the distance between each person's desk and the amount of space in cubic metres each can command. The lift in her building is able to carry sixteen persons or 1125 kilograms in accordance with the Boilers, Lifts and Cranes Act, 1950. She has seen a dozen secretaries get in that lift one day and the next, when three men from management stepped in, those same secretaries saw that the lift was full and waited in the lobby for the next one to arrive. Freyni's notebook is full of jottings: 1 m'ger = 4 sec's. If basic unit of space is 1 sq. m, then top m'gement = 20 u, asst m'gement = 6 u, sec's = 15 u, cleaners = 0 u. (This figure was later amended to .4 u when Freyni found the cleaners' tea room in the basement.)

Freyni's concept of the politics of space is constantly expanding. The discovery of the cleaners' tea room introduced the new dimension of height into her calculations. The managers' offices are on the seventeenth and eighteenth floors where their views of the harbour are unimpeded. Fifteen or so flights down, on the third floor, the secretaries' views are of other secretaries in the office across the road. The secretaries, she notices, wear tight skirts and high heels. The average length of their step, from back toe to front heel, is nineteen centimetres. The managers wear three-piece suits and shiny leather shoes. They cut the corridor into forty-four centimetre segments when they stride along. Freyni has no skirts, she only wears trousers. At home she practises doing the splits. Her current record is one hundred and sixty-five centimetres and she is always improving.

Freyni's work is not difficult to describe. ('My work is impossible to describe,' snaps Freyni. 'Let's just say I'm in research.') She has the sort of job that nobody believes anybody really does, like assembling light bulbs or designing tea towels, although it is neither of these. Her job is the sort of job that does not even have a name like fitter and turner, chef or home administrator but can only be defined by explaining what she does. Freyni compiles quotations for the company's numerous lines of appointment diaries and desk calendars.

She couldn't believe it was a real job either when it was first explained to her. The newspaper advertisement said *Graduate required for a key position which has become available in an energetic international company. Well developed knowledge of English language and literature essential.* Even her interviewer seemed overcome by the yawning gulf between the position advertised and the actual job offered. 'Language is a treasure chest,' he wheezed, teeth clinking inside his head like some foreign coinage. 'So valuable, such richness, don't you think?' Freyni agreed. In her mother's skirt, she was concentrating on keeping her knees together. She remembered his agitated proclamations on the wealth of the written word and the quotation's status as a market commodity but far more memorable was the way he rolled about in his chair, his breath hissing between his teeth. The interview was held on the fourth floor and, retrospectively, she recognised the symptoms of the bends.

Freyni's office is a windowless interior room, fluorescent lit. She has a desk, a bookshelf, two dictionaries and a thesaurus, a rubbish bin, seven volumes of collected quotations, a dead cyclamen and a headache. She spends the first three days of her employment looking through the company's old desk diaries while her heart sinks to some as yet unfathomed depth, more subterranean even than the basement tea room. She reads. March 22: *Discreet women have neither eyes nor ears.* July 10: *It takes two to make a quarrel.* December 7: *All colours will agree in the dark.*

Freyni was born in hospital on a Sunday afternoon. The night before, Freyni's mother sewed a medallion of the Virgin Mary and Infant Jesus to the inside of her nightgown and dosed herself with a medicinally measured twenty millilitres of holy water. The holy water came from Lourdes in a squeezy plastic bottle shaped like the Madonna with a removable screwtop head. After screwing the Madonna's head back on and replacing her in her carry case, Freyni's mother waited at the foot of the stairs to be driven to the hospital. If her case had burst open, as it was threatening to do, we could see strewn about the landing one nightgown (with medallion), one nightgown (plain), a recently witnessed Last Will and Testament, two wrapped sets of sandwiches, a notebook containing the names and addresses of her seven sisters now living in America, some moisturising cream, a photograph of her parents (framed), a string of Connemara rosary beads, a snapshot of her husband, an Our Lady of Eternal Succour holy water bottle, a brand new terry-cloth bathrobe, a couple of magazines, a razor and a first aid manual. In the event of an emergency, Freyni's mother was not relying on the medical staff.

Freyni's father would not have described himself as a religious man so he was surprised to find himself, with as practised a card hand as any devotee back home, setting out photographs of his wife and postcard-sized pictures of the bearded prophet in the spare bedroom. He lit several sticks of Mysore *agarbathi* and as he watched the columns of sandalwood smoke rise up to the ceiling he felt with a gentle tug the forgotten words of a prayer float up from some old memory like an easy fish on a line.

The most innocent, most public act of Freyni's mother is invested with a monstrous intimacy. There is something pornographic in her careful selection of two chops at the butcher's, her calm purchase of matching bedsheets and pillowcases in a sale. The moment the bulge that was to be Freyni became visible the pregnancy obsessed the town even while it feigned lack of concern. Dave Burns' stories circulate widely even among the children and soon everyone knows that over there a man would sell his sister for a couple of dollars. Everyone knows that once a month or so, Ron Fahey, the postman, delivers a parcel of strange-smelling foodstuffs sent down from Wellington. Everyone knows that over there when a man marries a girl he marries all her sisters as well, maybe her mother even.

Arriving early at work one morning, Freyni travels up in the lift with a cycle courier. He is wearing a baseball cap on backwards with the peak over his neck, a black T-shirt, black and neon green cycling shorts, red and black high-tops, unlaced. He carries a canvas bag. The reception area is empty and when Freyni realises that the whole floor is deserted she pokes her head back around the door.

'I can sign for you,' Freyni calls. The cycle courier is standing behind the reception desk, pulling a loose floral print dress over his shorts and T-shirt. He combs his blond hair with his fingers.

'Better get togged up before the boys arrive,' the courier says, kicking off her basketball boots and strapping on a pair of red stilettos. Freyni says nothing. She hurries to her office and writes up her first quotation for the day: *One's life is particularly one's own when one has invented it*—Djuna Barnes.

Her name is Alice and she tips Freyni's careful calculations into the fourth dimension. Alice applies her make-up before the rest of the staff arrive. She rouges her cheeks theatrically, gathers her mouth up in an elaborately pink *Love in Paris* cupid's bow, colours her eyebrows, raising one slightly higher than the other. There is something duplicitous about her, an edge of irony, that Freyni finds compelling. When the lift doors open the new temp secretary is already installed behind the reception desk, showing both rows of perfect teeth like a beauty pageant queen and vacuously answering the phones. Alice is a woman in drag.

At 4:17 pm, Freyni's mother is lying somewhere in the hospital on a bed with her feet up in stirrups. She has been in labour for six hours and is starting to mistake the clock's round face for her own. Her pale body is laid out beneath her like a wash cloth. An umbilical cord holds her a few inches short of the ceiling and she floats up there in the warm air, learning to swim. She sees her privacy carelessly displayed, hairless as a young girl, and observes as dispassionately the nurses' semicircular formation at the foot of the bed. They stand some distance from the bed, she thinks, as though afraid that through that smooth trapdoor may emerge some unknown beast, fanged or furred.

The heels of Alice's stilettos are never less than fifteen centimetres high. They end in a point so tiny every step threatens to go through the floor boards. The office carpet is pocked with indentations where she walks. Freyni makes some surreptitious calculations. Even allowing for the length of her shoe, Alice's average step is fifty-three centimetres long. Alice is an acrobat, a stilt-walker. Freyni is a woman in love.

There is a movement below. The nurses tighten ranks. A beautifully round head, dark with hair, appears between upraised thighs. On the baby's forehead a clot of black blood marks the position of the third eye.

'My black garbanzo,' thinks Freyni's mother. A second later the body follows, a girl's, slick as a tadpole and the colour of weak tea. She is perfect, unmarked as if hatched not born. The nurses are transfixed. The baby smiles.

'Wind,' say the nurses quickly and move in to gather her up, to clamp the cord, to examine the placenta. But not before Freyni (for her name is obvious from the start) fixes her impossible gaze on her mother flying overhead like a kite, their gazes lock and Freyni's mother feels herself being dragged down, spinning, like water down the plughole, back into the world, into her body, that tired glove. Freyni's mother feels empty, tired and empty, and her arms are light as helium balloons. They need a 7lb baby to weigh them down. She is up on one elbow, reaching out, but the nurses are all cool efficiency now as they move about briskly, reasserting themselves.

'Now, now dear. Baby has to be washed and weighed. It's a little girl. Perfectly healthy,' they say unnecessarily, more for themselves than for her. 'You just get some rest.'

Freyni begins coming early to work every morning. She asks Alice to lunch. Alice removes her make-up, throws her dress in a bag and they walk down the street to a café. Freyni becomes very aware of herself, the gap between her skin and where the rest of the wide world begins. Eating is beyond her. Alice has pumpkin soup and French bread, asparagus quiche, chocolate gateau, a black espresso. The inside of Freyni's head is as unfamiliar to her as the contents of a stranger's handbag. She briefly considers arranging herself appetisingly on Alice's tray.

'Been temping long?' Freyni asks desperately.

She is wondering how she can steer the conversation while not appearing to do so. Perhaps she should have asked Alice to dinner not lunch, somewhere quiet, just the two of them with hours to spare and a bottle of wine. She feels the twin spirals of her chromosomes unfurl as her body separates out into its constituent parts. Her mother looks across at Alice's broad face through her right eye, her father through her left. Her aunt, her father's sister, appears at her left shoulder. 'This must be his sister, nar?' she asks, reaching for her glasses. That grinding noise of enamel on gristle, like a dog with a bone, is Freyni's grandmother, her mother's mother, turning in her grave.

'Still I suit lots of places,' Alice is saying, pushing her quiche plate away from her. Freyni is confused. Alice holds out a few strands of her hair.

'Scandinavian,' she says by way of explanation, then seeing Freyni's blank look she adds, 'I go with all those white pine office fittings.' When Freyni returns to her office she spends the afternoon entering new figures in her notebook, reworking her former calculations.

Freyni's uncle is a movie maker in the worst possible sense of that word. That is, he orchestrates those filmic Indian extravaganzas which combine the worst excesses of the pantomime and the musical and whose monstrosity is only outweighed by their popularity. If he were directing this story, about now the narrative would be interrupted by a splice of film on which the lovers' images (here they eat together, here they dance in each other's arms at a friend's wedding, now they roll playfully down the slopes of a Kashmiri garden) are superimposed with the image of a calendar whose pages artfully turn, indicating the passage of time. If Freyni's uncle were directing this story, certain gender distinctions would also be introduced by way of a bushy moustache, a masterful gaze, perhaps a pilot's uniform.

Here, in the absence of any mechanised calendar, is Freyni in her back room processing appointment diary pages at the rate of forty per day. Alice comes in and hands her a piece of paper.

'What's this?' asks Freyni. It is a typed letter of resignation signed by Alice. 'You're leaving,' says Freyni, with a dullard's grasp of the obvious. Alice hands her another piece of paper.

'What's this?' asks Freyni. It is a typed letter of resignation awaiting her signature. 'I'm coming too!' squeals Freyni, signing her own name.

That night they have dinner with Freyni's parents. Their dark and light faces echo each other around the table.

'What will you do now?' says Freyni's mother, anxious that her daughter is becoming more and more difficult to describe. Freyni and Alice look at each other. They will travel around the country staying in out of the way bed and breakfasts. They will attend night school and retrain as journalists, as flame throwers, as heroes in their own stories. They will open a small soup and salad restaurant in the central city. They will leave this long white cloud behind and investigate their other locations on the world map. In short, they have no plans at all.

MATERIAL

Jan Hutchinson

Jan Hutchinson grew up on the southern
outskirts of Sydney but has lived most of her
adult life in the inner suburbs. When she
started writing fiction in 1985 it was as much
of a surprise to her as it was to anyone else.
Her work has since appeared in various
journals, magazines and anthologies including *Meanjin*, *New Woman* and *Fictions 88* as
well as more recently having been recorded
for ABC Radio's *Food Program*. In 1989 her
collection of short stories *Desire and Other
Domestic Problems* was published by McPhee
Gribble. For part of 1990 she was in residence
at the Literature Board of the Australia
Council's Writer's Studio in Venice, Italy.
Although she has worked at various jobs over
the years, since 1987 she has taught writing
part-time at the University of Technology,
Sydney. She is currently working on further
fiction.

MATERIAL

If you want to use any of this, he said to me, go right ahead. Just let me see it before you do anything with it. And whatever you do, don't use my real name.

We were down the coast and I was on his back. The next morning we'd be heading home. I was about to go away. He had to get back to work. And his course. We'd gone out for a walk, not so much for the exercise but for a final look round the place before we packed our bags ready to take off first thing. A huge, too yellow moon hung in the sky. We watched it come up out of the ocean, edge its way over the horizon and then appear to accelerate. Each night previous we'd stood on the little grassy slope out the back of the van, late, and looked at its craters through the binoculars, marvelling at how their colour matched that of the night sky. Tonight, however, we were relying on our own resources, though the capabilities of the human eye, as well as its failings, never cease to astound me.

I turned for another look. 'Sometimes,' I said to him, 'I could live here forever. Other times, I can't wait to get out of the place quick enough.'

He nodded, as if in agreement or at least understanding, but said, 'I'm staying put.'

We'd walked the long way, following the scenic route, a drive with a Hawaiian name. He'd been reading Joan Didion. I'd moved onto Judith Krantz. I was asking for it. At the top of the hill a group of boys clustered round a Kombi. I stumbled on the gravel in the gutter and came close to doing in my ankle.

'Recognise any of them?' X whistled under his breath.

'Nup,' I bit my lip. 'They're all the same in the dark.'

We stopped to admire the view. This was the highest spot in town.

43

If you could call it a town. It was one of those places where if you weren't into surfing or scenery or standing with a rod in your hands for hours on end then you were a goner.

I waited for Georgie to catch up, some instinct gnawing away at me. She was dawdling like a four-year-old, softly humming a tune that was familiar but that somehow I could not place. Her pace slowed further, creating even more than the obligatory distance between us that she'd set as soon as we'd arrived.

'Chip off the old block eh?' X glanced at me.

I didn't know whether to scowl or smile. I looked at him. This had been his idea in the first place. I said nothing. Ours is a funny sort of relationship. We don't fight. And we don't sleep together either.

We kept walking. As we rounded a bend, dark with banksias and mangrove, a curtainless window came into full view. A lamp was already on. Someone was getting ready for bed. Early. We watched him undress. He pulled the covers back and got in between the sheets. It was hard not to look. He adjusted the light and reached to pick up a book from a shelf on the far side. His back was the same colour as the moon. He leaned on the pillows momentarily, his hands linked under his head, and stretched.

'Should have brought the binoculars,' I said.

'I think I'm in love,' X sighed.

'Don't start that crap again,' I snapped.

'Tell you what,' he went on, 'I'll toss you for him.'

I shook my head. 'Nuh, he's not my type.'

Georgie caught up. And when I looked, she sang, her sudden self-consciousness giving her a hard time of it on the high notes, the moon had turned to gold.

Her phrasing was perfect. She turned to us. 'You two,' she said, in a speaking voice of unmistakeable tone, 'are disgusting. Haven't you anything better to do?'

'What else is there?' X hummed.

He suggested we cut across to the beach. I'd seen enough for one night too. When we reached the creek the tide was in. Loud white waves bucketed the shore. I knew this stretch from my daytime explorations and didn't fancy wading in invisible mud. I pleaded with him to carry me through, using my new sneakers as an excuse.

X held off. 'I wouldn't worry about those,' he said. 'You can pick up plenty when you're away.'

For not the first time that night I stared at him. 'People should hang on to what they've got,' I said.

'Go on then,' he said, bending over double from the waist. 'Before I change my mind.'

He looked like a kid playing leap frog. His Levis tightened across his buttocks. I held my breath.

He sat me down in the soft sand on the other side, beyond the line of washed-up blue-bottles that we could just make out. The hillocks of tough coastal grass inclined towards the barbed wire fence at the back of the beach. We could hear muffled shuffling sounds and stifled giggles coming from the shadows of the dunes. I sat down, trailed my fingers damp with salt and faint longing across my thighs. A mist was coming in. Things were fogging up.

'Sometimes,' I said, 'I think I'll feel like a teenager forever.'

He pulled me to my feet in one easy action and gave me a quick, awkward hug. 'Whereas I,' he hesitated, 'can't wait to start growing up.'

When we got back to the van something told me he'd been there before. I wondered why I hadn't picked up on it earlier. We'd passed Georgie near the entrance to the pathway. She hovered near the coastal stabilisation sign and seemed uneager to keep moving.

'I'm going to stay down here for a bit,' she'd said. 'Last chance I'll get. For a while.'

'I've heard that line before,' X had teased her.

I lent her my jacket. It was getting nippy. Sometimes he just couldn't help himself.

'Don't be too long,' I said.

Now we had the place to ourselves. I poured port into vegemite tumblers. It was all we had. Beggars can't be choosers. We'd said it often enough.

X grew sad. You know what men are like. 'To us,' he toasted. 'I won't forget these days.'

'Is that a threat or a promise?' I raised my glass.

'Neither,' he clinked. 'And both.'

They were mid-autumn days.

Days of standing on the shoreline up to our knees in salt water and casting out.

Days of getting tangled in green weed and conversation.

Days of forgetting and flirting.

Days of chancing the surf and finding it colder than either of us could remember.

Days of thinking that perhaps I should be staying at home and planting out bulbs. 'They're an investment,' X had said that day at the nursery. 'Like love they multiply.'

Days of thinking that since Mandela had been freed there might be hope.

Days of wondering about his wife and about long-term commitment.

And afternoons of walking, beach after beach, side by side, hands almost in each other's pockets.

Afternoons of padding over drenched rocks in old King Gees and faded singlets, trying not to slip on the hairy sea moss as we gazed into pink pools, into other worlds altogether.

Afternoons of cheap champagne and even cheaper shots at each other. We were getting closer.

Afternoons of Paula Abdul or the soundtrack to *Beaches*.

'Why is it that the music that reminds me most of you is disco?' I said one time.

'You didn't make that up,' he said.

'Yeah, I know,' I shot back at him. 'But I could have.'

One afternoon of wondering if things would ever really end. We argued about it for hours.

We never mentioned Steve. As if in not naming him we could obliterate his place in our lives as easily as a character from a book. Though that wasn't always so easy. We both knew what he'd come to signify. He'd done to X what he'd done to me and in the long run neither of us was willing to admit that was what had brought us together.

We'd woken one morning to teeming rain. It was early. The sun barely stood a chance. The pelting on the aluminium roof seemed a pretence at romance. I get toey these days when it's wet.

I tucked the curtains back into place. 'Sex or shopping weather,' I sighed.

Georgie rolled her eyes till the whites showed.

'Whatever happened to reading in bed?' she said.

'Let's go to the Bay,' X brightened.

He was at the stove, grilling the day-before's catch. We'd tried for salmon but landed trevally. I'd have fried them myself but X was keeping an eye on his heart.

It was tasty enough.

We went to the Bay. So did everyone else. 'Tourists in their own country,' X said.

'Yeah,' said Georgie. 'Just like us.'

I took X's arm.

In the big, new newsagents we looked at the latest glossies. It was hard to decide. X suggested *House and Garden*. I said *Follow Me*. We settled on smut. I paid for it. He knew he'd have to fight. Or bribe me. 'In any case,' he said, flipping through the last few pages, 'I think words open up more erotic spaces.'

At the cash register the assistant asked if my husband would like them in a bag. 'I'm not sure,' I said. 'I'll let you know when I get one.'

In the coffee shop at the end of the arcade we ordered strong cappuccinos. It seemed safe. We watched a woman order an entire meal, including dessert, for the man she was with. It was as if he didn't exist. He sat opposite her, the whole time barely paying attention.

'Isn't it amazing,' I said, leaning close to X's ear, 'how Australian women treat their husbands exactly like little children.'

I sucked froth from my spoon. 'She'll cut it up and start feeding him next.'

'Marriage is the same anywhere you look at it,' X said.

'I thought you wanted it.' I looked him straight in the eye.

'I do.'

I dangled a plastic bag before his eyes, changing the subject. 'I let them talk me into it,' I said. The shop was full of young things Georgie's age. And less.

The woman behind the counter said, 'They're not interested in how it looks or whether it fits. Only in the label.'

X reached across the table for it. I held on. 'Come on then,' he said, deepening his voice and shaking his hips slightly so that his shoulders moved, 'show us what you've got.'

It was then that I knew I'd miss him.

'Meet me somewhere,' I whispered. 'In the low season.'

But he couldn't be persuaded. 'That's your scene, not mine,' he said.

He called for the bill. I watched the waiter turn on his heel and head for the counter. On the back of his jeans was a label stitched in perfect symmetry across the centre seam. 'Closed,' it said.

X gave me a look I thought I recognised, a faint flicker in his eyes that I thought I'd seen someplace before.

I kicked him under the table. 'You're all the bloody same,' I said. 'Only interested in the one thing.'

He'd reduced me to cliches.

'And you,' he said, 'you're not? Don't you think we're covering the same territory? Aren't we in the same never-ending fucking story?'

He'd never raised his voice to me like that before.

'You wanna write a book about it?' I lowered my tone.

'That hurt,' he smiled. His lips twisted in the corners. 'Nuh,' he added, 'I've outgrown all that.'

On the way back up the highway he played his new tape. His speakers were fucked. His heads needed cleaning. I didn't say a word.

'You guys really like that stuff?' howled Georgie. 'I don't know,' her head moved from side to side. 'The older generation has no taste.'

She was listening to something else. She wanted to know if *Street of Love* was about cruising.

'At her age,' X muttered. 'What does she know?'

'Nearly everything,' I answered.

Georgie pulled her earphones out and pushed her pause button. 'Except,' she said, 'why would you want to fuck someone if you weren't in love with them?'

'Ask your mother,' X said. 'Mine,' he looked virtuous, 'would have washed my mouth out.'

'It's easier than answering questions,' I said.

'But not half as much fun,' Georgie grinned. 'You know, I always thought Steve was a bit of a poof.'

X nearly ran up the rear of the bloke in front. 'Plug yourself back in,' he choked.

'You're all the same,' said Georgie, changing her tape. 'No respect for the young.'

X straightened so he could see her in the mirror. 'Sweet Sixteen huh?'

'Do you ever see him?' I ventured, a bit further down the track.

We hadn't crossed that bridge before.

'No,' he said, 'do you?'

I shook my head.

We could have dropped him a line.

X grew quiet. 'The last I heard,' I picked up the thread again, 'he'd left the garbos and joined the Public Service. Some new section to do with cleaning up the shit on the beaches. They wanted people with hands on experience.'

'Bitch,' he said. 'You know, I could have loved him forever.'

We went up the next rise. 'So could have I.'

We came down the other side. The poplars along the gully were beginning to lose their leaves. A breeze had crept in.

'But he told me he wanted romance,' X said.

'Likewise.'

'As though you can sum it all up in one word. Could you come up with a single one for everything you want?'

I shook my head again. 'I could try,' I said, 'but I don't think so. Whichever way I look at it.'

'So where do we go from here?' he asked.

I clutched the map. The markings were blurred. I couldn't see the turn-off.

'Oh, for heavens sake,' said Georgie, 'this is starting to sound like *Gone with the Wind*.'

X looked interested. He swerved to avoid something dead in the middle of the road. There was a familiar light in his eyes. 'We could do a remake,' he said.

'Don't start that crap again,' said Georgie. 'Anyway, they've already done it.'

We ignored her. Even I knew about the sequel. X turned to me. 'How about it then, eh? We'd make a great team. Just you and me babe.'

'The public would never accept it,' I said. 'Not here or anywhere. They want old-fashioned values.'

X fell silent. 'When I get there I'll write,' I reassured him.

But I should have known I wasn't going to win him over with that one. He put the wipers on. Water squirted over the windscreen. Bird shit and insects smeared across the glass. I couldn't help myself. 'If you want to use any of this,' I said.

THE HARMONIC CONVERGENCE

Margaret Coombs

Margaret Coombs was brought to Sydney
from the country aged eight. She was
educated there then moved to London where
she finished an MA thesis and gave birth to
two daughters. With a grant from the Literature Board of the Australia Council she
began travelling with traditional circuses,
returned to Australia and worked as a publi-
cist and stage manager. In 1982–84 she was
involved in the setting up of the feminist
publishing co-operative, Redress Press. Two
further grants from the Literature Board have
helped enable her to complete two novels
(*Regards to the Czar* and *The Best Man for
This Sort of Thing*), stories which have appeared in a number of anthologies, and
various essays.

THE HARMONIC CONVERGENCE

August 16 marked the peak of the 'wave' of history that gave us civilisation—an event known as 'the Harmonic Convergence' which coincided with an alignment of the planets for the first time in 23 412 years.

The theory was that if enough people meditated, there would be a fundamental change in human consciousness...When this happens, the extraterrestrials will return to assist us and the world will be saved.

Sydney Morning Herald, 17.8.87

The trapped lightning of an electric heart
It's Sunday morning and you're bored. You should be working on your Futurism essay but you'd said weeks ago you'd go with Tom to his sister's 'family barbecue'—so that's what you're hanging around waiting to do.

Already you've spent an hour and a half putting on and then taking off various combinations of all the clothes you've got. What you want is: you want to look a way that will make Tom's family perceive you as 'artistic', 'a feminist', 'extraordinary', 'different from us'—but that at the same time will not make them think you 'arty-farty' or feel you're trying to put them down. It's not easy to find your balance on this sartorial tightwire and you've given up trying for a while. Now you're sitting in the old pink cane chair in the backyard reading—desultorily—a little book called *Cubism, Futurism and Constructivism* by J.M. Nash (Thames and Hudson, London, 1974).

51

You read this passage:

> More revealing even than the eleven points of the Manifesto is
> Marinetti's way of presenting them. He describes the events which
> led up to the moment of their proclamation. 'We had been up all
> night, my friends and I, under the Oriental lamps with their
> pierced copper domes starred like our souls — for from them too
> burst the trapped lightning of an electric heart . . . An immense
> pride swelled our chests because we felt ourselves alone at that
> hour, alert and upright like magnificent beacons and advance posts
> confronting the army of enemy stars staring down from their
> heavenly encampments. Alone with the stokers working before the
> infernal fires of the great ships; alone with the black phantoms that
> poke into the red-hot bellies of locomotives launched at mad
> speed; alone with the drunks reeling with their uncertain flapping
> of wings around city walls.
>
> This is very similar to the feeling of difference, of the artist's
> superiority, prevailing in nineteenth-century Romantic writing,
> typical of Edgar Allan Poe or Théophile Gautier. But, where
> Gautier uses similar images to present his account of smoking
> opium, Marinetti is using the ethic of Romanticism to attack
> Romantic values.

Sure he is! you think.

You think: *What wankers! 'Magnificent beacons'! Don't make you
puke, Boys!*

You think: *Of course stokers, 'black phantoms' and drunks are just
dandy, aren't they? As long as they know their place and don't feel free to
drop in and wipe their sooty feet on your ancestral Oriental rugs!*

Fed up with Marinetti and friends, you put the book down on the
garden table and go inside to change out of your worn-out Bloch's tap
shoes into your too-new $168 Doc Marten's boots.

*I am using the ethic of consumerism to attack consumerist values, the
ethic of woman as object to attack sexist values*, you say to yourself. It
sounds good. Maybe the Futurists *weren't* wankers.

The trouble is, your hair.

Last time you went to Lunatic Fringe, Sheryl hardly cut it. 'The
trend is towards longer hair,' she'd pronounced, and as you'd thought
at the time that the vanguard of the trend was what you were there to
be cut to fit, you'd agreed to 'just a trim'. On *you*, however, 'longer
hair' — especially when freshly trimmed — just looks *sweet*, like you'd

had it done at David Jones or somewhere. You look like Julie Anthony, for God's sake!

What you are tempted to do is to march into the bathroom and shave off your hair. That'd make everyone sit up! Inspired, you shove your discarded tap shoes into the bottom of the wardrobe and clump into the bathroom to stare at your head in the mirror. One theory you've read is that if you get the head right and the feet right, it doesn't matter much what goes on in between. With a shaved head and your steel-toe-capped Doc Marten's on, there's no way you're going to look like Julie Anthony!

But, when it comes to the point, you doubt your competence as a head-shaver.

Also, there's your commitment to not seeming pretentious to consider. Let's face it, bald heads on women do shriek 'LOOK AT ME! LOOK AT ME!' much more loudly than 'THINK ABOUT IT! THINK ABOUT IT!' A bald head would frighten Tom's family. It would not set them questioning the cultural construction of women as valuable only for their procreative capacity and/or as fetishised objects of desire. You don't believe they'd take one look at your baldness and think, 'Aha! Now I see! Fiona is a *desiring subject*, not a no-longer-desirable object!' You think they'd think, 'Christ, she looks ugly!'

Well, the truth is, you'd think you looked ugly with a shaved head. As you don't have the delicate features of the shaven-headed objects of desire in video clips, you'd think you looked freakish and pretentious, would slink around looking sheepish, defensive, self-conscious . . . It just wouldn't work. You're a wimp, you couldn't carry it off.

So, OK, you decide to forget the head-shaving. You decide you will 'go as you are', i.e. arbitrarily pronounce that, as an artwork, you are now complete. At this point, you are wearing the same old black Skin Deep skirt you always seem to end up wearing, and a Cherry Lane jumper from Grace Bros—well, at least it's black too—and, as I've said, your black Doc Marten's and your Julie Anthony hair. A bit of a cliché, all that black, but too bad. It'll have to do.

You take the bucket from the bathroom pedal bin and go out to the front of the house to empty it into the big grey-green garbage-on-wheels.

While you're busy disentangling yourself from sticky bits of the web that some enterprising spider had built between the rose bush and the gatepost, the woman next door (an immigrant from Vienna, aged eighty-three, kind but always ravenously hungry for 'drama') leans over the fence and asks you eagerly if there's been a death in the family. 'No, why?' you say, puzzled, alarmed. (There hasn't been, has there?) 'All that *black!*' she gasps, looking you up and down like you're some sort of loon.

Which means Tom's family, too, will fail to see quite the kind of statement you're making. 'Dowdy,' you suppose they'll think. 'Peculiar, isn't she?' 'Not very *feminine.*'

Well, isn't that the idea?

Yes, but you want to seem admirable as well. A *desiring subject*, not a *blob!*

Back inside, you look up Chris Weedon's *Feminist Practice and Poststructuralist Theory* to reassure yourself that you know what you're doing. 'Dress, for example,' she says, 'is open to many different readings. The effect intended by the wearer can never be guaranteed, but this does not negate the potential of dress as a site of conscious sexual-political struggle.'

You like that very much indeed. 'A site of conscious sexual-political struggle'. *See! I am subversive, not just a new sort of clothes-horse!*

'Are you ready to go yet, Fiona?' Tom calls out from the hall.

Introducing someone special

You set out with Tom in the van, a maroon Mitsubishi Starwagon, big and noisy, not conducive to chat even though the radio-cassette player's broken. Tom drives. He is picking up his elder brother, Michael, at The Old Ark Antique Market (Open 7 Days) in City Road on the way. You are not looking forward to seeing Michael. Michael bugs you. Michael's a misfit too, and so you feel he *ought* to be a kindred spirit—but he's *not*—which means you feel far more disappointed in him than in someone with whom you'd never expected any rapport. The trouble with Michael is (pot calling kettle black?) he's such a conformist! He's a person who's leapt at the chance to let himself be constructed according to a current Sydney stereotype—Darlinghurst gay—without even trying to question whose interests that serves. (*You come, you find a life, ready-made, you just have to slip it on.* Rilke.) It exasperates you that Michael sees his superficially eccentric lifestyle not as a spit in the eye of the whole heterosexist patriarchal capitalist culture but simply as a spit in the eye of one of its more obvious victims: his poofter-hating Granville working-class battler father who died, uncompensated, of asbestosis at sixty after a decade spent sawing up fibro in a factory to support a good Catholic family of seven. Michael himself gets on very well with the heterosexist patriarchal capitalist culture that so oppressed his unfortunate dad. He's discovered that, as far as the heterosexist patriarchal culture is concerned, most of the time you can be as gay as you like as long as you're a good enough *consumer*, as long as you *buy* enough *things*, as long as there's still enough *profit* to be made out of you. Though he doesn't, at present, own a car, he owns everything else he can get his hands on, including (he says) his own life.

Sure! It's the style-setters of Darlinghurst who own his life — or that's how it looks to you. He, however, regards you as the Lost Soul. He is frequently at you to buy into one of his 'self-realisation' courses; to be 'Totally Personally Transformed' and 'Own your Own Life' too; to acquire 'Insight'; to attend 'The Forum'. Indeed it's this nagging pestering that makes his company so uncongenial at times that you've come to dread seeing him at all! It's difficult and upsetting trying to convince someone who seems much more self-assured and at peace with himself than you are that you don't even want to become like that too — or anyway not at the price of your... er, vision. 'It's the *illusion* of controlling your own life these people are selling you, Michael,' you always say crossly. No you don't. I just wish you did, so I've got you saying it here.

As the van rounds the corner from Broadway into City Road, you prepare to defend yet again your refusal to be Totally Personally Transformed. You metaphorically gird your loins for battle.

'Le Must' If you want to be seen to be 'special' — This week's arcane knowledge
So it's disappointing when Michael fails to launch his usual attack. Today he has something even more important than your self-transformation on his mind: the transformation of the whole *universe*! He's bursting to shout at you, above the roar of the Starwagon's motor, that today is the day the Harmonic Convergence is scheduled to occur, tonight the night the world will begin to be saved.

You suspect Michael gets his ideologies from The Lunatic Fringe, along with his haircuts. (Of course you just get the haircuts.) Your impression is that while Sheryl snips, she tells Michael what set of beliefs the trend is towards this month — and if professing to believe in the Harmonic Convergence is what the trend is towards, then he'll cheerfully, uncritically profess to believe in it: he won't even pretend to have subjected it to any sort of critical scrutiny.

So, he says, 'Today is the day of the Harmonic Convergence' like you might say 'Musical underpants are the go this summer', and you can see that being 'in the know'—the proud proprietor of this latest piece of arcane knowledge—makes him feel (i) superior to, and (ii) 'a naughty boy' in the eyes of all run-of-the-mill, oppressed, obedient schmucks like you and Tom whom he sees as not daring to know about 'outrageous' things like this. There is a cheeky giggle in his voice. Like Bert Newton on daytime telly. Or Graham Kennedy at night. *Ooooh! Aren't I the wag you drab folks would never dare be!*

This irritates you something awful. You resent being pigeonholed with the dull and mindless by someone you see as too unthinking to see that it's precisely because you're *not* dull and mindless that you *don't* pretend to believe the sort of crap he pretends to believe.

You don't know what to say. Basically you would like to punch Michael.

'What?' you say.

'Today's the day of the Harmonic Convergence!' Michael repeats, still in that silly, giggly, guess-what, ooh-ah, bet-this'll-amaze-you-dags voice.

'Yeah, I saw a headline about it,' says Tom. 'On the front page of the *Sydney Morning Herald*.'

'Yeah, I saw it too,' you say boredly, yawning.

All three of you know, of course, that it's not the Harmonic Convergence you and Tom are refusing to find interesting; it's *Michael*. This is conversation as a competitive sport.

Michael, however, can't be knocked out that easily. Neither Tom nor you have actually *read* the article on the front page of the *Sydney Morning Herald*, he discovers. He informs you excitedly that this configuration of the planets occurs only once every 23 412 years.

'A-mazing! And how many minutes?' says Tom.

Michael regards Tom pityingly—as if thinking: *but what can you expect from a man with a ten-dollar haircut?* He doesn't dignify the interjection with a reply. Authoritative as a stereotypical academic, he announces that 'they' say that if you tune yourself into the energies and vibrations of the Harmonic Convergence, you will totally awaken your dream mind–body and help create the conditions essential for universal peace and harmony, and then the extraterrestrials will come back to help us.

56

'Extraterrestrials? Oh, goody!' you say.

'We're already here!' says Tom.

You ask a few questions, but there's a horrible patronising sneer in your voice all the time that distances you from your professions of interest and makes every word an act of aggression at least equal in force to any of Michael's. You say, well, Michael, if you Own Your Own Life, how come '*they*' tell you to tune yourself into the energies and vibrations of the Harmonic Convergence so that you may totally awaken your dream mind–body etc., and who are 'they', and what was their print run, and how many copies did they sell?

Michael pretends you are joking, and laughs. He elects not to waste any more time on you and Tom for now, not when it takes so much energy to shout above the noise of the Starwagon's engine. Evidently he's achieved his purpose, reassured himself that he's more 'special' than you are, more 'in the know', more attuned to what's 'hot'. He snuggles back into his seat and shuts his eyes.

You are still reluctant to accept this casting as 'not as special as Michael'. You have let yourself get thoroughly sucked into the game. In case Michael is not asleep, you make the effort to smile in Tom's direction a lot so Michael will be able to see how 'alive' your relationship is and how 'happy' you are despite not Owning Your Own Lives.

'Would you like me to drive for a while?' you say 'considerately' to Tom.

'No, no, I prefer to have control,' Tom says.

Manners of being

Time and kilometres pass. You tell Tom a story to demonstrate to yourself and Michael what an interesting and vivacious companion to Tom you are. Michael won't be able to hear the story, but (if he opens his eyes) he will see you 'chatting animatedly' to Tom, and that's what counts. The story you tell is one you were told at a Fine Arts Department function the week before, by a woman who worked for the Bicentennial Authority. One of the Bicentennial projects, she'd said, was to provide funds for the building of a community hall for the Aboriginal people of Blayney (was it Blayney?) who wanted it so they'd have somewhere to hold their debuts, twenty-first birthday parties and weddings. Although there is already a community hall in Blayney, the Whites, she'd said, refuse to let it to the Aborigines *even for debuts, twenty-first birthday parties and weddings*. Now, thanks to the Bicentennial Authority, the Aboriginal population will have a hall of its own in which to indulge in all these highly subversive activities. How about that!

You report to Tom that you'd said to the woman from the Bicentennial Authority: I hope these Aborigines don't *really* want it for debuts, twenty-first birthdays and weddings. I hope they're just telling you that. She'd said, 'Well, I know how you feel, but I think they really do want it for debuts, twenty-first birthday parties and weddings — and if that's what they want, who are we to say they shouldn't have it?'

You say you'd said at the time you weren't absolutely sure, and you're still not.

Tom says, 'For God's sake, Fiona! If the Blayney Aborigines *want* a hall in which to celebrate debuts, twenty-first birthday parties and weddings, you should be glad the fucking Bicentennial Authority's providing it.' He says it's the Aborigines' own business what they want. He says anyway the point about weddings, debuts and twenty-first birthday parties is that at least they get people together in a good mood, they 'foster camaraderie'. It's a start.

Michael, if he were involved in the conversation, would be sure to agree that it should be entirely up to the Blayney Aborigines to choose their Bicentennial gift but not in quite the same spirit of goodwill as Tom. Michael does not view subjectivity as a construct. Michael believes that 'the individual' is responsible for himself entirely, and that if people want ovens into which to shove their heads, that's their business. It wouldn't occur to him to ask what he or others or the world might have done to help drive them to this 'desire'. If pressed, Michael would be prepared to maintain that the Blayney Aborigines *chose* to let their traditional culture be undermined, *chose* to start wanting to replace it with what you, anyway, see as the 'worst' of White culture, and are lucky if some Whites, in 'reparation', choose to provide them with the means to get it. But then if pressed, Michael's prepared to maintain that his father *chose* to die of asbestosis at sixty, *chose* to work sawing fibro, *chose* to believe he had to support his wife and five children — which, of course, he *chose* to have. Further, Michael regards (for instance) the starving in Ethiopia as somehow *choosing* this fate, and 'not my problem'. Even when he thinks about it, he feels no anxiety about spending his money on musical underpants rather than, say, famine relief.

Oh well. Who are you to sneer? What have you ever done for the starving Ethiopians? Or the Aborigines of Blayney, for that matter. And at least Michael can't be accused of being 'paternalistic' or 'patronising' or 'invalidating' or 'over-earnest' or 'a puritan spoilsport'. At least he—how do people self-righteously phrase it?—'has the grace to acknowledge one's own individual responsibility to/for oneself'.

'Yeah, you're right I guess,' you say to Tom. 'It's the Blayney Aborigines' own business what happens to them. Except that's what Michael'd say about the starving Ethiopians too. *And* about your father!'

'That's different,' says Tom irritably.

'Is it?' you say.

End of conversation. You drive most of the rest of the way in silence. You think about Foucault and his faith in *manners of being* as forces for changing the world. You think of him writing a book called *The Care of the Self* and then dying of AIDS.

Lei Lines

You pass the house at Stanwell Tops where Tom says Lionel Lindsay used to live. Lucky Lionel Lindsay. Michael 'wakes up'. He starts lecturing you and Tom about 'lei lines' which, he explains, are the equivalents of Earthly acupuncture points and therefore good places to tune into 'planetary vibrations'. The cliff where the hang gliders take off at Stanwell Tops is an Earthly acupuncture point, he says. He informs you and Tom that there's going to be a ceremony there tonight, but that he himself is going back to Sydney to the similar ceremony at Bronte Beach, another Earthly acupuncture point. You ask why not stay here and go to the ceremony at Stanwell Tops, which seems to you much more beautiful and 'unspoilt' than Bronte Beach. He says because people he knows will be at the one at Bronte Beach.

The answer seems unsatisfactory. If tonight is going to bring about a fundamental change in human consciousness and universal peace and harmony, who will need to be with 'people they know'? Is this a party or is it serious?

'It's a party, for God's sake,' Tom says. (Who's side is he on?) 'It's like the Blayney debuts and weddings, Fiona. It's a chance for people to get together and have a good time. It all . . ."fosters goodwill".'

'With emphasis on the Foster's,' you say.

'I won't even groan,' Michael says. 'If you don't want to understand, Fiona, that's your problem.'

Tom says, 'I mean, it's not as if they're Nuremberg rallies, Fiona! They don't do any harm.'

You sigh. Because you think they *do* do harm. OK, they're not Nuremberg rallies but you think they're still doing their bit to reinforce bullshit and help to isolate and silence the people who don't believe the bullshit. You want to ask: where's the party on for the Blayney Aboriginal people who think debuts, twenty-firsts and weddings are a threat to everything they value? Where's the party on for the people who think all that 'Harmonic Convergence' stuff is a load of crap? And anyhow, *why* are Whites so busily involved in constructing a parody of an outmoded (?) version of Aboriginal traditional culture (large gatherings at sacred sites), and Aborigines so busy constructing a parody of an outmoded (?) version of White traditional culture (debuts, twenty-first birthday parties and weddings)?

'So where's the party for people who think all this "Harmonic Convergence" stuff is a load of crap?' you say.

'Well, why don't you give one?' says Michael primly and smugly. 'You're quite free to organise one if you want to.'

That shuts you up.

Parachute-jumping
At Stanwell Park, you find that Tom's sister Theresa's new house really is '*on* the beach'. It has the sort of view and location that you couldn't get for millions of dollars in other parts of the world. Nev's father is a Wollongong real estate agent who bought the place decades age, before Stanwell Park was anything more than a coal-miners' settlement, but still you're astonished to find yourself amidst such environmental luxury. You're also astonished to find that Tom's family are not astonished by it. They take all this glory for granted like it's air! Which suggests to you that even if we all do go to Heaven and there are cherubim, seraphim, holy virgins with golden harps etc., it won't transform our consciousnesses — not as effectively as a can of Foster's does, anyway. It reminds you of how people (you) can sit reading the *Daily Mirror* on Sydney Harbour ferries, ignoring the view.

Still, here you do all at least congregate on the verandah and cast the occasional glance at the billowing blue waves breaking along the hundreds of metres of sparsely-populated sand between the headlands.

'Did you know that today is the day of the Harmonic Convergence,' announces Michael.

'Here we go!' you say with a groan in your voice.

'Yep, Happy Harmonica!' says Tom.

Undeterred, Michael begins 'The Harmonic Convergence Story' all over again. You raise your eyes heavenwards. Tom starts to play with his sister's dog. 'Sit! Sit!' Tom keeps saying as Michael twitters on self-importantly about lei lines and vibrations. He moves on to Aztec prophecies and galactic energies. 'Shit! Shit!' Tom says, but you're the only one who laughs.

You watch the occasional hang-glider take off from the massive headland on your left and land on the sand right beside the house. Icarus inevitably springs to your mind. Breugel's painting thereof. Auden's poem about. But there's nobody here you can say that to.

'They make it look easy, those guys, don't they?' you say to the wind.

In a louder voice, you ask Nev — the guy who lives here — if *he's* ever tried hang-gliding. No, he says, but he's tried parachute-jumping; he and a group of his mates. He says it was terrifying and he wouldn't do it again even though the experience had left him high for hours afterwards. 'Too bloody risky,' he says. You quite like down-to-earth Nev.

As far as you know, there are only three other people you've met who've been parachute-jumping. Two of them run the wine bar in Balmain where your best friend, Lulu, a writer, works as a cook. This wine bar is notorious for being where drug deals are negotiated. The couple who run it (Lulu says) take cocaine 'all the time'. Cocaine isn't enough for them, however, they also go parachute-jumping every weekend. (Who else could afford to?) 'Addicted to their own endorphins,' says Lulu knowledgeably.

The other person you know who's been parachute-jumping — but only once — is your former husband's brother's former wife. She's another Owner of Her Own Life, and went parachute-jumping as part of an 'Insight' course. The idea was, her ex-husband told you, that you were persuaded in advance, 'brainwashed' was the word he'd used, to believe that if you could do a parachute-jump, then you could do anything. Then you did the parachute-jump and felt euphoric for hours afterwards — 'reinforced' — and took that to mean you could 'do anything', Own Your Own Life.

For your former husband's brother's former wife, it seems to have worked. She now owns a thriving Strand Arcade clothing shop and the sweated-migrant-labour-based 'design business' that supplies it.

You, however, it would not work for. If you went parachute-jumping and lived, you would believe that you'd been capable of jumping out of a plane with a parachute on. Once. Full stop. Nothing more.

'Have you been parachute-jumping?' you ask Michael.

'I don't need to,' he says in a voice that you hear as shockingly smug.

'I can eat fire,' you say brightly. Your two-bob's-worth.

But they already know. They're bored with you and your famous 'fire-eating'.

'Not much point in having a skill if you don't use it,' says Michael.

You feel crushed. You don't think to say, Use it for *what?* You assume he means 'to make money', 'get on', 'show off', compete and win.

The Scandinavian-looking wine flask

You drink a lot of wine from a strange glass jug on the table on this patio where you are all assembled. Inside the jug is a funnel filled with ice to keep the wine cool. The funnel is sealed with a teak lid. It is very Scandinavian-looking but 'Made in Taiwan', you notice. Otherwise it's exactly the sort of thing you used to long to grow up to own. There was a shop at Double Bay called Scandinavia House that used to stock items like this, only made in Scandinavia, and to you they symbolised the Perfect Life. That was a long time ago. You'd never actually go out and buy a Scandinavian-looking wine-jug complete with ice funnel, though you're interested in theirs. The ice looks as if it is suffocating.

Mavis, Tom's mother, and Nora, from Nowra—one of his sisters —start talking about what they call their 'charity cases'. Nora's 'charity case' is an ex-student of hers (she's a high school music teacher) who wants to be a ballerina and pretends to imagine this ambition can be achieved in Nowra. She calls herself Alicia Glenbrook, visits Nora wearing her tutu and converses in a posh accent that bears no resemblance at all to the broad Australian accent she had when she was Glenda Box at school.

Poor woman. You feel sorry for her. (Would Foucault have approved of her for 'creating herself as a work of art'?)

Tom's mother's 'charity case' is a woman called Mrs Cooper-Clarke who rings up but doesn't say anything. So that the only way Tom's mother *knows* it's Mrs Cooper-Clarke is by the silence on the other end when she answers the phone.

'What do you say?' you ask.

'Oh, I just chatter on for a while, then I say goodbye for now, and then I hang up,' says Mavis.

Christ!

'This ice looks as if it is suffocating,' you say.

Spineless Wonders of the World

You start leafing through a coffee table book you find a coffee table on your way back from the toilet. It's called *Spineless Wonders of the World*. 'Am I in it?' you say to Nev. Nev, the down-to-earth once-off parachute-jumper, is a roof-tiler who's a skin-diver in his spare time. He's the sort who makes you feel like Norm-the-Non-Participant in the 'Life, Be In It' ads. He shows you a photograph of a bluebottle, saying it's one of the best photos in the book. You stare at it dumbfounded, not knowing how to respond. 'It's certainly... detailed,' you say.

Then you proceed to study the volume as intently as if invertebrates were your special subject and this your first chance to peruse the definitive text. 'A creature which is both negatively phototactic (moving away from light) and negatively geotactic (moving against gravity) presumably swims towards the surface in darkness,' you read 'but in daytime moves down to the level where its responses to light and gravity are in balance, moving upwards or downwards as illumination changes.'

The metaphorical possibilites of the passage enchant you.

'This is fascinating!' you say to Nev.

Negatively phototactic Tom moves towards you.

'Soooo-per!' he says. 'Faaaabulous!'

Arvie/barbie

'I'm starving,' you say.

'Why don't you throw a few prawns on the barbie, Nev,' says Tom.

They always say 'barbie', Tom's family, instead of 'barbecue'. Also 'arvie' instead of 'arvo'. (Let's call the whole thing off.) Seriously, though, it's amazing how much it gets on your nerves when Tom and his family start talking of 'arvies' and 'barbies', reminding you how much he's 'one of us' and you're not.

By the time lunch is served, it's bloody four o'clock! (You, Tom and Michael have been there, hungry, since quarter to one.) Lunch is steak, 'snags', shaslick, fried onions, assorted salads. Lavish. (The prawns were an entrée.) You can't stop eating. The food, the manner of its cooking, the time it is served, the language in which it is spoken of—they all help to remind you of what an outsider you are. You're a pasta-at-Il-Rugantino-at-dinnertime woman yourself. You don't know the rules of barbies. You're petrified of seeming aloof and yet at the same time hurt at being ostracised.

Games on the beach

After lunch, Mavis and Theresa wash up ('No, no, there isn't room in the kitchen for more than two!') while everyone troops down to the other end of the beach to play touch football. *They* play touch football. Michael and you agree to 'watch'. It's not that you're not good at sport (though you're not), it's that you're not 'good sports'. You just don't have the knack of enjoying running around on the sand and not minding being duds. You'd rather not be involved at all.

You stand around for ages pretending to be an interested spectator while Michael pretends to doze on the sand.

Eventually, lonely, emboldened by alcohol, you saunter over to Michael, seeking to chat. He and you have a lot in common, after all. You both get your hair cut by Sheryl at Lunatic Fringe. You're both (it follows) growing your hair.

'I see Sheryl's bullied you into growing your hair too,' you say matily to Michael.

But Michael doesn't want a mate. He just wants to *win*. He wants to make sure you know he is closer to Sheryl and her dubious glamour than you are.

'Did you know Sheryl's pregnant?' he says, as delighted with himself for being the first with the latest as he was when he delivered the news of the Harmonic Convergence.

What should you say? Pregnant! Oh what fun! Like going blond. Or getting a flat-top. Or musical underpants. Or the transformation of the universe. Or extraterrestrials coming to help us. Or.

'Yes, I did know that. Poor Sheryl,' you say.

'She's delighted!' Michael says reproachfully.

'Yeah, sure,' you say. 'Christ, Michael! That's about as realistic as being "delighted" to be... growing up gay in Granville in the 1960s!' *Or an Aborigine living in a small NSW country town.* 'I mean, motherhood oughta be fun, but it ain't all that much fun, not in this "patriarchal society"!'

'But everybody adores mothers and babies,' says Michael. 'Look at all the ads!'

'Everybody adores people with money to spend,' you say.

'They don't have gays in the TV ads,' he says. 'Not *as* gays.'

'Shall we call a halt to the game while the score's one-all?' you hear Nora call out. 'Then there won't be any fights.'

Smutty bit

Back on the patio, Mavis, Tom's mother, is serving tea and coffee. There is a lamington sponge birthday cake for Nora's eldest daughter, Siobhan. Tom tells everyone it's also your birthday next week, so everyone kindly pretends the cake is meant for you too.

Siobhan and you blow out the candles together.

Then you spill your mug of coffee all over *Spineless Wonders of the World.*

'You could see that coming,' a voice says in your head.

Mavis, Tom's mother, tells you all about her new neighbour. She tells this story deadpan: 'Her name's Mrs Clamp. She's very nice. She even offered me her husband's services.' Everyone sniggers on cue. 'No, really, she said that! She said, "if ever the water's leaking in the middle of the night, don't hesitate to get him over. He's very handy with his tools".'

A helicopter buzzes past, noisy as the blimp and almost as slow.

Constructing the archive

At this point, the camera comes out. Michael wants to take photographs. It's strange, there he is — gay, partnerless, childless — and yet he's the one who, on occasions like this, is always desperate to take snaps carefully arranged to reinforce all the most traditional myths about how things *ought* to be. Why is he, of all of you, the most eager to reassure the future that nuclear families consisting of heterosexual married couples with kiddies are 'happy' and 'normal', and that 'family functions' are a barrel of fun?

65

None of you dare to ask. You all obediently pose in the lounge room as One Big Happy Family Group. You snuggle up to each other, clown a bit, smile to order. He shoots. *Bang! You're dead!*

But even then he isn't satisfied: the middle sister's youngest child, Sean, is asleep in the bedroom, not available to be included in the shot. Michael wants to wake him up. The recording of him as 'part of the contented group' is of course more important than his being content.

Sean's mother, however, vetoes this proposal. Michael may Own His Own Life, but he doesn't after all own the life of his middle sister's child. (Who does? Who should?)

This hitch in the proceedings is enraging to Michael. He sulks. How dare one of the cast not be made available when the director wants them! It's clear that, in his view, the absence of the middle sister's youngest child is like the absence of one volume from a new set of encyclopaedias: knowing what's missing severely devalues what he does have. (On gala occasions, weddings and Christenings, *your presence* in the picture spoils it, too! He actually asks you to withdraw from camera range if you're not quick enough to get out of the way unasked. He points out that you are not *real family*. Tom and you are not married. You are a stray volume that doesn't belong with the set.)

Not surprisingly, you feel there is something dreadfully wrong with the spirit in which Micheal takes his photographs. You feel he takes them so he can have the fun of being in control, so he can be the one who decides for once who 'belongs'. He pretends he's 'capturing the spirit of the occasion' but what you think he's doing is falsifying the records. You've concluded that he constructs these visual fantasies so he'll have something to look at later that'll make him able to think: *how could anyone who belongs with a jolly gang like that be lonely, isolated, outcast?* That'll make him able to persuade himself that life's just hunky-dory in the best of all possible worlds when it's bloody-well not. You feel that this activity, 'happy snap construction', isn't as 'harmless' and 'trivial' as some people think.

It seems to you the world is full of people like Michael, collaborators in their own oppression, busy persuading themselves they're delighted with things as they are when *you* feel they ought to be out there loudly questioning the perfection of the status quo. You know you're often one of them. You sit in the corner and drink more wine and wonder why.

The extraordinary line in the sky
'Look at the sky!' Tom calls out excitedly from the verandah.

Everyone makes for the verandah again. Wow! The sky is suddenly quite extraordinary. It is divided vertically into a carnation-pink half and a slate-grey-blue half, the boundary between the two contrasting sheets of colour as straight and definite as a vertical horizon. You have never seen anything like this before. It's awesome! You seriously wonder: is the end of the world at hand? Certainly your scepticism regarding the Harmonic Convergence abates: so this is what happens when all the planets line up for the first time in 23 412 years! The spectacle forces you into a thrilling awareness of human powerlessness and insignificance in the scheme of things and you helplessly await... What? Scenes from a Bernardo Bertolucci Apocalypse? Anyway surely something massively exciting is about to happen! You feel as high as a parachute-jumper. So does Tom.

Most of the others, however, ooh and aah about the sky as fatuously as they would ooh and aah over a phenomenon as common-place, though beautiful, as a full moon. They think it's 'very nice', that's all. ('Yawn. There goes Icarus. But let's get on with the ploughing.' Worse, 'Yawn. The world is about to end. But in the meantime, we might as well go on with the ploughing.') Fatalism rules OK. They seem not that impressed.

Whereas Michael, you feel, actively refuses to be impressed. Despite his claimed interest in the Harmonic Convergence, he's determined not to be interested in the staggering sight of the divided sky. You guess it's no use to him in his unremitting quest for power. He didn't spot it first. He seems to sees it as something that belongs to Tom, and therefore something he must pretend is worthless!

'East is East, and West is West, and never the twain shall meet,' says Tom's mother with a giggle.

You all laugh.

You try to remember a comment of Guy Debord's — 'The spectacle is not a collection of images, but a social relation among people, mediated by images' — but you can't.

The party breaks up
Then Michael, who feels he Owns His Own Life and anyone else's he happens to need, says to Tom it's time to go now, he wants to get back to Sydney because he has to be at Bronte Beach by 8pm. Your scepticism regarding the Harmonic Convergence returns, hitting like

67

a bag of cement hurled from a truck. Thud. 'Isn't it detrimental to harmony,' you say, 'to break up this harmonious group to rush back to attend a mere mass rally?'

But, as Michael probably knows, you and Tom don't want to stay any longer and you guess nobody's too sorry to see you go. In fact the ones remaining'll probably be glad to see the end of all three of you: it's some sort of genuine harmony you'll be leaving behind. You're the three disrupters of harmony.

Going home
Michael sleeps in the back all the way. You and Tom don't speak. The engine roars, or whatever it is that Starwagon engines do. You think.

You think: *Poor me! I would like to conduct my social life amongst people like Marinetti and Poe and Gautier, but I don't know them; they won't have me; they're dead. Instead I am forced to conduct my social life amongst people like Michael and Mavis and Nev.*

Then you think: *Oh Christ! Who do I think I am? I would have loathed Marinetti and Poe and Gautier. And Michael and Mavis and Nev are OK.*

Or anyway Mavis and Nev. They're kind and 'decent', just unsatisfactory company for you because... well, basically because you're unsatisfactory company for them! You don't share their preoccupations, do you? And they certainly don't share yours. Also, you feel they find you as intimidating in some ways as you, in some ways, find them.

Then you think: *Who does share my preoccupations?*

Most of the people you know who do seem, at first glance, to share your preoccupations strike you, when examined more closely, as competitive, pretentious, power-hungry shits whose overriding preoccupation is with trying to feel superior to other people and using you, one way or another, to help them achieve this state of bliss. Playing power 'games' with varieties of Michael is certainly no more fun than being bored and boring, threatened and threatening in the company of Mavises and Nevs! It's interesting friends who feel safe with you, whom you can trust, that you want.

Oh well. Count your blessings. At least there's Lulu. And at least there's Tom. Most of the time you love/feel loved by both of them. And trust them. And find them interesting. Two intimates isn't a lot, however. It would be nice, you think, to have more. Why is it people (you) are so much quicker to compete than to love?

'Will there be a fundamental change in everybody's consciousness tonight, do you think?' you say to Tom, 'or do you think you have to be at a rally at a sacred site to benefit from all this?'

Tom snorts.

The Harmonic Convergence

At home, tired, you and Tom flop down on the lounge and watch the first hour of *Call Me Genius* (Tony Hancock) on TV. You love it, especially after a gutfull of Futurists and an afternoon *en* Tom's *famille*. 'Tony Hancock — *c'est moi!*' you say. 'Talk about "the trapped lightning of an electric heart"!'

You can't seem to find *Cubism, Futurism and Constructivism* so you take the Dressmart thermal clothing catalogue to bed to read.

Dear Friend [it begins],

Spring is the season when the world stirs with the joy of awakening from winter, when all Nature seems to dress for the occasion.

'This is better than Marinetti,' you say to Tom. You read that bit aloud to him. You go on reading aloud in a 'Marinetti' voice:

Be someone's dream in lace-trimmed party pyjamas, entertain in sophisticated comfort in the Resort Patio Suit, or simply feel good all over in the flattering, floral Wrap Jacket. You'll feel poised, and in control, day and night.

Complete Satisfaction — or Your Money Back!

You and Tom giggle over that for a while. Then you clown around and make love and fall asleep.

Next morning, you wake to find no fundamental change in your consciousness, and (as far as you know) the extraterrestrials have not yet returned to help you.

You discover the cat has pissed on *Cubism, Futurism and Constructivism*, which you'd left out on the garden table all night. You relegate it to the garbage bin.

After you've scrubbed all remembrance of cat's piss off your hands, you sit down in the old pink cane chair in the backyard and skim through the paper Tom's bought to see what it says about the Harmonic Convergence.

It says that yesterday was the anniversary of Elvis Presley's death.

Somewhere else, it says yesterday was the anniversary of Buddha's birth.

There's a photo essay on the all-night party at Bronte Beach. ('Is that Michael? Yep, I think it is, you know!')

There isn't a word about the Line in the Sky.

WEDNESDAYS

Shonagh Koea

Shonagh Koea was the winner of the Air New Zealand Short Story Competition in 1981 and was awarded the 1989 Additional Writing Bursary by the Queen Elizabeth II Arts Council. She is represented in most recent anthologies of New Zealand fiction. A collection of stories, The *Woman Who Never Went Home*, appeared in 1987 and her novel, *The Grandiflora Tree*, was published in 1989. She lives in Auckland and works full-time as a freelance writer.

WEDNESDAYS

'I've married Yvonne,' he said, shouting to her from her little sitting room that was exquisitely Lilliputian even down to the Victorian children's tea sets she collected and displayed in a narrow vitrine. She was making tea in the kitchen—he liked to have a cup of tea when he arrived on Wednesdays—and came slowly through the narrow hall.

'I beg your pardon?'

'I married Yvonne,' he said. 'Last Saturday. Very quietly.' She did not speak. 'Only her mother and father were there.' Her reflection in the gloomy old mirror on the opposite wall looked much the same as usual, she thought. She had not turned to basalt, or died standing up, nothing like that. So she stepped forward and shook his hand while he laughed at her.

'May I congratulate you, then?' she said, solemn and erect as a little scholar and went back to the kitchen for the tea tray.

'Tôle,' she said when she brought it in. 'Quite a nice piece of Tôleware. I don't often get nice trays in at the shop. I brought it home.' She eyed the tray for want of anything better to do, then, somehow blinded, began to pour the tea.

'I must say you've taken it very calmly,' he said. 'I must say you've taken it well, my flower.'

'I never rock the boat. You told me years ago not to rock your boat. I'll have to go and get the milk. I've forgotten the milk jug.' In the kitchen, with the stove toad-like in a corner for company, she shouted, 'But you've rocked mine often enough.'

'Talking of boats,' he said when she returned, 'I'll have to sell the boat. Yvonne doesn't like boats.'

'Presumably,' she said, 'she likes bishops. I wondered why you told me you'd been to see the bishop. I thought you were joking.'

'Yes. I remember — you laughed.' And she had, she thought. She had doubled up laughing. That had been three or four Wednesdays ago. He always came to see her on a Wednesday.

'I'm going to see the bishop, petal,' he had said and she said, 'What? You? Going to see the bishop? Has the bishop sent for you because you're so wicked?' She twined one long pale leg round his stocky tanned left calf and whacked him with a lace pillow.

'So the bishop must have been there when you got married to Yvonne? Last Saturday? There must have been you and Yvonne and her mother and father and the bishop, this bishop you mention?'

'And just a few others.' He sipped his tea. 'It was quite small. We just had a very few family friends and her sisters came over from Sydney with their husbands and children and there were a few other relatives and the bridesmaids and her colleagues and all my directors and a few chums from the yacht club.'

The yacht club, she thought. Ah, the yacht club.

He had a little sloop and sometimes on Saturdays he took her sailing. He took on a jaunty air on the boat, seemed laconically confident, and his eyes, faded to the palest blue from glaucoma and executive stress, suddenly looked like those of an accomplished seafarer who coped with the great waterways of the world.

'You can look after the ropes, flower,' he used to say but it was only a kindly brand of politeness, just a seagoing courtesy. She knew nothing about sailing. In the course of the day, though, out sailing on the harbour she made tea and sat neatly in the corner she had allocated for herself, walked carefully so she did not rock his boat in any way at all.

'You're a good girl, flower,' he used to say when she boiled the kettle, brewed up in the late afternoon. 'A very good girl, my flower.'

'Yes, I'm a good girl,' she said as she grew older, and older. 'I don't rock your boat.'

She used to sit, in her little corner of the sloop, and watch the day go by and half the world as well, or so it seemed. Families bucketed past in little mortgaged yachts while the father held the tiller and the mother held the baby and a little boy or girl might be jumping up and down on that debt-ridden deck with a teddybear under one arm, red sunhat atop the head. Over the years she watched the children grow up, the teddybears fall into the water, the fading of all the sunhats and her own evolvement from being a plump and pretty girl to a sleek beauty, not young, who read biographies of the Duchess of Windsor.

'Was that nice, flower?' he would say as he moored the boat in the farthest corner of the marina. He never took her to the clubhouse. She noticed that. Never. Not in seventeen years had he ever taken her to the clubhouse but he always came on Wednesdays to see her and sometimes he took her yachting on a Saturday in the summer. So those weeks it was Wednesday and Saturday.

'He's just someone I know,' she said vaguely to her friends in the beginning, when she first knew him. 'He's just someone I met once in an art gallery. He just comes to see me on Wednesdays. We have a cup of tea. I tell him about the auctions.' She was an antique dealer and he collected Sévres so the link was there. They had a lot in common. Her friends said that but he never did, and she noted that as well.

'When are you two going to get married?' her friends used to say, years ago. 'When are you going to introduce us? When are we going to meet him?'

'It isn't like that.' Always, she fended them off.

'But what does he look like?'

'Oh . . .' and she had to think then, 'not like anything. He's just a neat sort of man. I mean, he's always very tidy. Probably,' she said, 'you wouldn't even notice him.' But she knew they would because they must have read about his meteoric rise on the finance pages of the newspapers.

'*We've seen him.*' How triumphant they were that day, her two old school friends. 'We saw him on television last night, on the news. We rang each other straight away.'

'Show me the pictures of the children.' They were usually easily diverted. 'Tell me about the farm. Tell me about Harry getting the prize for Southdowns at the show.'

They laughed then, rather embarrassed, and she had to persuade them to get the photographs out.

'But you lead such an interesting life, with your friend and everything. You don't want to see all this?'

'I do. I think it sounds lovely. I think you all look lovely. I want to see. Show me.' She envied them and they never knew.

'*We've seen him.*' They were so pleased, radiating hope and congratulation in the doorway of her shop. 'We both rang each other up and all we got was an engaged signal.' And they fell about, in her chic little shop in one of the better suburbs, laughing so much she thought the chandelier might fall down on to the very fine Heraz she was displaying on the only available piece of floor. There had just been a huge consignment of large furniture from England and the place was jammed tight. They sat on a chaise longue, waiting for her to close the shop for lunch, and she saw clearly that the gleam of old Waterford and the sheen on the silver had blinded them to the actual fact that the place was as empty as her own hopes. They sat, like two plump ducks, on the little sofa and waited for her while she fobbed them off again.

'Seen him? Oh yes, well you probably would. He's often on those things where they're talking about shares and companies and what have you. Are you coming? Don't you want any lunch?'

So they trundled along beside her, ripe and plump as big birds in the shooting season. They had all been brought up on farms at the back of beyond, had gone to boarding school together. She had been the naughty girl, nearly expelled for going into the nearest town on the bus, completely naked under her school raincoat. It had been a dare. Betty had been the head prefect, Wanda the tennis champion. They still, she could tell, saw life in terms of the country.

'How lovely,' they would say, 'to be in a shop all day.'

She thought of everything as a harvest.

'Oh it was lovely,' she would tell him after a day out on the harbour. 'Such a yield of loveliness out there on all that glimmering water.'

He saw things in nautical terms.

'Now, my flower,' he said the first year she knew him, 'Now, don't rock my boat will you, my lily?' They lay, with her pale limbs entwined with his, one of her white hands on his tanned arm. He had a little P Class yacht then, before he made all the money.

'Of course not. I'm not a boat rocker.' So she never told him she loved him or that she was glad to see him (on Wednesdays) or that she was always afraid Wednesday would come without a ring on her doorbell. Never told him any of that.

'You're a good girl, flower.' Sometimes he said that.

'Yes. I never rock the boat,' she used to say and was careful not to do so. Even when they were out sailing she walked with meticulous care.

'It's my birthday next Thursday,' she might say to him some years, as a test, waited for his reply. But Wednesday was his day and he

76

always said, 'I must remember, then, to wish you a happy birthday next Wednesday, my lily, ready for your big day.'

The little brass clock, newly mended, chimed four from the mantelpiece.

'I've had the clock fixed,' she said. 'More tea?' He never ate anything. 'I suppose you got the usual one million chiming clocks for wedding presents, did you? You didn't? How lucky. What good management. I suppose you wouldn't like a biscuit?' He was on a low-caffeine, no-alcohol, high protein, low-cholesterol diet, had been for years and years of Wednesdays.

How many Wednesdays? she thought and drew her little calculator forth from the drawer of her desk.

'I've just thought of something,' she said. 'You'll have to excuse me for a moment. I want to work out something.'

'Profit and loss, flower?'

'Something like that.' They often talked about business, just in a general way.

The total came to 884, plus Saturdays on the boat.

'How many times would you have taken me out on the boat?'

'What was that, flower?' He had wandered over to the rosewood card table and picked up a plate.

'I'd forgotten about that,' she said. 'I brought that home from the shop for you. I thought you might like it.' It was Sévres, a nice armorial piece, plain but lovely.

'I'll go out to the car and get my glasses.' He always wore jeweller's glasses to consider the finer pieces.

'What was that you were saying about going out on the boat?' He had returned and, glasses firmly clapped to his eyes, now examined the piece of porcelain.

'I just wondered how many times I'd gone out with you on the boat. I've worked out that seventeen years' of Wednesdays comes to 884. With the days I've spent out on the boat I estimate I've spent, possibly, two and a half years with you.' He continued to look at the plate. 'But not consecutively,' she said.

'How much did you have on it?' The Sèvres seemed to have his complete attention.

'Oh sweetheart,' she always used to say, 'have it, have it.' She liked to give him things from her shop. 'I can't be bothered about all that. Keep it, sweetheart.' And she would cuff him fondly on the chin.

'I'll have to look it up in my stock book,' she said now. 'Have a look at the clock while you're waiting. There's a new man in that complex down town. He mends old clocks. He's got it to chime for me. I'm very pleased,' she said and sat down at her desk again to consult her records of buying and selling while outside the cicadas screamed because she was not able to. Far away a siren wailed. 'I was very pleased,' she said, envied that screaming and wailing outside her pretty windows. Two and a half years, she thought, of Wednesdays and some Saturdays.

'I seem to have paid rather a high price for it.' She picked up her black pen, poised its fine nib over the entry. 'I wonder why I did that?' She carefully wrote a figure one in front of the price. 'I couldn't let it go for less than twelve hundred.'

'God,' he said. 'That's a bit stiff, isn't it? I'd have thought two.'

'I entirely agree with you. Sèvres seems to be on the up and up. It's getting rarer with every passing minute.' She waited. 'I'm terribly sorry—I can't give it to you. I'm so sorry. Two hundred isn't realistic, under the circumstances.'

'It doesn't matter, flower. You've given me lots of things. The coat of arms,' he said, 'is not elaborate.' He put the plate down. He had a reputation for being tough in negotiations.

'That's what makes it so fine. It is,' she said, 'so discreet.' So had she.

'Do you think I should take it, flower?'

'I do.'

'But it isn't an unusual shape.'

'It's condition is superb.'

'Shall I write you out a cheque, flower?'

'Yes,' she said. 'That would be fine.' She watched him do so while outside the cicadas screamed louder than ever but the siren had died.

'Yvonne's mother and father must have been pleased,' she said as he signed his name, 'that you fronted up at last and married her. How long have you lived with her?' Then she answered herself. 'Centuries,' she said. 'You've lived with Yvonne for centuries.'

'But you're still my flower.' He placed one insidious arm round her waist and tried to waltz her between the secretaire and a gilded chair.

'There isn't any music.' She stood completely still. 'And you can't dance with me. You'd better take your plate and go home. To Yvonne.'

'Don't be silly, flower. It's Wednesday. I never go home on Wednesdays till midnight. I'm never expected home on Wednesdays till late. Everything's still the same, flower. We'll still have our Wednesdays. Don't get all old-fashioned on me now. Don't make a fuss.'

'Don't rock your boat. No, I won't do that, but it's all different. It's quite different being a bit on the side of a bit on the side to being a married man's girlfriend. It's quite different.'

'That's a very old-fashioned way of looking at it.'

'You forget,' she said, 'I deal in antiques. A lot of my stock is Victorian and so, obviously, are my ideas.' A small chair, hand-painted with roses, held her lightly and kindly — its silk cushions had been stuffed with feathers from the breasts of dead geese. The carriage clock struck a quarter hour, the sound of the quavery chime like the noise a heart turned to china would make if struck with a small bone.

'You mean I can't come to see you any more?'

'I don't think you can. It's all different now. You're mixing sentiment with expediency,' she said, 'and someone will get crushed.' The silence lengthened. 'It will,' she said, 'be me.'

'Flower.'

'Go away.'

'But flower—'

'It's all different.' She persisted with that idea. 'You've married Yvonne. Everything in the world has to be paid for. You wanted the plate. You paid for it. You wanted to be married to Yvonne. You paid for her,' she said, 'with me. It's not always money.'

'That's archaic.'

'I deal in things that are archaic.' She waited. 'I've got a sixteenth-century table in the middle of my window at the shop right now.'

'I see.' He sat down very slowly on the sofa that matched her chair, perched there like a huge human bee amid the rosy trellis. The painter had stencilled the flowers with a naively enthusiastic but romantic hand. 'If you had a price—' he put one hand on the arm of the sofa, seemed about to stand up again. 'Is this safe for me to sit on? Will I break it?'

'I don't care if it breaks into a million pieces. I don't care if the house catches fire and I burn with it. I don't care,' she said.

'I'm sure you would, flower, if it really happened.' The sound of her own coughing shivered in her ears again. 'Flower, if you were to put a price on yourself, if you had a price, if your roses were to be priced—'

'My roses have gone into seclusion.' She watched her own reflection in that murky mirror again while she buttoned her shirt to the neck, turned the collar up.

'But if they were to be priced, how much would they be?'

'You'll come to a bad end, my girl,' the old headmistress had said all those years ago, regarded her with distaste as she shivered on the mat, naked except for her school coat. 'A good name is above rubies in price.' She thought of it now, in that lovely little room, while the chime of half past five trembled in her ears.

'There you are.' The figures she scribbled on a scrap of paper looked like haunted eyes, there were so many noughts.

'God,' he said again. 'That's a bit of a poser, isn't it?'

'Isn't it enough? Is it too cheap?' She snatched the shred and added another nought.

'This is terrible, petal.'

'It's just business. You paid for having me by not marrying Yvonne. Now you have to pay for Yvonne by not having me, or you have to buy me in a separate commercial transaction. It's very simple.' She coughed again, a dry sound. 'As a matter of lack of interest,' she said, 'how many bridesmaids were there?'

He mumbled something.

'What was that? I didn't hear you.'

'Eight,' he said. 'Eight, eight, eight. There were eight bridesmaids. Is there anything more you want to know?'

'What did they wear?'

'Pink satin. With sweetheart necklines and panniered skirts. Matching shoes. Dyed the same colour at Stone's.'

'At Stone's. Well, well, well,' she said. He spoke as if he had listened carefully to all the arrangements over a long period, had committed them to memory, had them off by heart. 'Eight bridesmaids,' she said. 'In pink satin. It sounds as if it was very official. There couldn't be any mistake about it, if there were eight bridesmaids. In pink satin. And a bishop.'

'They went a bit overboard,' he said, 'the parents.' She coughed again like somebody who had become suddenly and inexplicably ill. 'He's a judge. She's their only daughter. They wanted to do it all properly. They were keen on the idea.' She waited. 'The grandfather was a judge too. He's a dear old chap. I get on well with him.'

'My grandfather was a horse dealer,' she said, sad as a lost sixpence. 'We're a family of traders. We always traded,' she said, 'in horse flesh.'

'What shall I do about this?' He waved the piece of paper. 'What will I do, flower?'

'Perhaps it might be better if you went? Do you think?' She did not watch the departure, did not stand in the frills of her chintz curtains to wave goodbye as she always did.

When the clock fluttered six, like a sparrow dying on the mantelpiece, the doorbell rang but she remained curled up on the floor with one of the feather cushions held as some might embrace a small child for comfort. The light in the room held a curious aqueous translucency, filtered through festoons of indigo double ruffles like the mark of a distant and brilliant sun far above the floor of the ocean. I am drowning, she thought. I have drowned.

'Flower?' He had come round to the French doors, must have waded through spills of blood-red geraniums that splashed the side path. 'What are you doing on the floor, my lily? Lillian, answer me. Lily, are you dead?' Very slowly she licked the tip of her right index finger and placed it on the toe of one of his shoes, amidst the day's dust. The mark remained there, clear as a fullstop or a decimal point after dollars. 'Lily? My lily? Will you take a cheque?'

KENU

Wendy Pond

Wendy Pond grew up in the swampland of
the Waikato, and learned to swim in Lake
Karapiro. Leaving her cousins to carry on
farming, she embraced the arts of the Austro-
nesian seafarers and began an enquiry into
the affairs of their descendants. Reports of
her scientific investigations are circulated
through her short stories.

KENU

Tevita Maka keeps watch through the morning dark. At intervals he uses the compass to fix a star in the ship's stays. Rigel is ensnared in Orion above the three stars of Māui's carrying-stick.

Prostrate bodies stir with the light, dreams despoiled by the heat of the ship's engines and soot from the funnel.

Against the mast a young man stands unshielded in the tropical sun. The youth stands still through the heat of the day. His wrists are lashed together at his groin, his shoulders bound to the mast.

'Stowaway. *Faka'ofa*, pitiable.' The crew carry on work in the galley, peeling yams and taro.

By mid afternoon, a volcano has risen from the sea fished up by Tevita Maka, navigator of the *'Otu Fetu'u*. Small waves scale the backs of the running swell as the vessel is swept towards the windward shore.

Now low atolls appear across the foot of the volcano. The southern swell runs onto the yellow reefs. The crew can discern no human presence on the white sand beaches footing the coconut plantations.

Rising and falling, born on the swell, the vessel clears the windward reefs and continues on its course to Pagopago.

Siaki Tali and Sione Moli, coming down to the lagoon shore during a night of kava-drinking at Mele's place, watch the lights of the fishing rafts along the reef. The wind is from the sou'east, bringing a low swell in from the back of the land.

They share a cigarette, sitting on the log under the futu tree. During the afternoon women passing with brooms have swept the leaves from the sand.

The two youths part company for the night.

'Mohe ā!'

'Mohe ā!'

In the dry grass along the foreshore the crickets are calling, *lingo-lingo, lingo-lingo*.

The tide is on the way out. A spring refills the coral pools with fresh water. From Mele's house on the lagoon shore a child is sent out onto the reef to fill the water bottles. Inland, women carry water from the well in galvanised buckets.

Grey herons follow the edge of the retreating tide, picking up sprats in the shallowing pools.

Mele has gone down to the fish fence on the low tide flats taking her kenu, a basket trap constructed from a lattice of coconut ribs. She wades out to the barricade where coconut fronds are held weighted down with coral rocks. She stands at the outlet with her kenu, waiting for the fish that retreat before the outgoing tide. With a quick jerk she lifts the basket out of the water, trapping the fish before it can see the end of the enclosing funnel.

In the cool morning air the blossoms of the poison-fruited futu rest open on the swept sand, delicate and perfect before wilting in the heat.

A chorus of shell trumpets sounds from the back of the village. Songo and his work-team are diverting domestic life with a call to work on the village fence. The young trumpet players blow in chorus, orchestrating the different tones of each shell.

Until last century the families of Fatutui had lived in fenced gardens dispersed through the bush. Then they were relocated in a village formed round their churches and school. They fence the communal yam garden with skilful walls of interlaced saplings, but since the break-up into nuclear households few families have had the labour to fence their own bush allotments. The contradiction of household pigs getting into other people's gardens has plagued the people of Fatutui for a century.

At first the Government Representative gave orders for each pig-owner to build a fenced sty beside his house, within the village boundaries. The householders obliged and then let their pigs loose to forage in the bush. Now the order has been given for each householder to contribute a thirty-dollar roll of barbed wire, and labour to construct a fence around the entire village.

Siaki Tali strolls along the lagoon front swinging his bush knife and joins Sione Moli in a cigarette on the log. He grins at the sound of the call to work. The outcome is foreseeable. Since the pigs are in the habit of going to the bush and his countrymen are not in the habit of shutting gates . . .

Sione slices at the log in a silent and desultory gesture.

'Our chiefs do the thinking for us,' he says. 'You lead the way.'

The first work-day had been for the men only. The young men walked along the coast to a bush allotment on the foreshore and cut down hardwood trees, while the old men prepared the food. The owner of the allotment wanted his land cleared for a coconut plantation, and gave the wood for the posts in return. At kava last night the plan had been to load the posts on a barge and float them along the coast opposite the village. Men and women would carry the posts ashore from the barge.

Tauvaka calculates the distance across the low-tide flats from Mele's cookhouse on the seafront to the line of coral rocks marking her fish trap. How far out will they take the fence to stop the pigs rounding it at low water? He wears a ragged work-mat round his waist tied with plaited sennit. The overlapping end hangs down in a triangular point, like the clew of a sail, marking the seafaring traditions of his forefathers.

'Too much influence coming from the landward side of the village,' he mutters to his brother, Limuloa. Limuloa hoists a post onto his shoulder and strides inshore, singing the opening line of an old rowing chant. Tauaka joins in after the first phrase, and other men take up the wry refrain.

Want to fight? Then go aboard
Set sail for Nukulei! Put up a fight!
Scratch like cocks and leave our land
Alone, abandoned by its warriors.

Tauka sings recalling the leadership that came from prowess and far sight. Looking shoreward he sees the landing where his father hung his nets, usurped by the copra store, the wireless operator's shack and the shipping agent's new block house.

Lusiane works in a pair with the shipping agent's wife, Caroline, carrying a post between their shoulders. The young men and women are wearing necklaces of sweet-smelling flowers.

'It hides the smell of the sea,' Lusiane tells Caroline.

In the course of the morning someone has the idea of stripping bark off the hibiscus trees, tying a strand round their log as a halter, and floating the log along behind them in the water.

The change of technique brings new energy into the enterprise. The young people laugh and shriek, exchanging remarks as if they have travelled from different parts and have news to recount. The event becomes a carnival. The purposelessness of the fence is forgotten. The cooks turn to preparing baked pork and yams and packets of breadfruit pudding in caramel sauce.

The village officer announces that a kava club will be held after dark. The money will be used to buy wire on behalf of those households who have not met their obligation. The workers go home to rest and groom themselves for the evening.

Rectangles of yellow light fall onto the coral pebbles outside the new catholic clubhouse. Inside, kerosine lanterns have been hung from wire hooks in the rafters and workday mats of unbleached pandanus spread over the concrete floor. Groups are forming round each eligible girl, who sits crosslegged with an enamel basin of prepared kava between her knees. Members of the group take it in turns to pay twenty cents to have the bowl refilled.

Siaki looks in through the window, keeping his head hidden amongst the young boys who gape through the louvres at the kava drinkers. When he comes in through the doorway he is ready to slip into Lusiane's group without any hesitation of choice that could betray his plans for the evening. He tucks up his vala and claps his hands with a commanding percussion. Lusiane picks up an empty cup, fills it halfway with kava, and passes it to the drinker beside her. The cup is handed down the line. No direct glance passes between Lusiane and Siaki.

Siaki throws back his head and drinks his portion in one breath. He twirls the cup back across the centre of the circle and sits with his head bowed as if absorbed in the effects of the kava. He is recalling the view of Lusiane through the louvres: her hair newly braided in a single thick plait, the freshly made necklace of flowers. Her bare arms gleam with scented oil. He can distinguish her particular perfume in the medley of tobacco, kava and oiled bodies.

The group around Lusiane begins to sing a favourite love song.

When the sun sets, thoughts of you arise
And I recall the path where we walked
Picking gardenia flowers for your hair.

The singers take different parts, some of the young men adopting a high falsetto, a wheedling plea to the woman of their heart. Talking stops as the song resonates in the still air.

A rival group puts up ten cents to stop the singing. Lusiane's followers promptly pay out twenty cents for the right to continue, and begin another song.

Oh peak of Nukulei, how I long again
To see terns tumbling in the up-draughts
Pigeons flying to their favourite berry tree.

The older drinkers in the kava circle know that the pigeon berry is a metaphor for some woman courted by the composer. They recount episodes from the composer's life and speculate on actions which might give a clue to his meanderings.

Siaki passes round his tin of tobacco which he has received from the shipping agent in exchange for a basket of taro. Each man takes a modestly small portion and rolls himself a cigarette. As Mini Kafa reaches into his shirt pocket for a cigarette paper an amount of tobacco falls unseen from the palm of his hand.

A new group has purchased a basin of kava and formed a circle of its own. They put up twenty cents to buy Lusiane to serve their kava. She keeps her head lowered modestly but manages to communicate a triumphant arch of eyebrow to Siaki as she bends forward to straighten her vala.

The drinker nearest the bowl takes over as server for Siaki's group. There is a prize of a suckling pig to be won by the group which buys the most kava.

Lusiane serves kava to her new group of suitors. One-eyed Songo is sitting beside her. He takes a cigarette out of his shirt pocket, having a good look inside to indicate to his fellow drinkers that this is the only one he has left. He smokes the cigarette until he gets asked for it by his older cousin.

Outside the clubhouse people are sitting on the coral paving watching the lights of the fishing rafts along the reef. They are waiting to claim their share of the haul as the fishermen come ashore.

Songo joins those taking an adjournment in the night air. He pulls a cigarette out of his back pocket and discovers to his chagrin that it is the only one he has left. He hasn't a cigarette to offer anyone else, so he just smokes his own.

Lusiane's elder sister arrives to replace her. This outwits the young men who have sat through the night to be last in her company.

At mid-morning a policeman from the government headquarters in Hihifo cycles over to Fatutui village, coming by the main road along the lagoon shore. The white sand road is mottled with shade from the coconut palms. The policeman finds the village deserted, except for the Australian shipping agent and his wife who are sitting under a sun umbrella on the grassy foreshore.

It is 'Aho Niu, 'Coconut Day', a mandatory day of work in the coconut plantations whether one is a land-owner or not. The government representative closes down the wireless office, the government store and the copra store. From 8 am onwards the villages become deserted. The people walk away, ostensibly inland to their bush allotments.

The policeman returns along the coast road. Had he only continued through the village, following the inland road through the open gate in the village fence, he would have found the bush allotments deserted and as silent as the village. Had he then returned curiously and continued up the coast, he would have found the seaward allotments thronging with householders picnicking. The children coming home from school at one o'clock head straight for the seashore in time for the opening of the ovens. So people cope with the alien authority of the government: not a word of protest. Their own chiefs are wilier: when they need people's labour they kill a pig and feed the workers before the task begins. Whoever has eaten is obliged to lend a hand.

There is a craze on the island for flying kites. Kites are called 'frigates'. The frigate birds soar over the island ahead of storms, crooking their wide-spanning wings to reduce speed. The kites have coconut rib frames and skins made from the fibrous spathe of the coconut frond. The owner of a kite runs along the road to get it airborne, a stream of children chasing after the tail. The children use reels of cotton for their kite strings. Their kites soar away over the palm trees into the blue sky, until the cotton breaks.

It is full moon. On the uninhabited windward shore land crabs leave the plantations and crawl down to the sea to lay their eggs. People from Fatutui come across the island to wait on the beach, for that moment when the moon believes it glimpses its own image, appearing on the eastern horizon as the sun sets in the west. Lusiane lies in a hollow of the sand watching the red sun set into the sea. The waves in the sun's path are capped with blood. The sea turns black.

Lusiane yearns for Siaki. Today he went to Nukulei to help his uncle clear land. She said goodbye to him at the end of the wharf, her cotton vala wet from swimming in the lagoon, her long hair unloosed from its plait. One-eyed Songo followed them out to the end of the wharf on his bicycle.

'Looking for fish, Songo?' Lusiane had asked.

Lusiane's brother had prepared a basket of cooked food, with a roasted fowl. Her sisters brought it down to the wharf and gave it to Siaki's uncle when he came alongside in his open boat. Siaki stood sheepishly on the wharf looking like a lover who had just got out of bed, transmuting his nature into meekness and compliance. His uncle had accepted the basket of food with repeated thanks as if honoured by an unexpected offering. The food was passed from hand to hand and eaten on the voyage home without ceremony.

At moonrise the tide is full in. At midnight the moon will be overhead and the tide full out. The moon's path of gold light will shine across the lagoon flats, straight to Nukulei.

In this hot land the trees flower all the year round. Each morning flowers of the poison-fruited futu lie like waterlilies on the lagoon sand.

Sly Songo leans his bicycle against the futu tree and falls into conversation with the shipping agent's wife.

'Poor Lusiane. Siaki doesn't really want to marry her.'

'I should think it is Lusiane who doesn't want to marry that wild-haired mongrel,' Caroline says.

'The Nukulei boys have rumours about the Fatutui women,' says Songo coyly. 'Mosquitoes.'

'Mosquitoes?'

'They say the women of Fatutui keep their legs covered because they are swollen with elephantiasis.'

'Lusiane is the most beautiful young woman in the village,' retorts Caroline. 'As for that Siaki, I have seen the Nukulei men in silhouette on the wharf. They walk with a jig with their knees bent, as if they are still carrying a load on their back down the mountain-side.'

It is Sunday morning. Caroline is seated on the coconut log which bars the pigs from crossing the doorway, legs astride a bowl, skirt pulled up over her thighs. She is the only housewife in the village who hangs out washing on a Sunday.

Along comes Mini Kafa, lean-limbed like other fishermen of the village. He has brought a snail shell with a double turret.

'It's very interesting,' says Caroline, 'but collecting shellfish is not part of my work any longer.'

'Have it anyway' says Mini, tossing the shell onto the floor of the tent. Caroline does not like talking to Mini with her legs astride. She calls to the shipping agent. He comes out of the house.

'Anything I can do for you?'

'No thanks,' says Mini. He sits under the futu tree. Caroline goes on with the washing. After a while she looks across at Mini with a wry smile and says, 'What's up, Mini?'

'Just watching the cloud-cover on Nukulei.'

Mini's come for something, thinks Caroline. Tobacco probably. I'm supposed to feel obliged now he's brought me the shell. Since Mini has discerned my need, I'm supposed to discern his. I should give him some cigarettes so he doesn't have the embarrassment of asking and I don't have the embarrassment of saying no. After a while, Mini casually wanders off.

'I thought,' the agent says, 'if Mini asks for tobacco I'd say I'd just given away my last packet and I was miserable to think of him drinking kava after church without any tobacco to share around, but there was nothing I could do to help. Then he would have left with a sense of my good will towards him.'

'I'd rather be frank.'

'Humourless you mean.'

'We'd both rather have given him a cigarette.' Caroline says defensively. 'But we've scared of being caught by everyone coming and asking.'

It is full moon again. The last glow of orange fades in the west. Instantly an immense red ball shines through the black coconut palms. The full moon rises and pales. Bands of silver light are cast across the village between the black shadows of the palms. Figures run through the shafts of light. Then the village is silent.

A voice calls out, 'Give me a whistle, you bush-birds.' Falsetto squeaks come from different parts of the shadows. A figure runs through the trees, another runs out of a house, and soon there are figures all round the village criss-crossing in and out of the black shadows, giggling and calling out to each other. The whole village, adults and children, is playing hide-and-seek in the full moon.

The shipping agent makes an expedition to the volcano, Nukulei. There is no sheltering lagoon and no flat land for settlement. The open boat comes in over the coral shelf. The travellers leap out to haul it ashore on the waves. The people of Nukulei show the agent 'Ivory-Rock' which they use as a landmark for the boat landing. The rock is large and black, composed of gnarled conglomerate. On the way up the cliff face to the village, they show the agent 'Horse-Track-Path' which descends vertically to the beach below. The island everywhere is too steep for horses. Loads are carried by men and women on shoulder-sticks. The party crosses to the northern coast and continues along the beach. Coming round the eastern headland it encounters three gigantic, volcanic pedestals in the sand.

The agent's companions explain to him that the first two outcrops are the burdens Māui carried fore and aft on his shoulder stick and deposited hastily at Nukulei when the sun rose. The third is the burden Māui carried in his arms. But then they show him a depression high on the side of the third outcrop and explain that that is really where Māui inserted his carrying stick, which he afterwards threw away so that people would believe he had carried the immense burden in his arms. The young Nukulei people lean on each other's shoulders, laughing at the cunning of their gods.

On this same afternoon Pule'ota walks to Fatutui from Hihifo. He is a renowned choreographer. Already people of Fatutui have heard that the other villages have begun rehearsing for the opening of the Agricultural Show. They are waiting for their own chief, Fulimai, to give the order for them to start. Some say the delay is because they are tired of performing their old dances and they want a new composition. They say their old dances have won them reputation but have lost their excellence through being seen so often. Others say the delay has occurred because Fulimai wants to avoid the burden on his household of feeding the choreographer and supplying kerosine for the rehearsals. Whoever calls for the village to begin rehearsing will bear these costs.

Before people leave to work in their gardens next morning the village officer, Taki, holds a public meeting. He speaks about the contribution the village will make to the opening of the show.

Then the chief's orator speaks, standing upright, his stocky figure bow-legged. He wears a ragged mat to designate his humility in the village of his chief. He berates the people for their slowness in meeting their responsibilities.

'It is the same every year. The responsibilities of this village are not heavy but you delay. You don't pull together. I am fed up with you all.'

The village officer speaks again. He too is forthright.

'I am continually being asked to carry the burden of an undertaking that ought to be led by our chief, our greatly respected chief to whom we all owe our well-being. We will perform a new composition. Pule'ota has arrived with it. But the decision as to time and place is Fulimai's.'

Taki's speech closes the meeting.

That afternoon, when people of Fatutui have returned from their gardens and are sitting outdoors in the peace of the weakening sun, the wooden gong is beaten. They end their conversations and go indoors to wash and change for the first practice of the new dance. The verses are written up on a blackboard. The place names in the composition belong to Hihifo village, not to Fatutui.

In the course of the practice, word reaches Fatutui of the death of Longo, the wife of a Hihifo orator. The practices will cease. The lanterns are taken down and people disperse.

Two days later Longo's family beats a kerosine tin and announces that this action completely ends the period of mourning. They respect the pressing responsibilities which people have to meet.

Pule'ota returns to Fatutui and sleeps overnight so that two days can be spent learning the new dance actions. The rehearsals are all-day affairs. Pule'ota stands with the women in a circle around him under the shade of a breadfruit tree. Because it is daytime the women are in work clothes, but already the beauty of the hand movements is emerging as the dancers in their circle sway rhythmically from side to side, singing the verses they mastered at the first practice.

In the afternoon people go away to eat in their own homes, returning for the evening practice in fresh garlands of flowers. Fulimai is not present. At the end of the practice, the choreographer must be thanked. The village officer stands up.

'The presentation by this village of its dance is a matter for the chiefs. I am not a chief and it is not right for me to come forward. It is only so our village can preserve its reputation that I have stood up to thank the choreographer.'

Then he continues, 'Our choreographer has come from a village famed for its dance performances. There are not enough people of Fatutui attending our practices. When the day of the Show arrives our voices will not sound strongly. We will be ashamed of our short rows.'

The choreographer sits with his head bowed, his black padded windbreaker zipped up.

The women have decided to teach Caroline the new dance. They sit in a horseshoe with Caroline in the middle, singing the words very slowly so that she can follow the hand gestures. The old men who are seated under the verandah of the clubhouse call out to the women to stand up so they can watch the foreigner learning. The women stand in a half-moon on the loose coral pebbles. Each woman elaborates the basic gestures differently, confusing Caroline. The dancers stop for a while.

The village rests in the heat and the still air. Out on the reef the grey herons stalk and pause.

In the evening Fulimai attends the rehearsal. The women put a spike of feathers in Caroline's hair to show off her head movements. Fulimai demands that she stand in the front row so he can see her. This is the first time the men and women have put their parts together.

The dancers kneel, paying deference to the chiefs. They rise as the singing gains momentum and begin the slow elaborate gestures with their hands, swaying from side to side.

Caroline follows Lusiane's movements. Suddenly Lusiane spreads her legs with bent knees, flicks her head, and gives a double stamp with her feet. Caroline does likewise. The onlookers dissolve in mirth. The dancers continue with composure.

During the performance it begins to rain. The dancers raise their level of exuberance. The rain sets in. Finally there is an onrush into the club house. The two pressure lamps are hung from the rafters and everyone sits down on the concrete floor. Taki, the village officer, stands up and speaks against the rain beating on the tin roof.

'Deference to our chief who lifts up our reputation.'

Taki's speech is lengthy, to occupy the interval of rain.

'I'll take this opportunity to remind the young men that tomorrow is our work day on the show grounds and we have been asked to provide posts for the fence. The posts have not yet been cut, so that should be done first thing in the morning before the copra board tractor and trailor arrive.'

Siaki is sitting against the side wall. By keeping his gaze directed steadfastly across the room to the window opposite he can catch any movement of the white feathers in Lusiane's hair.

The rain stops and the dancers go outside into the night air for a last run through. Lusiane slips back into the second row. She stands on the inner end of the women's line where she can dance beside the men, enjoying the contrast of style and dash, and the exchange of head flicks.

The dancers are gaining command of the dance. The old men drinking kava in the clubhouse call out words of recommendation. The dancers respond with shrieks of excitement.

WE DID IT THEIR WAY

Pat Mathew

Born in 1947, Pat Mathew is the eldest of
ten children. She was brought up on a mixed
farm in north-eastern Tasmania, attended
school in Launceston, then worked for an
accounting firm until her marriage in 1967.
She and her husband now run a 67-acre
hobby farm where they have cattle, sheep,
goats, chooks as well as children aged between
15 and 22. *We Did It Their Way* is the first of
her fiction to be published.

WE DID IT THEIR WAY

'Let's do it,' he said. And he didn't mean sex.

This was a marriage proposal.

We didn't believe in marriage really; didn't consider it necessary. But in the mid-sixties, in rural Tasmania, it was the only way to be socially acceptable. We'd been sort of living together for a couple of years. He spent a few nights a week, and most weekends, at my flat, but he didn't keep any of his things there. We felt we had to keep up the pretence of being 'respectable'. When we did decide to get married, we rationalised it by saying we were doing it for our families. So we decided we might as well go all the way—church and bridesmaids, the whole bit.

What he actually said was, 'I suppose you might as well stick a curtain on your head and grab a bunch of flowers.'

So I did. That was for Mum really. She was a war-time bride in a navy blue dress and sensible shoes; something she'd get a lot of wear out of afterwards. Most of her ambitions were for her sons, but she hoped that at least one of us girls would have a 'proper' romantic wedding.

Once we'd definitely decided to 'do it', we had to let people know. My Dad was old, as well as old-fashioned, so Tom thought he should make a formal request for my hand. During the hour-long drive into the country he got more and more nervous with every mile, and changed his mind twenty times about what he'd say. Dad was feeding the pigs when we got there. By the time Tom had walked halfway across the farm he'd forgotten all the good speeches. He thinks he said something like 'Me and Tammy reckon we might as well get married.'

Dad pulled out his pipe, filled it, lit a match, then puffed hard for a while.

'Well,' he said, 'That's OK by me boy, but you'd better ask her mother.'

Mum said she thought we would get round to it sooner or later.

Mum and Dad were busy on the farm. Mum didn't drive and they didn't have the phone on, so we had to make a lot of the arrangements.

Half his family didn't talk to the other half. Eileen wasn't talking to Margaret, Lorraine didn't talk to Eileen, and Frank doesn't talk to any of us. When we tried to sort out who to ask, and where to sit them, he gave up. 'Stuff this,' he said. 'You arrange it, tell me when and where, and I'll be there.'

Years later he said to me, 'I was a pig wasn't I? I don't know why you didn't say 'stuff this' too.'

Neither do I!

I was in trouble at home because I wouldn't have my sisters as bridesmaids. I didn't particularly like them, and anyway they're all taller than me.

'Not a good enough reason,' said Mum.

We couldn't settle on a time. Nothing suited Dad. Whatever we suggested he'd say, 'Well, that counts me out.'

It was either too early for him to have the morning milking and other chores done, or too late so he wouldn't be home in time to start the evening lot. Eventually we settled on 11 am, and he grudgingly supposed that that was the best we could do.

Then Mum started to panic about the kids. When I showed her my dress, my four-year-old brother said, 'Jeez, I fink she looks like a fairy.'

Mum decided to send the five little ones to a neighbour in case they 'said something' in church.

The big day arrived. We had a few relatives staying, so we rostered the baths to start at 6 am. I escaped the chaos and helped Dad feed the pigs. Grandma was horrified. But no one else was going to and he wouldn't hurry.

When I finally got my dress on, a lacy thing with a full skirt and three hoops in the petticoat, I got an attack of nerves and wanted to pee. Our dunny was across the yard, so the girls went across with me to hold the dress out of the dirt.

We couldn't fit the bloody hoops through the door, so Mum fished the jerry out from under her bed, and they held my skirts over my head while I went.

On the way to the church my Dad cried. In the church my sisters cried. Brenda cried because I had beaten her to the altar, and Annette cried if anyone else did, while Doreen was bawling because her 'beloved' was at that moment in the church round the corner marrying his pregnant girlfriend.

The reception was horrible. Tom's sisters carried on a cold war, mine cried, and Uncle Leo got drunk and kept disappearing into the kitchen to chat up the CWA ladies who were catering.

Mum censored all the telegrams, so it appeared that twenty-nine people sent identical, unimaginative messages saying 'Congratulations and best wishes.'

We left. Mum said later it was with indecent haste. We put on our jeans and went camping.

That was the best bit.

We had a wedding for our families. I wore a romantic dress for Mum.

I hope they enjoyed it.

Do

Sue McCauley

Sue McCauley has been writing 'professionally' for thirty years. She has written three novels—*Other Halves, Then Again* and *Bad Music*—one stage play, numerous radio plays, a few short stories and several scripts for film and television. Married with two grown-up children, she enjoys her work, her family, animals, children, friends, gardening and various aging rock stars.

DO

'Hobbies?'

The man looks at his wife before answering. 'I do the garden. Vegetable garden. And...' He tries to imagine a day, any day. The things that fill it in. The others are waiting. He moves on to the weekend. 'Rugby,' he says. 'I mean I watch it. Our boy plays. And on TV I watch it.' The interviewer notes this down in careful lettering. Then she will look up and wait. The man tries, desperately now, to think of what else he does.

'And cricket,' says his wife.

'You play cricket?'

'No,' he says, 'I watch that too.' He smiles wanly, ashamed.

'Clubs?' prompts the interviewer helpfully. 'Do you belong to any?'

The man shakes his head slowly. He is a dull person, and his life is humdrum — he sees that now, and it makes his movements heavy.

When the Works closed they set up a Resource Centre in the canteen to help people adjust to redundancy. We went there a couple of times to see what was on offer. We sat around drinking the free coffee and chatting to the others who were in the same boat. The mood was almost jovial, as if we were all starting out on an adventure. But that was early on.

At the Resource Centre they had all the appropriate officials — Employment Service, Social Welfare, Iwi Authority, Inland Revenue. They also had leaflets on how to handle redundancy, and a Job Vacancy screen with cards for experienced computer operators, bookkeepers and door-to-door salesmen. The Resource Centre committee was applying for money from the government so that in the new year they could start up work schemes for all the people who hadn't managed to find jobs by then. Because of that—the safety net—we told each other things weren't so bad. *It was the Job that was made Redundant Not You.*

Let's hang on in, we said. For the sake of the kids as much as anything. It wasn't even three years since we'd moved here, and they'd hate being dragged away from school again.

'I fish sometimes,' the man says. 'Go fishing.'

But the interviewer, daunted by the silence, has turned to his wife and speaks at the same time as he does. 'What about you?'

'That's right,' his wife says. 'He goes fishing. And we do a lot of things together: family stuff—picnics, visiting. Most of our friends live in other places. We haven't been here all that long.'

'Of course,' says the interviewer. She grimaces. 'We've been here eight years and we barely know our neighbours. Unless you join things...' She bites her lip and looks at her questions. 'Are you in any clubs? Committees? Groups?'

The wife shakes her head, smiling at the very thought. 'I'm not that type,' she says. 'I sew a bit but I don't enjoy it all that much. I like gardening. And dancing. I used to like dancing.' She gives her husband a small glance of rebuke. 'Music. We both like music. And reading. Watching telly when there's something halfway decent on, though with kids you tend to end up with what they want. Anyway I don't supposed those are *hobbies* exactly?'

'If you enjoy doing them, they are.' The interviewer is hunched over her papers, getting it down. The husband stares at his wife, impressed by her ability to make dullness sound so energetic.

He was a permanent seasonal worker. That means he'd been laid off six months before, at the beginning of winter. *Work out a weekly budget by looking at how much you spend.* Even then there were rumours that the place would close but no one really believed it; there had been such rumours every off-season for as far back as the old hands could remember. Most likely we'll lose one chain, they told each other. Even though factories and freezing works had been steadily closing throughout the country they were certain it couldn't happen to *theirs*.

I was a bit surprised that my husband would go along with such unreality. He had reason to know better. It was less than four years since he left his forestry job because of the rumours that they were all about to be laid off. He'd been offered a job with a trucking firm. We talked it over for a week. It seemed too good to turn down.

When the forestry men got their redundancy pay most of them headed for the city. *Managing Your Redundancy Pay: hope for the best — but plan for the worst.* The trucking company lost business and had to put off drivers. Last on, first off. No redundancy agreement. You live and learn, we told each other. *DO — think in terms of how you can make the most of it. No 'chips on the shoulder'.*

I did a horticultural course at polytech. I couldn't get into the computer course or media studies, so I took horticulture. At the end of the year I got a cerificate. This would give me a better chance of getting into horticultural college if we could afford it. At least it's something to put on your CV, they said. I thought, at least it got me out of the house. I've never wanted to get away from him before.

While I was out he put in an asparagus bed and tended his cabbages and broad beans. *DO — keep yourself busy.* Then he began going down to the pub and playing the machines though he'd never been a gambler. It fills in the day, he said. And it's only till the Works open.

Some weeks our neighbour, Veronica, gives me a few hours work in the gift shop. She pays me cash so it won't affect our dole payments. We tell people I just help out because she's a friend. But now she's offered me a regular job four days a week and late night Thursday. The shop barely makes a profit but Veronica's husband is working and I think she feels sorry for us.

I'm not sure whether to accept. Not because it feels like charity, but because it might seem a betrayal. In making dole payments Social Welfare divides the money equally between us, but *he* is the one who is registered as unemployed; *he* must report in, fill in the forms, sign the declarations. If I earn the money even that token sense of contribution will be gone. He might feel he had no substance.

'It doesn't even need to be things you *do*,' says the interviewer as if she's just remembered her briefing. 'It can be things you'd *like* to do if the opportunity was there.'

'Anything?' says the wife. She looks at the interviewer with suspicion. 'Regardless of cost?'

'As long as you'd like to do it. Some people have said "travel", things like that.'

I keep remembering school. That's how it feels. The playground and the teachers shoving you into teams; c'mon you, over there and get rid of that long lip you've got an attitude problem know that better start shaping up make something of yourself.

Then I escaped to the real world and it was so good, like landing on cotton wool. No attitude problem, not out there. Fell in love and she wanted me. We had a boy, stillborn. But then a girl and a boy and another girl. And despite the kids, or because of them, I kept falling in love with her every six months at least. Making comparisons and feeling fortunate: happily married, family man, content.

Lately her movements have got sharper. Her head jolts when it turns. Her voice has a thin black outline. The children have noticed; when she's in the room I see them think before they speak.

At first I only took five dollars a time. Twenty-five chances. The first time I went down the woman before me won a hundred and fifty dollars. Last week I won a hundred and twenty. Now I allow myself ten dollars a time. When I wake up in the morning I look forward to pushing the button, watching the numbers spin. At least it gets me out of the house. The day I win two hundred I'll take it home to her and I won't ever play the machines again.

I keep remembering school. The teachers always had to be right, to have the last say. It's as if they've been lying in wait for me all these years.

Personally, I can't see much wrong with Australia, but she's against it. We're New Zealanders, she said, and our kids should be New Zealanders. Why should we have to crawl away from this country like refugees?

I thought, every refugee must have asked that question, in petulance or despair. What makes us think we're so different? But I didn't say this. Instead I peeled back the petalled layers of her words to find the hidden accusation and slipped it into my pocket with all the rest.

'Well, travel, of course,' says the wife. 'Everyone wants to travel. All the same I don't see the point of information like that.'

'They must have a reason,' says the interviewer, 'though I'm not sure what it is. Perhaps if a lot of people want the same thing they'll try and organise something along those lines.'

The wife laughs sourly. 'What? Take us all to Europe for a couple of weeks?'

This upsets the interviewer. She squares her shoulders and looks primly at the sugar bowl. The wife sees and tries to make amends. 'It might be to do with personality,' she offers. 'To give some sort of guide on what kind of potential...' Her voice falters. The three of them sit there in silence, stifled by a gust of futility.

The Resource Centre organised a house-to-house survey of all the redundant workers. *DON'T — harp on about it to everyone around you.* Then they went to the Minister of Employment to ask for funds to set up work schemes which could utilise the skills of those people. At least that's what we were told.

And the Minister of Employment has REMEMBER *first impressions count* announced in the paper that the government does not believe in creating jobs. However she has promised the Resource Centre enough to pay for a full-time co-ordinator and two social workers.

DON'T — worry about it to the point of losing sleep.

'Bungie jumping,' says the wife suddenly. 'I think that would be amazing. And hot-air ballooning. Imagine that.' She smiles across at her husband.

The interviewer snatches up the ballpoint and bends over her papers with relief.

'Water skiing?' The wife tries to tempt the husband into this game. 'Gliding. On a perfect summer day with just a few feathery clouds...'

The interviewer finishes the list and looks, hopefully, at the husband. His wife is also watching him, her smile collapsing slowly as she waits. He tries to think of something, if only to restore the smile, which had been for an instant so... *unlimited.* But all his imagination offers him is flashing fluorescent lights and that little mechanical tune of success that plays while the coins spill out into the tray.

ARCTIC RABBIT

Gillian Mears

Gillian Mears was the recipient of the NSW
Writer's Fellowship in 1989, the 1990 Martin
Bequest Travelling Scholarship and the 1990
Australian/Vogel Award for her manuscript
entitled *The Mint Lawn*, to be published in
1991. Of her writing, Gillian says: 'I come
from a family of storytellers and readers but
was never very good at speaking my stories. I
think I've always noticed extraordinary or
slightly peculiar aspects of ordinary events.'
She is currently writing full time with an
Australia Council Literature Board Fellowship.

ARCTIC RABBIT

Man on Tightrope has a piece of grass coming out his penis. Or is it a thick strand of floating spider web? He's more bent forward than before: about to fall and who would catch him? If my father wasn't in such a vivid mood I'd wander away from his stories to crouch for a moment beside the waist-high garden bronze I made so many years ago. *Boy Across a Gap* was his first name but time has aged his skinny arms.

Each afternoon, the storms. They charge the air and something like confetti being scattered, rustles along my belly and down. When my father was a little boy is such a long time ago. In these NSW north coast summer storms that remind him so strongly of his growing time in South Africa's Natal province, his stories of childhood multiply. He is a good story teller but sometimes I ask too much I think: about how he loved and hated and one day had to abandon his mother. To accompany the easy, laughing stories, there are albums full of black and white photographs. From the smooth lawns of his childhood, his round face has a way of gazing straight into your eyes. Sometimes his mother is with him, sitting on a square of cashmere with her knees tucked under her. She watches him dotingly. His black nanny, all dressed in white, stands by in case of accidents.

Storm light from the west moves closer. It glances for a moment across *Man on Tightrope* and he falters again, outstretching his arms to balance on the thin twist bridge across a spindly vortex. Today, for the first time, I notice how the vortex looks female: like a womb with a damaged and delicate umbilical cord trailing for earth. As if the storm has already picked the statue up. As if damage has already happened. My parents are proud of this early effort from my past to

107

cast bronze. I have heard them boast in whispers to visitors who do not know me. *Julia made him. She is our arty daughter.*

My father comes and leans on the kitchen counter with me. From a bowl he picks out the glossiest tomato. 'Your mother grew these. Look at the size of them would you.' He bites and one seed lands like a red tear on my cheek. We laugh. I pick up one too and, after the first bite, begin to sprinkle the torn skin with salt. As the salt's slightly damp from the weather, my tomato ends up badly over-salted.

'Oh darling,' he says sorrowfully. 'That's White Death, that is. You'll never see forty if you eat salt like that. I don't know why I even let your mother keep it in the house.' Tomato juice spurts again from his mouth. Though he has never been fat, he has always loved food. I can remember how in floods, when my sisters and I were children, he'd always cook confectionary: treacled pan scones, stickjaw toffees, coconut ice and a variety of fudges. If they were slightly on the side of runny, he'd blame the humid rains. The waft of burnt sugars would bring us out of our bedrooms and out of the books we had buried ourselves in. Nothing exasperated my mother more. For days after her kitchen was sticky and her daughters complained of pimple crops and sugar ulcers on their tongues. Once, in the big flood of '76, he borrowed a machine and made pink fairy floss on sticks. Spun sugar. Our father's enthusiasm made it as extraordinary as the volume of Icelandic fairytales I was in the middle of reading.

'Look. Look at this Julia!' My father moves over to the door. 'Watch the light now.'

The storm clouds have moved to let late afternoon sun stream down the side of the house. 'What?'

'Everything's almost lining up. It's how we designed the house. Lineal. Everything aligning itself. The shadows. The light. On the equinox.'

'Like Stonehenge?'

'Sort of like that only...' He gives his rueful laugh. 'We got it slightly wrong. We're about twenty-one days out. The parallels are not quite straight.'

We stand watching the slightly crooked shadows. I think how the past stretches like a kind of shadow, a dark tangent or fairytale to the present. Just for a moment the light seems to throb a deeper gold. So *Man on Tightrope's* hands seem to be brushing something precious.

Even the air smells yellow as the approaching storm sends eddies of air out to us from the old stand of mangoes. It makes me feel strange, watching the hover and haze of fruit flies over the mangoes. For they give the appearance of a frenzy, as if the trees are about to revolt.

'Phew, those mangoes smell bloody rotten.' My father waves his hands.

'Couldn't we make them into chutney?'

'Nup. Too watery. Riddled with disease. The cattle've been eating a few. Next time you go past a cow pat you have a look. The seeds come out all sucked looking.'

'Really?'

He grins. 'You have a look for yourself. In Africa,' he says, 'they used to make carvings out of them sometimes. When I was little. The African workers on my Dad's farm. And they made small clay oxen for me to play with.' My father yawns. 'I think we drove your mother away with all this talk of Africa.'

'She took the dogs for a walk, didn't she? Do you think she'll be all right if it storms?'

'I'll go and meet her in a little while. After a catnap.' He disappears into the bedroom and shuts the door. When my father was a little boy is a long time ago but his stories dispense the distances. He was an only child with a lonely mother is one story but there are many others.

When my father was a little boy he clutched a handful of nettles at the edge of a Cornish garden and sprang back shocked, thinking they'd bitten him. He cried and cried. On the passenger liner going home to South Africa, he sat on his mother's bed, examining the rash fanned out along the soft skin between his thumb and first finger. She was dancing. He hoped she was dancing. When she waltzed in the long crimson dress, she looked taller and laughed a lot. It was 1938 and he was four and a half years old: easy to lever open the porthole window and lean out. It was like looking up at London. All the lights! Layers and layers of glittery colours. But instead of the sound of dance music and tinkled laughter, it's the sound of the dark sea below he remembers most: the swooshing wake pointing back to England. He perched in the oval window and thought if anyone could see him they'd think he was The Man in the Moon. He waved, imagining layers of laughing ladies. If he really craned out, the real moon appeared like a cut out in the sky. *Hey diddle diddle, the cat and the fiddle.* He sang his favourite song, shivering because he'd taken off his pyjamas.

Over on his bed he had moored the Madeira boat his Great Aunt Barker had given him to help stop him crying. *Those naughty nettles* she'd fussed, as if they were her Jack Russel terriers, and had bent to show him how, next to any clump of nettles, the soothing green docks also grew. The leaf she picked was like a dark green hankie. She showed him how to fold it over the stings so all pain soon disappeared. *Oooaahh, it's one of those coddly Cornwall days,* his rich maiden aunt said and from behind her creaking back took out the Madeira boat. Probably it was her bone corsetry creaking but my father thought at the time it was her bones and looked alarmed. *Ooohh, he's a nervy little fellow Elizabeth,* the aunt told his mother. But at the sight of the present his fright turned to pleasure. It was a perfectly made ship with canvas sails, frail riggings, a polished wedge of wood for a rudder in perfect proportions to the rest. His mother loved it too. She'd marvelled over the invisible joints and the white and red jib-ropes. So it was hard to know why she didn't understand him dropping it into the ocean. When he did it *for* her: wanting to leave something behind because she'd cried so hard at having to leave England.

I saw her sailing back. He put his hand on the underflesh of her forearm. *Mumma. I set the rudder.* She let him unzip the dress. He loved the fast sound of it. He was half glad she was crying. Her heavings were like ocean swells of white water beneath his brave little England-going boat. *I set the rudder for the home country Mumma. Elizabeth?* He used her real name, the way Budge his father did and felt very grown-up, his arm on hers. Her crying tipped her forward. He was amazed to see breasts like a pair of creamy moons, rising his way.

In the darkness under his blankets, he took out his torch and his miniature magnifying glass and began to count the pattern of tiny puncture marks left by English nettles from the garden of his Great Aunt Barker. Would they last until Africa? He hoped and hoped they would so he'd hear the soft cluck grow in his nanny's voice. His mother's crying had changed now: it was just as tiny and endless as the red dots swimming into his eyes. Dog nettles had little teeth, he marvelled. One way and another, it had been a wondrous night. He pulled the little tassle between his legs experimentally. She hadn't even noticed he'd thrown his pyjamas into the sea as well. He dreamt of them: threadlike and fast, moving in the under currents, the tops and the bottoms. They were his Peter Rabbit ones. The flannel would be as warm and salty as when he wet the bed. If they drifted into the open mouth of a whale, it would be the story of The Pyjamas, not Jonah, in the Whale. He went to sleep chuckling because his head was so full of jokes.

This afternoon lantana sprays and his short sleep have made my father's face puffier than usual. He stands back at the kitchen bench again, pouring tea, as he watches the weather blot out his favourite view.

'Think it'll hit?' I ask.

'I don't think so darling, no.' He swirls the ancestral pot that is the shape of an elegant oil can. 'I think it's a Wanderer that one. Not that you can ever really tell.'

We watch the storm coming in a swoop from the west. It dims the day. At the bottom of the hill the river has grooves but further away, whole lines of foam travel and travel in lines so neatly spaced you can imagine swimming fast straight laps between them.

'It's quite incredible,' says my father, 'how this hill acts as a pivot for storms. I think we built our house under some kind of meteorological playground.' He studies the dark clouds. 'I wonder where this bugger's off to?' He resumes his teapouring. 'My poor old Mum hated storms.'

'Did you ever ask her to visit?'

My father sighs. 'It wasn't easy, Julia. Remember she wouldn't even recognise that I'd even married, let alone had four daughters. You see she was living in England again, Budge died in '54. And your mother and I would send over photographs and she'd send them back with my face cut out of them. I mean, my darling, she'd never acknowledge the present.'

'It's sad, isn't it?'

'I don't know. I don't think I could've trusted her with small children. Not that I think she would ever have done anything violent. But in later life she'd developed this rather unfortunate fixed stare. It was terrible really. It had the effect of making people flinch away. As if she carried a knife or a pistol.'

'Could she shoot?'

'Oh yes. Budge would've taught her soon after she first arrived in South Africa, but she never liked killing things. She loved painting. I often think you owe your talents, your eye, to her. But she was never much good at drawing animals. She liked landscapes and still life. Watercolours. I mean she would've loved Australia. She would've loved the birds we get here in the mornings.'

The storm hits suddenly. It gusts the house and out of the earth we see one of the pink grevilleas torn free. Like a tumbleweed, it cartwheels away. My father groans. 'That's the third one of those to do that. Your mother insists on putting them in the most exposed position.'

'Will she be all right in this?'

'She's probably cowering terrified somewhere under the most dangerous tree. I'll go out in a moment. I don't know though Julia. You always seem to be like a terrier for the nitty gritty details . . . for the past.'

'I'm sorry.'

'Don't be sorry. Anyway, I'll be back soon if you want to talk about anything else.' In the laundry he takes off all his clothes and puts on my birthday present to him: a large sized goretex coat. From underneath the red hood, I hear his voice take on a mischievous note. 'I'm going to give your mother a real thrill,' and he disappears into the rain.

Time spent in reconnaissance is seldom wasted has always been my father's favourite saying. Even into my teenage years I believed reconnaissance must mean the past. And I used to plot my own future with exacting attention to early childhood, and further back even, into his and his own strange mother's.

In my parents' house, in a storm, you could almost be on an ocean-going vessel. The logs down the hillside look like they've rolled out of some very high sea. They look sea smoothed. I imagine a saltiness, curls of seaweed, pink shells inside the logs: small and hidden peninsulas of white sea sand. They are huge twirled driftwoods that could sink a ship the size of this house on an unlucky voyage. The hill itself seems set on a swoop of blue. I squash at a line of ants suddenly penetrating into the cutlery drawer. My father's memories involving water often have a particularly poised feel. I wonder how it would feel to have had such a mother. A mother who named her only child after Peter Rabbit but who for years called him Mouse, then Muffin. As though he was her lover.

On their way home from their English holiday of 1948, my father turned fifteen. His mother organised a ship party. He had to wear a paper crown and blow out fifteen blue candles. Strangers cheered and sang *For He's a Jolly Good Fellow*. As he stabbed the knife through the immaculate layers of royal icing, marzipan and fruit cake, he caught sight of his mother. She'd painted a pair of eyebrows on too high and each not quite even with the other. Beneath them her eyes went crooked. She was drinking pink gins.

—Mother?

—Muffin?

She had no sense of right public behaviour.

—Mother . . .

—Make a wish Muffin. Make your lucky wish.

Against the side of her glass spilt bitters looked like watery blood. He twisted the knife and the pearl handle snapped from the blade. Please stop calling me Muffin, he wished, and tried to wipe the blush invading his face away with the back of his elbow. Then he whispered his ghost of a wish again.

—Hip hip Hooray.

The passengers at his party clapped and looked merry. His mother came close to tweak his tie straight and someone took a photograph.

—My Muffin.

She held his hand, tickling all the pale places that used to make him laugh for *Walkie round the garden like a teddy bear*.

Her doctor at the time was an authoritarian Durban psychiatrist. He had her on a certain tonic in an effort to hold off her depressions. For years she'd been on similar cures. The taste of citrovescence was always on her lips. After his birthday kiss it was like a thin and bitter moustache above his own mouth. She nibbled at her corner slice of cake and peeled all the icing off for him as though he still was her own tiny son. On deck it was a clear day. They walked as if promenading until his mother scrunched her face up against the breeze and began to imagine pebbles caught between her shoes and stockings. He crumbled his cake over the railings. His fingers felt sticky and useless.

—Look, look!

His mother had forgotten the invisible pebbles.

—Isn't that cloud just like England. The exact same shape?

He made another wish, staring into the sky: that she be as calm as the clouds—the tufty ones that seemed teased apart.

—Now it's a little girl in jodphurs. You used to love this game.

She was full of accusations. He kept on walking. He knew that to look back would make her cry. But when he did turn around, she was undressing.

—You can't take your stockings off here!

At that time she wore her hair unfashionably thin, in a pale ponytail latched up at the back with a butterfly pin. To see her from behind, my father has often said, would make you think of autumn fires and the colours of a sad winter ahead. Sometimes a strand of hair unthreaded from the clasp and looked like a candlewick against her nape. He imagined striking a match and lighting it. She would burn: fast like a party candle but no one would blow her out. Her buttons would melt into her throat. Until all that would be left would be her favourite locket and the chain that clink-clinks now against my own neck.

Back in the cabin, after he'd unwrapped his present—a Madeira card box full of ten pound notes—and they'd laughed stiffly about what he'd done with his last present from Madeira, she made him brush her hair. She held the card box. It was decorated with a hand of aces in every suit, made of inlaid timbers. The heart held the catch to opening and shutting the box. He watched her pressing it in and out, in and out. He hated brushing her hair. It was the limpness of it. She sprayed it each morning with a lacquer that did nothing to disguise its lack lustre qualities. Across his fingers, he could feel the smudge of oil. The longest hatpin, part of the Butterflies of the World set, lay by a large hat in front of the mirror. After a while, she put down the card box from Madeira to begin slicing the pin through the straw of the hat. Her fingers, he remembers, looked lethal. The metal pin went through the straw as dangerously as it sometimes did her hair. Sometimes he'd be sure she'd miscalculated the angle and that the long thread of metal had punctured her scalp and kept on travelling: to pierce the seething oddness of her mind. As he brushed her inadequate hair, as she told him the strange story, he imagined her mind as a crazy spinning top. It would have corroded edges and an off-key squeal.

On his fifteenth birthday, she told him why it was that for the past decade she'd treated his dear father Budge as a Russian Sleeper, an imposter in the midst of their Natal wattle farms. How the soldiers who'd sighted her touching herself and sighing at the tickle her fingers made across her breasts and then lower and lower down, had spirited him away. You were only a child, she told my father. You weren't in the room but your kaleidoscope was. After the soldier's faces had left the window, she'd looked between her legs with this. What she saw spun at her eye like a flower that grows in rocks. Deep pinks and darkness. Flower shapes. As she filled his head with the frightening and pretty patterns, he stopped brushing her hair. The soldiers, she told him, had smelt of monkey cages at the Durban zoo as well as some kind of motorcycle fuel. They smelt . . . as she searched for the right word, her nostrils flared . . . inflammable. And they had Budge taken away. To Mt Querboo, she believed, which in Zulu meant, 'Place where they find gold'. Mt Querboo was the perfect blue peak that sunsets fell around. There is a photograph of Budge looking towards it on a cold winter morning. It lives permanently on top of my father's desk.

My grandfather is a lean, sad man in profile. 'Imbegabuzalu' his Zulu workers called to him. 'Sukaborno Imbegabuzalu'—Good morning Man Who Looks to the Sky. As if it had become too painful to look anywhere else, let alone at his wife who was not the lively, laughing English girl from Chester she once was.

In winter holidays, home from boarding school, my father loved to go riding through the wattles. They were like cathedrals, he said. Light sprang in arcs. Through the mist they'd just be able to make out the tips of their horses' ears and the thin blue tip of Mt Querboo where Budge was meant to be hostage.

There are photographs of my grandmother, but never on my father's desk. She liked Darjeeling tea, cream for her scones very warm and slightly on the side of ripe, watercolour painting, badger hunting and other blood sports. Looking through the half-full album of the 1948 trip back from England makes me feel sad for mostly it's full of pale oceanscapes. Sometimes there is another boat in a corner. Apart from the birthday party, no other events are recorded.

Every now and then, the last puppy left over from the litter of pups lets out a high scream. I can see my parents coming up the hill now. They are frailer than when I last was here. The word sprightly springs to mind and I hate myself for that. They veer away from the easiest track up the hill in order to walk along the long fallen gum that points towards their favourite range of mountains.

They come through the door laughing.

'The mountains, the air — an African-blue!' my father says. Their wet weather gear brushes against *Man on Tightrope* but they don't notice him: how, during the storm, the cobwebs have flown free. Rain has darkened him and tear-sized drips fall from his outstretched arms. My parents infect the kitchen with laughter. So that I too begin to giggle: at the way my father's penis tip keeps bobbling out and then back. As if the new coat is a red curtain and his penis a comical puppet.

In the morning I wake up still thinking of parents. About my father's, but also about mine. How last night they became so flippant about death. I'd been trying to tell them how Virginia Woolf had filled her pockets with stones and walked into a small English river.

'I think that's what we'll do,' my father said. 'Yes darling. Let's just fill up our gumboots with topsoil.' He'd poured more red wine into the tall tulip glasses that had been his mother's and laughed at his reflection in the curtainless windows. The sky outside looked dyed. A small silver gravy boat sailed between us: all curves and glints.

'I wouldn't even have to do that,' my mother held her glass up. 'I'd just have to try breaststroking and I'd go under.' Their laughter, and the smell of summer lantanas and their sprays, floated a peculiar pain under my ribs. It felt hot there. So I rolled the silver serviette ring that is initialled with my grandmother's name under my shirt. But it just made the pain feel colder. I look under the sheet and stroke my ribcage as if something is lodged underneath there still.

Mist like steam rolls off the hill. Everything is glimmering. My mother walks outside the window and past. She's chattering away to her puppy like he's a child. I feel like her child again when she comes into my room a little later with a tray. In the middle is a freshly squeezed juice. The glass is still warm from being washed but the juice is icy. She comes over and kisses me in the middle of my forehead. 'Well,' she says, apologising for it. 'You're still my little girl. And we worry about you.' She sits on the end of my bed. 'You're not still with that man with the wastrel eyes are you?' I am but I shake my head. 'You should see your father this morning,' she goes on. 'He's doing his exercises. He thinks he's a real turn on, jangling up and down.'

'He's irrepressible isn't he?'

She doesn't answer. Her pup's snorting around in the basil beds below my window. 'You must remember to take some basil back with you.' She leans against glass. 'Your father won't eat pesto anymore. Says it's too full of salt.'

I step from bed. Tomatoes shine up through edges of the basil.

'Look at your ribs Julia!' My mother pokes me under one. 'Like a little fishbone. If only you'd stay longer we could really have a good go at fattening you up.' I hold my hands up over my breasts that have recently begun to lose their structure.

'I'm not too skinny,' I say, but I am. A blue light nestles in the dips about my collarbones. And away from the man with wastrel eyes, it's a bony, alone feeling, hugging myself to sleep each night.

'I hope my pup doesn't get sold today.'

The potential puppy buyers are an overweight, one-child family. My mother hates them on sight and her conversation is very rude. She intimates to the wife that she must be expecting her second child any day now. The wife looks confused and then turns bright red for it is only fat beneath her cotton dress. 'If she didn't have skin she'd spill!' my mother says in a loud whisper to me. The overweight child has taken off all his clothes and runs up and down, up and down, in front of the shed, watching his rippling shadow on the tin corrugations alongside. Already it's late afternoon again and up in the meteorological playground invisible storms are pivoting. The puppy, in for a game, leaps up on the child and he bursts into tears.

'Hey,' consoles the father. 'Did he nobble your nuts son?' He picks up the child and tips him upside down. The child half giggles, half cries. When his legs fall open a bit, his father says fondly, 'Little arsehole,' and his wife laughs dutifully at the joke.

'No way are they buying my last darling,' my mother snorts. 'They're thick as butter.' And ups the purchase price, just like that, by two hundred dollars.

'But the ad in the paper said fifty.' They whinge and cajole. 'The little kiddy's had his heart set on a pup just like this.' At that moment the little kiddy's tormenting the puppy's tail. They are easy to disappoint.

We can almost see the chips and chiko rolls lodged in the flesh of their elbows and arms as, reluctantly, they get back inside their Kingswood. But my father, who must have overheard all this from

117

the kitchen, comes rushing out at the last moment. He is waving a knob of his salt-free soda bread at them.

'Oh my god,' says my mother, as he pokes his bread enthusiastically through the wife's window. 'So you won't get hungry on your trip. It's a bit hot, just out of the oven.'

We stand watching the car — its turquoise glitter disappearing round the bend — as my mother begins to tell him how they live in town, only fifteen miles away.

'Well,' my father laughs sheepishly. 'They were so disappointed weren't they? You didn't even ask them in for a cup of tea.'

The warm waft of my father's bread. There are two more loaves cooking as, outside on the long river veranda, I begin as promised to cut his hair. I chop the scissors in front of his face. Hair falls down his bare shoulders. Meekly he perches on the stool, his hands held together. Dough is caught under his thumbnails. He smells of yeast and hand hot milks.

'Oh, look at this hair,' my father takes a tuft into his fingers and examines it sorrowfully. 'I'm like an Arctic Rabbit.'

'Don't be silly.'

'No. Look at your lovely mother's hair.' His hair is very thick and sometimes my scissorblades slide across it. 'Is it your hair in the back of your mother's old locket?' I ask.

'I didn't know there was hair in it.'

It seems inconceivable I've never shown him or asked. I unclip it from round my neck. The old soft gold's full of dimples and dents. I imagine her nervous fingers pressed them there over all the unhappy years.

Behind a picture of my calico cat is a plait of baby hair. At least it feels soft enough for that. I put the plait into my father's fingers. He holds it against the silvery tuft. 'Oh dear,' he groans. 'I think I'll buy some dye and restore my youth.'

'Dad...'

'No. I feel old today.'

'The Old Couple.' My mother comes out and titles herself and Dad.

'Do you know, Julia, that I'm older now than Budge was when he died.'

I take the plait back and lock it again into the gold heart. 'The puppy's having sleep screams,' I tell my mother. She prods his tight belly with her toe and he pokes his tongue out.

118

'Soon he'll be poking something else out that's little and pink. He'll be a horrible adolescent then.' She keeps stroking him with her foot.

'I expect I was a horrible little adolescent,' says my father cheerfully.

When my father was an adolescent, Budge his father stood up one day and fell back into his chair dead. It was a cool morning. He and his mother had to carry the body out together. Did she weep? It is one of those questions that resists being asked. He carried his father's ankles and was the one to walk backwards through the door. If she cried, did her tears fall onto her dead husband's face? Did she look down?

— Muffin . . .

Her pet name for him muffled his shock. From across the expanse of the heavy body she began to call out. She kept calling out for years. Long after my father had abandoned her, her letters and cards called out. My sisters and I squabbled over who got to hoard the beautiful cards, unaware or careless of the messy sorrow inside.

My Muffin.

Only one card seems to have survived from her frantic correspondence.

Cancer of the heart. Her handwriting creeps with sadness I think. Some letters, especially small-case vowels, are lurched at such a slope they've formed frail blue lines instead of words. Old perkins paste in the shape of a cross obscures the rest of her card, because, since 1973, the picture on the other side — of English horses wandering through an English mist — was stuck to the cover of my third class composition book. I tried to peel it off carefully but, inevitably, words were lost in the paste. A dead silverfish, lying between My Muffin, Cancer of the heart covers the gap with a dusty sheen.

She died enormously fat. Her legs puffed up and her face, and the rings on her fingers had to be rubbed with melted lard before they'd slide off. The Mrs Brummel who supervised her death wrote a letter saying it was arteriosclerosis but maybe it was cancer of the heart.

My Muffin, she called him, even after he tricked her into thinking he would send for her soon. Instead of abandoning her on a railway platform and never seeing her again. Muffin. To make English muffins, you need a good strong flour and two good hours. My father makes them sometimes, without salt, using her old recipe in her old

119

edition of *English Bread and Yeast Cookery*. He says he can't remember why he burnt all his letters to her. He made a huge bonfire, trying to turn the past into smoke. All his four daughters were there. But we weren't paying attention. We were gambolling about and I was eight years old. We only interrupted our play to watch the way our father burnt his childhood teddybear. He threw him suddenly on to the top of the burning boxes. When only that morning we'd all admired him: such a fat little dumpy teddy called Foxy, because of his fox-coloured eyes and pointy nose. It was sad watching him burn. The heat made his front paws move together like a plea. 'You shouldn't have . . . in front of the children . . .' but my mother's voice had trailed away. For when I chanced to look sideways at our father he was crying, though maybe it was smoke in his eyes. He wept as the boxes of letters crackled open and gave Foxy's passing a more festive sound. A crooked snowman we'd made from sleet melted nearby. Watching the toy burn reminded me of Indian wives going up in flames in the colour pages of the *National Geographic*. My father's crying reminded me of nothing I had ever seen before. Our snowman had ears. They fell off simultaneously and then the heat caved in his tummy. Later I saw my father scraping through the ashes with the tip of his shoe. Of Foxy, there were no traces.

As the apostle birds begin to hop on the lawns in front of the veranda, my father brings out a loaf of warm bread and we demolish it all. Butter and heath-honey dribble from our fingers and chins. Apostle birds are clowns. They like to travel in one-dozen flocks like biblical messengers. The food lifts my father's mood. He begins to insist on trying out an old gymnastics trick he used to play with all his daughters when we were small, thin girls. It involves gripping ankles and arms, holding your breath and dive somersaulting for the ground between my father's legs.

'I'm scared,' I laugh, and stand poised above him. It's like being in a very athletic mood with a new lover. This thought must occur to him too because his laughter is suddenly uncontainable.

'Come on Julia. *Dive.*'

'I can't!' I look between his legs and my father's testicles are mossy with hair. Unlike my wastrel-eyed lover whose legs are hairless and thin, my father's thighs are a pattern of tight black curls.

I dive. The ground hurts my head but the trick, once in motion, cannot be stopped. Our limbs are locked into a continuous, caterpillaring somersault. Grass clippings stick to our sweat and the sky is a twilight tilt every half second. Like memory-stories there can be no known ending. I hold tighter and hope I don't snap as the slope increases and my father's white head tucks and hits the ground between my legs.

RAG BAG

Fiona Farrell Poole

Fiona Farrell Poole was born in Oamaru in 1947, and studied English at Otago University and Drama in Toronto. She is presently living with family and friends in Palmerston North where she teaches and writes poetry, short stories and plays. A collection of poetry, *Cutting Out*, was published by Auckland University Press in 1987, and *The Rock Garden*, a collection of stories, by Auckland University Press in 1989.

RAG BAG

I've been thinking about the rag bag.

It was faded and floral and it hung from a hook behind the wash-house door. Mum kept old sheets there to rip up for handkerchiefs when he had colds, and old dresses, trousers, shirts and shorts: a tangle of houndstooth, gingham, flowers and stripes too threadbare even for the Corso box. When we were sick, at the convalescent stage when you had to stay in bed with eucalyptus on your chest and a cardy over your pyjamas, restless and itchy-eyed with too much reading, and you'd joined all the dots and lost Master Bun the Baker's Son and the nine of diamonds down behind the mattress then Mum brought out the rag bag. 'Here,' she'd say, up-ending it. 'You can tear me some strips for The Rug.' The Rug was one of her winter projects, along with The Jersey and The Firescreen. Winter after winter for as long as anyone could remember Mum had been knitting a fairisle golfing sweater for Dad, tingling rows of green and yellow lozenges from a pattern in the *Weekly* called 'Rugged and Handsome', and she had been embroidering a firescreen and she had been hooking a braided rug. None of the projects ever seemed to alter or approach completion. The sweater remained a migraine mass in the knitting box, endlessly knitted and unravelled ('Tsk, darn look at that...'), the screen was stored behind the sideboard, an outline of windmill Dutch girl and boat over which a blue and white lichen crept from top right, and the rug was a disc eighteen inches across where you could detect bits of Karen's old slacks, a navy striped skirt and several pairs of Dad's trousers. Sometime or other, when she had a minute, it would expand into a mat big enough to cover the worn place in the kitchen lino, but in the meantime, Mum said, at least those old clothes weren't being wasted. So we tore away happily in our beds

123

after mumps, chicken pox, measles (German and English), scarlet fever and an anonymous series of colds and flus, reducing our cast-offs to strips or plaiting them after Mum had stitched them into bundles of three. Another bag in the wash-house held a coiling mass of our braided worms, and nothing was going to waste.

That was important. Drawers in our house held string, wound into figure eight knots and kept in case they came in handy, and crisp yellow bundles of recipes clipped from magazines; there were tobacco tins of rubber bands and safety pins, buttons and tacks. When we went on holiday and stopped at tea-rooms, Mum took all the packet sugars, swept them grandly into her handbag, saying, 'We've paid, and more than we should have for just a scone and cup of tea. We're entitled.' If there were teabags she took those too, though she didn't trust teabag tea, said it was just the dust swept from the floor after they'd packed the real stuff, the leaf variety, into boxes in Ceylon. Dad seemed not to notice but Karen and I cowered. 'Don't, Mum,' we'd say, looking round furtively at the other diners who were merely pretending interest in their asparagus rolls, at the basilisk behind the till. 'Everyone's watching.' 'Nonsense,' said Mum. 'They've got better things to do than take any notice of us.' So we'd eat our dry scones, fearing the heavy hand, the ultimate humiliation: our mother stopped and her bag opened, spilling a rattling hail of packets all over the floor while people who were better-off and better-mannered stared and stared and stared. We grew up with a firm resolve never to take a thing: not a beermat, not a coffee sachet, not a complimentary soap. As adults we waste on principle, throwing out clothes before they are even slightly faded, clearing our shelves regularly of unused packets and medications. We scorn the doggybag. I write copy: ten years freelance, three at Lundy's Advertising ('We Hit the Target, not the Fan!'), and now for a Sunday freebie, extolling the virtues of shopping malls and garden centres and rejoicing in the knowledge that it is all destined for the tidy bins of the city. Karen travels for Vandenberg Bread, living out of a suitcase, scooting from motel to motel and home occasionally to the bare white box of a flat in Lyall Bay which she bought after her husband left her: on the Saturday she sold a dinner set, three casserole dishes and a ten speed to a man who'd arrived at their house by mistake thinking they'd advertised a garage sale. 51 Patea St, she'd said, not 53 — but they did have a lot of stuff cluttering up the place if he was interested . . . Don said when he got home that she was crazy, but she said, and I think reasonably, that there was no point in hanging onto things they never used and he liked only the idea of getting fit by riding to work, not the reality of slogging up the hill amongst the traffic. We call our clean shelves and empty cupboards 'puritan' and 'minimalist' and we laugh about it, feeling pity for our mother who hoards because they lost the farm during the Depression and she has subsequently no faith in replenishment. We think we are different.

But this morning I wonder if I am really so different after all. I may throw out clothes and unused food and magazines — but I hoard some things jealously: scraps of conversation, odd episodes, inconsequential gestures, the bits and pieces that some time or other, when I have a minute and have lost interest in malls and garden centres, I intend to tack together into a novel, properly finished front and back, something firm and permanent.

These oddments, for example, collected in England two years ago.

Here. Rip them up. Braid them. Twist them to form a circle. Can something be made of them?

We went to England for six months. To Cambridge. To Hawthorne Close. My husband is a musicologist. He wanted to finish his book on Baroque opera. He needed a decent library. I'd had a muddled year, a tangle. I needed a break.

When I say a tangle I mean that in January, my father died, passed out at the twelfth hole after his first eagle.

In March, Stephie, who is seventeen and, as her father says, quite capable of looking after herself, poured tomato sauce onto a slice of bread and butter and said she wasn't going back to school, had spoken to the principal already and was going to Taradale to learn how to blow glass. 'But what about university?' I said. 'What about bursary and being an architect?' 'It'll keep,' she said. 'Where are those sausages from last night?' 'Cat got them,' I said. 'And what are you going to live on? Mrs Waters didn't agree did she? She's always saying you're so gifted.' Stephie arranged chippies in overlapping rows on her sandwich. 'She says that to all the mummies and daddies,' she said. 'I don't want to go back to school and Misty Kerehoma's uncle's got a bar restaurant in Napier and he's got a job for me if I want it, so stop fussing.' Crunch. Crumbs pattered on the bench. 'I'm not ready for this,' I said. 'Oh Mum,' she said. 'I'm seventeen.' She is. She is seventeen and much, much taller than me. When she hugged me I said, 'You used to draw such beautiful little houses' against her smooth young neck, and she laughed, said she would again and not to worry, and she left in February.

In May Michael said he needed time out and I suspect he had an affair with Jenni Winkler who was first violinist in the Albinoni Ensemble for which Michael played continuo. He moved into a flat in Kelburn anyway and it was quiet at home so I worked late. I worked late and went into Lundy's early which is how I found Gary from design tucked in a sleeping bag under his desk at 6.30 one Monday morning. He was embarrassed, dragged on jeans, hopped about trying to deflate a lilo which bounced and writhed under his feet like a live thing, rolling his sleeping bag and stuffing clothes into a sports bag. At morning tea he said he'd rather it didn't get around, specially not to Lundy, but things weren't going well at home, Gina was pretty keen on a guy she'd met through PSA, said he was spontaneous, made her feel alive for the first time in years, would you bloody believe it? To which I of course replied with Michael and Gary said he'd read that taking time out sometimes revitalised mid-life relationships, he could lend me a book about it. So he did and we talked about it over a drink at Bardinos one evening after work and within the month I was in Gary's bed (Gina had gone with the spontaneous Union delegate to Invercargill), sliding about on Gary's sheets while Gary tried out positions 5 to 8 from Good Loving: A Guide to Gourmet Sex which lay open on the bedside table and which he consulted from time to time like a kid figuring out a slot-car assembly.

In August Michael rang and said would I like to get back together again and I said yes, and put the copy of Creative Divorce Gary had given me for my birthday on the bottom shelf of the bookcase.

In November I lost my job: went into work, found the telephone cut off and a Kleensak by my desk. Lundy's were trimming back and though my Kupe Resorts brochures had been terrific, first-rate, it was last on, first off, sorry. So I gave Gary my rubber plant and dumped my mother-of-thousands upside down on Lundy's desk and walked out. I needed a rest. Michael suggested Cambridge. He had six month's leave due, March–August. It would be quiet. I could have a trip overseas, write my novel at last, find a job when we got back. It sounded like a good idea.

Hawthorne Close was a square of fifty-four urban dwellings constructed from creaking pine and fake brick in 1972, lvng. rm/kchn down, 2 1/2 bdrms, bth.w.tlt. up, garage at rear and precisely 6 square feet of lawn bordered by 14-inch strips of bare earth from which some residents were able by constant watering and attention to conjure up sweet peas, marigolds and runner beans. Our garden remained empty till May when if flared suddenly with thirty scarlet tulips, budded bloomed and fallen within a fortnight. But when we first arrived the borders bore no hint of this approaching glory: not a blade, not a weed, not a flower.

So Michael went off to the university library and I set up my typewriter by the standard issue picture window and looked out at my new view. The centre of the Close was a lawn circled by a wagon train of cars. There were no hawthornes of course, any more than there are lilies in a Lilybank Gardens or the waters of life in a Paradise Place. It's a townplanner's idea of irony. There were two plane trees popped on top of two symmetrical hillocks of builders' spoil like the holly on a couple of puddings where the kids from the local high school sat to smoke or eat their lunch. Their uniform was navy and the fashion was for pale make-up and spiked hair. They sat puffing seriously, malevolent and impassive geishas, unless driven off by the two drunks who stopped there on their way through to the vicarage on the next street. There were two regulars: Fergus, a morose Irishman who walked with an odd step hop hop step and carried his bottles in a smart leather handbag, and Bert who was bald as Buddha and wore a sort of sarong of old curtains. As he strode through Hawthorne Close to take his place beneath the plane tree he swore at his left shoulder and punched the peopled air.

The Close backed on to a row of shops: newsagents, shoe shop, Chinese take aways, fish and chips and Philippe of Kensington with mirror tiles and Clairol posters, and the air was a pungent bouquet of diesel, chip fat, soy oil and hair spray.

I settled down on that first morning and waited. Wound a clean sheet into the typewriter. Could New Zealand take another novel about a young girl coming to maturity in a small town? Or should I try for something futuristic like *The Handmaid's Tale?* Through the wall, two alsatians thumped up and down the stairs or barked, scratching at the picture window and exposing petunia-tipped cocks at the passersby. Their owners, a small man like a spud on a stick and a doughy woman, had whined out of the Close at eight on a black moped. On the other side was silence: a short Korean man had left at 8.30 carrying a brief case, followed by three small girls, with square satchels, square legs and square fringed faces who dawdled away hand in hand with their mother and a thin child in a short pink dress and pixie boots. Should I abandon art and go for the money with an historical romance? I made myself a cup of coffee. Something contemporary, set in an advertising agency perhaps? A woman with a camera was crawling across our six-foot yard. I opened the door. 'Shh,' she said, winding on. There was a hedgehog by the garage eating a snail. Click. 'I'm Laura,' said the woman. Click. Click. 'This town's the pits, but some of the animals sure are cute.' Slup slup went the hedgehog and crawled through a hole under the fence. Laura knelt back and rewound, said she was new too, was from Massachusetts here for the whole year and sure, she'd love a cup of coffee and she should have known she'd hate Cambridge after *A Room of One's Own* but she wanted her kids to experience life in another culture and she and Don had only just gotten together and he had to get this book out for tenure so she thought, what the hell? She'd built up a good veterinary practice back in Salem but she thought she could leave it for a few months safely with Cory who was her assistant, but Cory had gone bananas. Was fighting with all the clients, ringing her at three am wanting advice on every teensy thing and generally driving her nuts. Don's opinion was that Cory was in love with her and was punishing her for moving in with him and for leaving but what could she do? Nothing, except write Cory long letters to try and keep things calm and hope that there would still be a practice when she got back in December. The kids hated the place too: the endless teasing about accents and being wealthy Yanks and the people in the shops were just so damn rude and she couldn't believe how long it took to do the simplest things like having a phone installed or washing clothes. The one thing you could do better here than at home was read: had I seen the bookshops yet? She'd show me the bookshops.

I hadn't seen the bookshops. I hadn't been into town. I didn't want to shop. I hadn't shopped for a year.

I didn't cry at my father's funeral. Nor did my mother. She didn't believe in making a spectacle of yourself. Karen wept like a gargoyle, mouth stretched wide and soundless, and after the minister had rattled his way through there is a season and dust to dust and my father had been dropped into a slit in clay and the RSA had sprinkled poppies like clots on the coffin, we went back to the house for a cup of tea. My mother's sisters had arranged cakes and sandwiches and sherry for the ladies and a few whiskies out the back for the men. Dad's golf bag was on the hall stand and his chair still bore the print of his body. Auntie Rene clasped me in a damp embrace, then held me at arms' length. 'You'll miss your poor daddy, won't you?' she asked. Her pink marshmallow hat had been knocked sideways with the force of emotion, and coconut from a lamington spattered her bosom. I escaped into the bedroom. The bed was covered with clothes and on the dressing table was a pile of brown paper and some twists of string. 'Sort out what you'd like,' said Mum in the doorway. 'They're hardly worn. This, for instance.' She picked up a jersey, a green and yellow fairisle sweater. 'He only got a couple of months out of this. It'll come in handy for Michael to knock about in.' 'I don't want it,' I said. 'And some cakes,' said Mum. 'The girls have made far too much as usual. You can take some of those sausage rolls home for your tea.' Karen was out in the hall holding Rene at bay. 'I've got to get out of here,' I said to Karen and she moved fast. She'd driven down in the Vandenberg Bread car, so we drove into town labelled on all four doors 'Naturally the Best!' and shopped. We tried on dresses and hats, jeans and skirts and sweaters at Mademoiselle, Slick Chick, Arcady and Formosa, where I stumbled against the bamboo walls of the fitting room while dragging on a pair of skin-tight jeans and fell out into a rack of summer dresses. That's what I remember most about my father's funeral: lying on the floor in Formosa in a tangle of muslin, my knees locked in a pair of Levis and both of us, Karen and me, laughing. We laughed and we laughed. We laughed till we ached. Till we cried.

I hadn't wanted to shop since then. But Laura took me into town that afternoon to Heffers and we stopped off at one of the colleges on the way. She wanted to take a photo. 'Do you know this used to be a nunnery?' she said, stepping across the Please Keep off the Grass sign and backing away to focus on the gatehouse. 'The nuns were thrown out on trumped-up charges of indecency. There are colleges all over this place that were endowed by women...' ('Hoi' said a voice from the porter's lodge.) ...'and when the vote went against them in 1921, some of the jerks actually stormed over to Newnham...' ('Hoi,' said the voice. 'Can't you read?') Click goes Laura's camera. '...testosterone poisoning,' she calls from the middle of the college lawn. 'The whole place reeks of it.' Click. A little man, very irate, emerges from the porter's lodge. Click. She has him at long distance. Middle distance. Close up. Too close to focus. Laura smiles her sweetest smile and we leave for Heffers where she says you should read this. And this. And this'll blow you away . . .

Next door to Laura lived Hodda's mum. I met her the next day. She knocked at the door. (A novel about a woman in middle age and the complexities of her relationship with a grown daughter perhaps? Stephie had written that morning: the glassblowing was the max, the bar restaurant was the max, the weather was the max. I felt abandoned.) This woman knocked, opened the door, came in and took one of the dining chairs. I followed her along the street to her urban unit where she stood on the chair, pushed open the fanlight above the door and pulled herself up. She was plump but surprisingly agile, through the gap in a thrash of petticoat, stockings and grey knickers and unlocking the door. 'Thank you lady,' she said. That evening, the child in the pixie boots arrived with a handiwipe full of crumbling sweets. 'I'm Hodda,' she said. 'Mum says thanks for the chair. She's always losing her keys. Here. She made these for you. They're horrible.' Once or twice a week after that Hodda's mum stopped by for the chair, usually after her driving lesson. The narrow-hipped sleek young man from the Acme Academy, his hair clipped from black plastic, flustered her. On Tuesday and Thursday mornings he sat bored and elegant in the front seat of her Toyota, Nasi her oldest daughter sat in the back like a pale princess and they bunnyhopped out of the Close, gunning from first to second to first. The Toyota squirted purple smoke and Hodda said, 'Mum's hopeless. She's had fifty-four lessons.'

We talked as best we could. Her husband was a soldier somewhere, she stayed in England for Hodda and Nasi who was training to be a hairdresser, she came I think from Baluchistan. I looked that up. There was a drawing in the encyclopedia of a hairy hornless goat beside a stack of double decker buses. 'The Beast of Baluchistan' said the caption. 'The largest mammal ever to have existed.'

Michael fretted. 'You're not bored?' he asked over and over. 'You're not lonely?' He was completely happy with Rosmene torn between love and duty and establishing a meaningful relationship with Imeneo in the course of 36 da capo arie. From time to time a thin blue aerogramme slid in from The Hague where Jenni was studying with Kuijken, to which Michael I presume replied. Gary sent cards of pohutukawas on the Coromandel where he had bought a section with his redundancy cheque and was trying to live more in accordance with natural rhythms as advised in a book, *You and Your*

Biorhythms; he recommended it. I sent in exchange Kings College Chapel from the Back and Ely Cathedral. But Michael and I took care. We were a couple in convalescence, living quietly and hoping the spots would go away. We were solicitous. Michael tried not to be too happy and to soothe him I wrote a few pages, left the paper about as evidence of creative disarray. He relaxed and I was able to return to looking out the window undisturbed.

There was Zoe who lived at 22. Tiny. Dark. Leeds Jewish, 'and I still feel foreign here,' she said. 'We've been here since the eighteenth century but people still make you feel foreign.' Her husband Paul was a fastidious computer technician, his hands raw and pink from allergies and repeated scrubbing. They all had allergies. That was Zoe's job: Daniel had to have non-dairy foods, Anna reacted to wheat and Paul had both plus house mites and synthetic perfumes. They weren't kosher, but it took time just the same to maintain a preservative-wheat-dairy-and-chemical-free, scrupulously clean environment. On the kitchen bench were two large bottles of naturopathic pills, administered daily with elaborate ritual, not touched, but laid reverently on the children's pink pointed tongues with sterile tongs. When she wasn't cleaning or cooking or shopping, Zoe was driving the children to their school or to computer club or to their Suzuki lessons forty miles away. She stopped by sometimes for coffee, kicked off her shoes on the dusty fluffy carpet, curled amongst the mess on the sofa and took two teaspoonfuls of sugar. Paul couldn't tolerate sugar.

There was Claire who worked as a dentist's receptionist so the children could go to boarding schools: not the top drawer exactly but proper schools just the same with housemasters and the lumpy ill-fitting uniforms which in England signal expense. They returned at holidays and occasional weekends to stand uneasily on the edges of the multinational scrum who played each night in the Close till it was dark. Claire and Peter had fenced off their garden and paved it and instead of marigolds they grew two spindly bay trees in pots and the walls in their living room were painted dark green and hung with sporting prints. Claire said their friends were always asking why didn't they move? But the Close was so convenient for town and they'd formed a Residents Association to keep the area up to the mark. They could have moved eight years ago when Peter had the chance to go out to Australia but they chose to stay so the children could have a good education because you needed that extra polish these days to get anywhere and colonial schools might be very good, but perhaps not quite as successful when it came to polish. Peter wore a shiny grey suit and drove a 1976 Austin Princess because he thought it was important to patronise the old store and besides, Austins might lack the electronic razzamatazz you found on the new Japanese cars but he knew what he'd prefer to be driving in a head-on. He called in once or twice soon after we arrived and in between chatting about rugby, which he'd played at school, with Michael who'd been too short-sighted even for cricket, he enquired whether we'd got proper cover for the second-hand Ford we'd bought. Even for a short visit, he said, it wasn't wise to be underinsured.

Next door to Claire was Margo. An Australian. A radiologist. She'd come over on a visit fifteen years ago and decided to stay. She had a son called Alan and three lovers, a matching set: all short, all dark, called Hugh, Jake and Richard. They moved through Number 20 in rotation. 'She's so casual about it,' said Claire. 'They even know about each other. And none of them is Alan's father. He was a pilot or something on West Indian Airways. I don't know how she does it.' Claire twisted a blonde curl into a corkscrew. 'She's not even pretty.' Which was true. Margo had a heavy good-natured body and her bum spread amply over the narrow shaft of her bike seat. 'And I don't know where she gets the energy.' Margo smoked incessantly, a heavy blue pall clouding the picture window. But she had the energy, went each August on strenuous cycling holidays in Spain or Greece with Alan and Hugh or Jake or Richard. The Mediterranean was a sump, she said, but blue and wet and the closest thing she could find to the beaches back home, which were the one thing she missed. She'd never go back. No way. She'd got off that Qantas flight fifteen years ago and walked through Heathrow and thought nobody knows me here, nobody gives a damn. She had attained anonymity at last and she wasn't about to give it up.

There was a Japanese family at number 18. Their son Ken jumped in batman cloak and with laser sword from our garage roof smashing the last of the tulips and cutting his knee wide open on a stone in the dry earth. I carried him home dripping tears and blood and scarlet petals and that afternoon Akiko brought me a doll caught like a butterfly in a lacquered box. Next to her were Ann and Bob from Winnepeg, both Lutheran, both preoccupied with spirituality. Bob was writing a PhD about Kierkegaard, Ann took slides: Stonehenge,

Tintagel, Cadbury, Cerne Abbas, Glastonbury, caves, hills, circles and menhirs. 'Do you know they're in alignment?' she said. 'They're part of a huge grid and the intersections possess special power.' We visited an intersection near Huntingdon. It was a hillock in a field of rape. We pushed our way through and lay spreadeagled on the earth east to west to pick up the vibrations. The air was insect buzz, planes from the American base and cars on the A604. 'Listen,' she said. 'That's the pulse.' I wasn't sure. Our clothes when we got back to the car were gilded with pollen.

The six months passed. Nothing happened. Hodda's mum had her driving lessons, Laura wrote to Cory, Ann went to Brittany for the Carnac lines, Akiko showed me how to make rice balls, wrapping the sticky grains round an inner sliver of sweet pickle. I wrote to Stephie and to Mum who replied on In Memoriam notepaper; she'd bought more packets than she needed. In July the aerogrammes from The Hague stopped and Michael mentioned at dinner that he'd heard that Jenni was going to Florence in the autumn to marry an Italian musicologist: he'd written on Paolovicino for the Grove, but not with any special flair. Michael was restless that night, the bedroom stuffy and the air thick with chip fat and diesel. He turned and turned, dragging the bedclothes round him in a tight ball till I put out my hand and touched his neck. He turned suddenly to me and held me so tightly that there were faint bruises on my upper arms next morning.

Nothing happened. We flew out four weeks later. Laura wrote a couple of times, once with a photo of some otters and once after she'd flown back to Massachusetts a month early because Cory had tried to gas herself in the operating room at the clinic, and was found by the receptionist on the floor with a samoyed in her arms. 'She's OK,' wrote Laura in sloping purple. 'She's gone back to Vermont and is having counselling. People do such weird things.' And she mentioned Hodda's mum who had driven into the bonfire the Close Residents Association had organised for Guy Fawkes. Just lost control of the brake pedal, apparently, bounced over the verge straight into the flames and had to be dragged out before the Toyota blew up. Nasi had moved out and was living somewhere in town with the driving instructor. She'd seen them together in Bridge Street: beautiful, impassive and arm-in-arm. There were new people in our old flat, and the Koreans had moved home as well. It was good to be back,

Laura said. She was going to get the clinic on its feet again and in the spring she was booked to go on a women's expedition to the Galapagos, had asked Ann to come too. She'd write.

Nothing happened. I got my job with the *Sunday Advertiser*. Michael finished his book.

I wonder still about that novel: perhaps a tragedy like *Anna Karenina* or *Madame Bovary*. Something filled with powerful human emotion. Something destined to become a classic.

But I don't seem to have the temperament for it. I collect scraps instead. I'm hooked on ephemera. I prefer the glancing contact.

IN WHICH MANY CENTIMETRES OF PROSE RUN ALONG BESIDE THE FACTS OF SEVERAL DEATHS, SOME TOPIARIES AND TWO KINDS OF PESTO

Cathy Peake

Cathy Peake was born and educated in Melbourne. During the 70s she lived in the shade of the Cafe Danton and, since 1981, in Sydney where she sleeps under a jacaranda tree (in a house). She has published wrapping paper, cartoons, book covers, three small children's books and a great deal of arts and literary journalism. As well as writing and editing, she has worked as a projectionist, a colourist, an architecture gallery director, and in glass houses full of cattleyas, African violets, mist machines and sphagnum moss.

IN WHICH MANY CENTIMETRES OF PROSE RUN ALONG BESIDE THE FACTS OF SEVERAL DEATHS, SOME TOPIARIES AND TWO KINDS OF PESTO

Apparently without a backward glance, Herschel always said, his mother remarried, and there was very little in her former life, or in Herschel's, that carried over to the new. His father's funeral — and its dismal, dusty sequel at the Eltham cemetery — was not long over when, one by one, the old friends stopped calling. The subscriptions to the French magazines were cancelled, and the Persian rugs which once had sailed from the sitting room to the scullery were swept away, perhaps sold, and replaced with sisal squares.

Did his mother choose these changes, or was his stepfather's will already so rapacious? He said he remembered very little, that he was terribly confused. There were nights, he said, and then there were weeks on end, when the sitting room door across the passage from his study was shut with a click, and he swayed on his elbows, distressed by the sly but saw-toothed evidence of his exclusion.

One day he returned from school and found all the photographs of his father had been swept from the ledges and mantelpieces around the house. He supposed that there had been some discussion about their removal, but nothing had been said to him, and in turn he said nothing either, at first feeling sad, and then with a rising confidence realising he had committed their images to memory.

They had appeared fairly soon after the funeral, as is the custom, and he remembered quite clearly, he said, how he peered into their frames and that now nebulous world where his father sat on the garden bench and he, still a baby, lay across his lap staring straight back into the eye of the camera. At first he had been startled by the difference nine years had made to his father's face — how much older he had looked propped up on pillows at the Royal Melbourne Hospital, where he'd struggled through *The Silver Dove* just before he died.

Years later, an aunt whom he had not seen for a decade or more gave him one of these photographs and the memory of that difference came flooding back. But the curious thing, he said, was the way it came back as a memory of difference. With the passage of time he knew as a simple fact that his father had not looked like that when he died, though he could no longer remember exactly how it was that he was different.

In Kashmir one winter I noticed the local drivers set fire to kindling beneath the petrol tanks of their trucks, before cranking them to life each morning. The passage of a stray spark in that dawn light is hard to contemplate — but it could never be confused with the fires of creativity — and nor should these few pages. Something quite different is taking place, though what it is . . . is hard to say. The petrol tanks and Kashmir are quite beside the point, which is that Herschel too, has died, in his sleep, at the age of sixty-three.

Ever since he died, I have been more or less constantly in a state of anxiety, and restlessness — like a weather satellite, Douglas says, which signals back its findings without interpretation. I had no answer to Douglas's probing questions. I walked, and I looked at nothing in particular, and I struggled with diversions, as I still do. I know I am not alone in that.

Last week I took my neighbour to the Blue Mountains, but found, when we walked out to Pulpit Rock, there was little to see that was not immediately beneath our feet because the day was cloudy. When it started to rain, he offered to go back to the car to get his umbrella.

But he took so long, I was drenched by the time he returned. Before the afternoon was over we had both started to snap, and when we finally got home, the fire smoked, and a leaking wall behind my bookcase formed a large bubble underneath the blue paint, and then exploded, completely soaking *The Palm at the End of the Mind*, which bulked between its covers to nearly twice its size.

I last saw Herschel on his birthday. We talked about birthdays then, I think, because he was somehow embarrassed that I remembered, and knew very well my ambivalence about such occasions. 'I have always wondered,' I said, 'whether if we knew that on the 24th of January say, in such and such a year, we were going to be born, and that subsequent to that gruelling event, were going to have to endure seventy, even eighty years, perhaps more — would we chose to be born, or might we not just go on procrastinating about the time and the date forever? And go on sliding down the rainbow?'

'The latter,' he said, laughing. I think he wanted this train of thought to end and I am not sure why I persisted. 'And if we really had the choice, and nobody noticed or minded how we chose, once born, would we choose to remember the date at all, or just continue as best we could, letting the passage of time continue as best *it* could, as only it can... without the aid of our anniversaries?'

We were silent for a while then. He had set a small table for us out in the studio with a green batik cloth and serviettes and he asked me suddenly, as if he was impatient, to sit by the door where I would get the best view back up through his garden. A new path had been laid — so straight, so scrubbed and bare of moss or lichen that my spirits sank when I looked, though of course I said I admired it. Just near the back door of the house, two plastic bags of wild bird seed were waiting for the currawong. Herschel said Bill was going to build something for it to feed from high up in the Moreton Bay fig.

We waited a while for lunch, and he poured us some coffee he had made earlier that morning and talked about Tristan and Isolde. He told me Bill had taken him to see it last week, and that he had done some study before the performance with a borrowed copy of the libretto. I took out the pesto I had brought with me and said rather hurriedly I thought I had used too many pinenuts, and that I hadn't had time to go to David Jones for the potato gnocchi I had promised, but had bought dry pasta in Cooper's at Five Ways instead. We discussed coriander pesto and eggplant chips too, I think. We often talked about food, and it wouldn't be the first time we'd watched the morning sun move across the verandah and agreed that coriander pesto was really for winter, when basil wasn't available.

Somehow that dinner at my place, when Jill had arrived late with her daughter, bringing a huge bowl of raspberries and vanilla sugar with her and directing the whole conversation into an argument about Gide and Montherlant within minutes of her arrival, came up, as it had done before, and again we laughed. I can remember thinking at the time how it was our habit, and quite a comfortable one, to behave as if we were locked *in perpetua* in rehearsal.

Around the studio in which we were sitting, Herschel's canvasses were stacked against the walls, sometimes two or three deep, and he said he wanted to show them soon. I stepped outside to smoke a cigarette. 'It is often hard to find a good gallery,' I said. An old friend of mine, a ceramicist, had just exhibited his work in a country town where it had been arranged by the local council on red velvet, and the room had been lit by chandeliers. No matter how hard he tried, when his pots were set up like that he didn't feel as if they were his anymore.

Herschel said how lucky he felt he had been with his last exhibition and then we fell silent again. Now and then, I remember, we both looked out into the foliage of the flowering tree near the double doors, and across the lawn to the corner of a neighbour's shed which was nearly covered by a potato vine.

After a while we picked up our lunch things and went back into the house. As we put them away, we talked about the anger many people we knew felt for their parents, and their past. I said that as a habit of mind, I found it irritating. He agreed, then looked at me closely with that quizzical expression I knew so well which somehow expressed his doubt that he had heard me properly. 'I've had a wonderful life,' he said, wiping out the china salad bowl, 'though there has been a lot of sadness in it.'

It was at about that moment, I think, when the garden gate banged, and we heard steps, and greetings from Chip who materialised in the doorway with a grin and a large white plastic bag full of video cassettes which he stacked up at one end of Herschel's table. We made more coffee, and listened to him telling us about Deliah, his daughter, who is eleven, and is doing gymnastics, recorder, violin and Amnesty International after school. He said they'd got a poster in the house now saying 'Get rid of the noose!', and every time he looks at it, he wishes they hadn't agreed to put it up.

Herschel passed around a plate of almond biscuits, and Chip asked us whether we remembered the Hammersmith flyover in London. We were talking about topiaries. I remembered some in Bairnsdale in Gippsland, and Herschel had seen photos of a famous topiary in America in which a group of hounds and a fox are leaping over a hedge. Chip said that in Hammersmith he thought they were trying to make a topiary of the Crucifixion which would be clearly visible to the traffic on the flyover. 'So far they had only just got the wire netting under-structure in place, and now they were trying to encourage ivy or something to grow up it,' he groaned, 'perhaps to spite the pollution.'

Herschel insisted on coming up to the gate with me when I had to go, leaving Chip to wander in the garden. As I stepped out into the street, he looked in his letterbox where two identical red and yellow flyers lay folded on one side. 'I never get personal letters now', he said, and left the flyers lying in their corner.

And that was the last time I spoke to Herschel. There were other ways to remember it, but they all miss the point with equal facility, so that really it is a question of which strategy fails better than the others. For instance, I might have spent more time on Douglas, who lives with me on and off, and who keeps finding me titles for my notebooks from a book called *Fizzles* like *Imagination, at wit's end, spreads its sad wings*. (It gives Douglas a kick sometimes, to be witty at my expense.) But he was fond of Herschel too, they used to work together, so more about him would not have been inappropriate.

I might have told you how my musings had led . . . but that's the problem, I don't know where exactly, and perhaps 'led' is the wrong word since it raises expectations of consequences. And there aren't any. Not really. Not now when I try to walk around these memories as if they had been carved in stone and sometimes find I stub my toe. Memory and difference. I have not mastered them as Herschel had, and wonder if I ever will?

It is raining as it rains in the tropics, plunk, pause, plunk. Plunk. It is the 24th of January again, and the morning sky fits over Sydney like a lid of tarnished stainless steel. Over the road, Hestia waves as she sweeps across her tiled veranda. Much closer, a late cabbage moth settles noiselessly into my neighbour's Avon rose.

PARTICULAR FRIENDS

Margaret Sutherland

Margaret Sutherland has published several
novels and collections of short stories since
the mid 1970s. A new short story collection
will be published in 1991. She has been
awarded a New Zealand Scholarship in Letters
and was writing Fellow at Auckland University in 1981. A qualified comprehensive
nurse, Margaret has worked in the area of
migrant health since moving to Australia in
1986, and, more recently, has set up a music
teaching practice with her husband.

PARTICULAR FRIENDS

En route to New Zealand from a three-year stint in New Guinea, I saw Morgan again recently. We met in Sydney for the day. I was spending a week there while a specialist checked me for giardia, and Morgan came by train from the Central Coast, where she had settled. As we used to as students, we took our sandwiches to a green and shady park.

'You're thin,' she said. Well, a diet of rice and kaukau plus the tropical trots soon put paid to overweight. She on the other hand had gained weight and looked relaxed. Her new life and marriage seemed to be beneficial.

She asked me about the mission hospital and I showed her my photos. That was my life — the flooded river plain, the stilt huts, the dark, wary men, the women coming at dawn to gather fallen leaves for fuel. I told her about our work. The maternity complications are horrendous. People come too late, with eclampsia, prolapsed arms, dead babies that have to be sawn to pieces to be removed from the mother. Mind you, we deliver many a healthy, bawling infant to suckle those strong nipples that often share their milk with a prize piglet or two.

In those conditions, which quickly become the norm, it is the little things that send you crazy. Batteries, in my case. They never last in the climate and we have no electricity. We all dread night emergencies. I explained that I wanted a solar-powered torch. Ever-practical Morgan walked the legs off me for the rest of the day and when our enquiries led only to deadends, she promised to see what she could do. There was a scuttle at the end to get to the station on time. We parted there, as we seem bound to do, the mysterious bond of friendship still firm. What fastens it, I wonder?

145

We met in New Zealand, ten years ago, as students in the new comprehensive nursing course. I was twenty-six (it had taken me that long to make my vows as a missionary and discover I wasn't cut out for teaching) and Morgan was older, with a husband and teenagers. It wasn't only our role as 'mature students' that drew us together. A lapsed Catholic, Morgan wasn't mystified by a nun. We rarely talked about religion, though I knew she had joined some sect which acknowledged all creeds and prophets. It sounded a muddle to me, while I think she saw my faith as a straightjacket. It didn't matter. Unless people wish to argue or defend, what is there to say?

Our first day at college was a shock. It was hard to go back to school at my age. The introductory tutor told us to stop talking, called the roll, appointed a fire warden and addressed us on discipline. The class responded with giggles and whispers. Earnest in dowdy clothes and a plait, Miss Moss scolded and dismissed us for morning tea. I stood in the quadrangle, absorbing the atmosphere of the red brick institute that had once been a theological college, and seeing my classmates define their roles — the clown, the loner, the leader. The only religious symbols I wore with my ordinary dress were a half-veil and crucifix, but not many girls spoke to me. Perhaps they thought a nun's only topic of conversation was God. I was glad when Morgan offered to share her thermos of coffee. We walked back together to the class room. It was set up as a ward with linen trolleys, shelves of medical equipment and several iron beds, in one of which lolled a dummy with an expression reflecting the indignities we were to inflict on various parts of her anatomy.

Miss Moss, dashing about with bowls and towels, kept up an arch monologue as she removed the model's peach-pink nightgown to demonstrate a sponge bath. 'These are the new girls, Mrs Chase. Roll over and I'll rub your back. I'll just wash down here. All comfy now?' My amusement ceased when I heard we were to sponge one another. I was grateful when Morgan subjected herself to my clumsy washing. The soap was too soapy, the water dripped, and when Miss Moss dipped a practised elbow in my bowl she frowned. 'The poor patient, Sister Jane — get her dry!' Morgan had goose pimples. I dabbed and scrubbed and still Miss Moss shook her head. Morgan and I had to change places. I hid under the flannelette rug, blushing in a way that must have looked horrible with my ginger hair. Morgan was far more comfortable than I with others' physical aspects.

The coming months brought lectures on anatomy, physiology, microbiology, biochemistry, epidemiology, demography, pshychology and sociology. I even welcomed any opportunity to lay hands on Mrs Chase as tests came and went with never a sick person in sight. We stripped off spotless linen and made unoccupied beds. Miss Moss scolded, crisping the corners. Her compressed, frenetic energy earned her the apt nick-name of Mozzie. It was used in her hearing more than once. She looked at us like silly children, lectured us on untidy hair, laddered stockings and bad breath, and said we were off to the wards in a week's time. And so we went forth. The system let us in reluctantly. How could we be nurses, wearing blue and capless? I wore the light veil I had permission to retain in public, but it did not help my confidence. We did not belong, though our tutors were with us and we were well drilled in ward procedures and theoretical human needs — comfort, hygiene, nutrition, exercise, mental stimulation and the rest. We hated those classroom dossiers called Care Plans, for they took hours to write and revise daily, but they were teaching us to make instinctive care-giving into a method — not a bad exercise, as I've learned as a nun bound by the routine reading of my Office. Instinct isn't an objective guide; not in winter, not in the small hours!

We make decisions lightly until confronted by our choice. On that first day our brightest student found she didn't like nursing and withdrew from the course. The sights and smells of sickness had been missing from our classrooms. For myself, I knew I'd found my right work. I took out my ruled columns headed *Assess, Plan, Implement, Evaluate*, and sat down with my patient, ready to consider any problem from ill-fitting teeth to disquiet of soul. She was a mother of several children. She answered my questions while she knitted. I wrote my first plan of care-giving and took it away, privately, to come to terms with helplessness. For a doctor had just explained to us both, as kindly as he could, that her cancer could not be treated. 'Thank you,' she said. 'Desmond starts at the convent next term — he counts and prints his name, you know.' I saw the half-made little sock, suspended.

Morgan found me in tears, and tried to comfort me. 'She wouldn't accept that diagnosis,' I explained. 'I don't know what to do for her.'

'If I had to die and leave my children, I couldn't bear to know, either,' Morgan said.

When I returned next morning, my patient had died in her sleep. I was assigned to a teenager. His leg was in traction and he was bored stiff. We played cards and checkers and I learned about heavy metal through his earphones. He wanted to know if I dyed my hair. Had I ever had a boyfriend? Before the week was up, I knew he feared he'd be left with a limp, and wondered if he'd have the courage to ride another motor bike. 'I'm *bored*,' was his catchcry. I felt sympathetic for I have the nature that is said to go with red hair. Temper and impatience may not run away with me these days, yet, secretly, I abhor meekness, that virtue praised by Christ. I don't want to inherit the earth — it is heaven tugging at my soul!

We all had our problems that first winter. Some were dealing with homesickness, budgeting small bursaries, finding their way around an unfamiliar city. Getting to distant hospitals for a seven am start was no joke. I was delighted when my Order bought me a motor scooter, and my nick-name, *the flying nun*, helped lay the ghost of spiritual pretension, I felt. In fact my vocation felt very dull. These days, nuns who claim miraculous visitations and heavenly voices might end up in the psychiatrist's office. Still, I was in an empty state, without an ounce of joy. I recited my Office like a laundry list, prayed mechanically, picked up books supposed to help. *When The Well Runs Dry* was one. I flicked its pages. I knew my problems were trivial compared to others'. One girl had to leave because of illness and another, who loved nursing, because her marks were poor. Classmates mentioned private pains — a sister with leukaemia, a friend killed in a car accident. I felt gauche, for my family life was an uneventful and a happy one. While girls gossiped about love affairs, I went back to the little community house I shared with two sisters, both retired from the mission field. Sister Elspeth made the altar breads for the district. Sister Bertha was a chronic invalid who spent a lot of time in bed. We had a stray cat.

Morgan seemed immune from our winter depressions. The colds and coughs we harboured, as draughts, eddied in the stairwells and through the classrooms, did not affect her. She did not miss a single day. She said she often studied late at night. I could not see how she could do justice to husband and family, but marriage is not my thing. My relationship is with the Faithful One, expressed through each one of his creatures. I had enough to attend to without speculating on my friend. She seemed to have her life sorted out and I grimly clung to my own handlebars, negotiating those treacherous winter passages.

A new tutor, Miss Gould, joined the staff. She was an experienced paediatric nurse, said Miss Moss. We would be grateful for her long years in the field. Miss Gould accepted this introduction with a quiet smile, and I was struck by the transforming kindness and warmth that altered her plain looks. Miss Moss was in her element that term. She told us about the birthday party her parents had just given her. 'Heavens, girls! Another year gone, and I haven't had my babies yet.' She believed, as I have never done for myself, that her fulfilment lay with children. While she could sweep upon the wards, wiping grubby faces and singing off-key nursery rhymes that made her little patients stare and forget their tears, I found the going hard. Hard to witness innocent suffering—equally hard to put up with tantrums and grizzles. Counting the weeks to the end of term, I failed to notice Morgan's look of strain. One day she told me her husband was suggesting a separation, and one of her sons was in trouble for truancy.

'It's all my fault, I'll have to pull out,' she said.

I resorted to my own way of warding off emotional scenes. 'Theory has to be of practical use, Morgan. Write a Care Plan for your family.'

We both smiled, and a few days later she had followed my flippant suggestion. 'I've really had to think about things, Jane. The principal is giving me a few days off. I have to make some changes.'

She came back a week later. It wasn't long enough, she said, but things were better at home. 'How can we become so out of touch, Jane?' I knew how she felt. Wailing, homesick children were not my thing, never mind Mozzie's cries of, 'Oh, the little ones!' I was delighted the end of the year was at hand and grateful Morgan hadn't left. My affection may be undemonstrative but I would have missed her very much.

I used the summer holiday for a visit to see my parents and a long private retreat that watered my spirits. And then, on a hot February day, I was a second-year student sitting on the museum steps beside Morgan. 'Dry sandwiches and gossip—never again, Jane. Let's walk at lunchtime.' It was pleasant in the Domain. Joggers exercised and tourists chattered in foreign languages. We followed them past the white pillars to look at Maori artefacts and meeting houses. Perhaps it was the spirits Morgan claimed to feel that made us late for afternoon lectures. The tutor neither acknowledged nor reprimanded us. Childhood was over; Miss Moss had new fledglings under her wing. I glimpsed her in corridors or on the wards. Her hair was cut in a modern style now and she dressed smartly. Those in the know (how this occurs I cannot say as I am always the last to hear) said she had disagreed with her parents and fundamental church authorities on some private issue and left home. She'd taken a flat with Patsy Gould.

I suppose shelter has to be outgrown. In convents of the past, as well as families, its effects all too often included a stifling ignorance of the self. Now we are sent out into the world to learn about ourselves and others. We are expected to develop insight. To see one's nature is to be made humble. Until then, pride will tinge our service. These days there is more responsibility and less fear in being a nun. How suspect were human affections in convents of the past! Novice mistresses warned against 'particular friends'. I have never experienced that intense bonding myself, although for a certain kind of emotional nature it does not seem to me surprising, for loneliness is not a sought-after state. Am I defending myself against a charge of coldness? I am not cold, though at times I am a person filled with self-doubt. As the term wore on and I watched classmates and tutors plough through their various friendships and love affairs both happy and tragic, hearing murmurs of a pregnancy here or a triangle of jealousy there, I felt more and more alone. As always, I got on with my work.

Morgan quickly ceased to mention lunchtimes with nature. We crammed our sandwiches and withdrew to the library. No doubt we were regarded as all swots are, but Morgan had confided she was determined to keep home and work life separate, while I, still touched by the grace of that time spent alone listening for the barely audible Voice, felt the same. I would take more of myself to prayer than a ragged and exhausted shell.

Our second year of training had an even heavier weight of learning than our first. Once, nurses went their separate ways like fishes at a river's tributaries — caring for the sick in body, or the handicapped, or the mentally ill, or the new-born. But we were encouraged to cease counting conditions as though cutting up a health cake, and to think about the wholeness of each person in our care. Hence our second-year curriculum explored the fringe areas that gave the course its Comprehensive title. Soon, even the most fun-loving students showed up more often in the library. I suspected their extracurricular activities might become as restricted as my own — a pile of books, a cup of Milo, and strains of Sister Bertha's favourite 'Coronation Street' wailing through the wall.

Humanity dons many cloaks. In the chronic wards of mental hospitals, the fact was hard to face. We would all select a fairer and more pleasant world, devoid of ugly sights, bad smells, inhuman noises that could have been communication or a grunt of anguish. I choose extremes to make the point that quite often I was afraid of my patients. Sometimes I would look into eyes which seemed to reflect my deepest conventions, most entrenched fears. *I am like this — what are you covering up?* Is it that we need a model to find certain hidden aspects of ourselves? When all is controlled, so are we, for socialising is a powerful process. These cast-off people showed up my glaring conformity. They did not know or would not use the tools of propriety, discretion or politeness. I hated the yelling or the throwing, the blatant scenes. Emotional excess freezes me. Reserve sets in my inner channels, inhibiting compassion and forbidding love. I did not know how to relate to these people who wanted neither my counsel nor my pity.

I began to endure deep loneliness. At group meetings held for the students as part of this psychiatric training period, I sat miserably apart. One by one, the others spoke of doubts, fears, mistakes. I had no idea how to share myself this way. I could not even show that I admired their openness. Mouth clamped, I sat week after week in their circle. I had an inkling of those states of clinical isolation we studied in textbooks and observed in the wards. Sometimes, overwhelmed by the memory of some early shame or trauma, a girl would break down and weep. Our tutor was not afraid of tears. She would place her arm around the girl and wait.

Why did this part of the course uncover the hurts and wounds so many of us carried? Perhaps our interaction with the psyche and its suffering witnesses was reflecting a journey within each of us. Certainly I hated the atmosphere. There I was compelled to be, day after day, my head down and my hands twisting and turning bitten nails. Everyone contributed but me. No one questioned my silence. No one commented on my evident uninvolvement. They were accepting. I found this most painful of all.

That pain had its effect at last. I had had a dreadful day. The patients had been dreadful and the nurses on that ward had been dreadful. I had been part of a scene of violence, control and retribution . . . oh, a very subtle control, there was no ball and chain nor even the old-fashioned paraldehyde to quell and silence. Yet I seemed to find myself part of a universal madness. Everything seemed gross, all faults distorted. By the time I arrived at the group, I knew I must try to share my confusion and upset with the others.

It was a rainy day. I came in late, still in oilskins for I was working on a remote ward and had ridden my bike back to the meeting room. I sat down and thought of what I needed to say. I could not say it. Not a word would form. My mouth would not formulate a sound, not even a groan as inarticulate as any helpless patient could express. The deepest sadness filled me. I grew heavy with it. It overpowered me. I felt my body crumple and lose resistance and I was on the floor, weeping. In the depth of this shame (it felt shameful) I was also conscious and relieved. My self-containment was taken from me. I was like a catatonic woman whose silence is at last plundered. There on the floor I wept and waited for the comfort of my friends.

It did not come. They did not know a nun can weep, that she can need the comfort of a human touch. My kind tutor, who could so readily slip her arm around my classmates, did not know how much I wanted a similar confirmation of my flesh-and-blood humanness. I suppose they all stared and felt sorry for me, wondering if a nun was allowed to be comforted.

Perhaps I was weeping or perhaps I had stopped, knowing I had asked for something that would never be shown to me. I thought I would have to remain there on the floor for ever, for how could I lift up my head and look at them? Then I felt a touch. It was distant, for my oilskins were thick. I could smell their ugly, greasy smell. A hand was reassuring me. It moved to my hot, sweaty face and began to stroke my hair kindly. I felt the deepest gratitude as I accepted the unknown hand. Then I sensed it was Morgan's as I recognised the wedding-ring, and said, It's you? She went on stroking my hair. Eventually I must have got up; we must have all gone home. I don't remember that . . . only the insight into the meaning of that much used word, loneliness. Patients often mention it. I became a better nurse that day.

On we trudged around the spiral of study, exams, wet weather, strange wards, weariness and those unique, gifted moments that made it all worthwhile. Suddenly it was spring again. From the tortuous passages of the mind, we progressed to the straightforward anatomy and physiology of childbirth. I was very interested in this part of the course. I knew my future work in the Pacific would involve midwifery and maternity experience and I took good care to learn. I like obstetrics. It was quick, with a clear outcome. There was an excitement to the delivery phase and a satisfaction at seeing mother and child safe and well. I was willing to rub backs, sponge foreheads and give encouragement all night long if necessary, and the women were touchingly grateful for my tiny services. I felt I had a gift for sensing when things might not go well, for several private assessments I did not dare share with qualified midwives and doctors turned out to be accurate. After the trials of the previous term, I was granted a most welcome respite.

For weeks I lost touch with Morgan, who was gaining clinical experience at a different hospital. On our next joint study day she was away. I thought she must be sick, and phoned her that evening. She sounded stunned. Her son had been involved in several acts of vandalism with other schoolboys and she'd been summoned to court to attend his hearing. The magistrate had said that, juveniles or not, their offences were serious and that a repetition would see them in a remand home. Some hard words had been directed at the parents for failing to exercise proper control.

'Control! What do they want me to do? Tie him down, lock him up? He's bigger than I am.'

Poor Morgan, who tried so hard to manage life and be a success, had met her match in the child of her body. I'd met the boy and liked him; reminded of myself at his age . . . that is, without the restraints of different times and a father with a leather belt!

'I'll have to give up my training. The meals aren't balanced and there's dust and it's true, I don't talk to the boys enough but what can you say to teenagers with earphones?'

I felt sympathetic yet irritated. Though I'm no mother, I sensed the role could create a lot of negative definitions. I am glad I will never be a parent. When people tire of blaming God for the world's free will, they shift their judgments to parents and their offspring. In a few stern sentences, I told Morgan to advise her rather spoiled son that a stretch in a remand home would do him the world of good, if he so chose. She sounded horrified.

'But Garth and I have to be interviewed by a social worker, Jane.'

'That should be educational,' I said firmly. 'Compare their technique with your own in counselling patients. You might learn something.' Personally, I would be a hopeless counsellor. That was more up Morgan's street. She could cope with tears and dramas; any astute teenager would discern and play havoc with that.

She and her husband weren't on speaking terms, Morgan said. She blamed him for lack of discipline, he said she was over-protective. I thought I'd like to administer a few red-head's boxes to the ears of that shrewd young expert in divide-and-rule. 'Morgan, your son will be off and away in a few years. Go and make it up with Garth and get back here to work. Really, you're a good mother.'

She latched on to this, of course. Why are we so insecure, and so ready to take on the definitions of others? At least she came back to work. She looked ill and her work had an automatic quality. Some idea she'd needed to believe in had been destroyed and she looked lost. I've had to shed illusions of what I thought I was, too. Such times are desolate but we go on and one day confusion drops away. I don't know what Morgan had to shed (some false ideal of motherhood, perhaps); I only recognised a process I will know again, for self-deception is an endless series of skins.

We finished out the term. At the annual presentation ceremony and ball I watched her with her husband. How lightly they spun on the dance floor, and how little their inner struggle showed. I sat with a few others who had no wish or opportunity to dance, thinking that a year earlier I might have envied them.

Throughout the three-year training it was often pointed out to us that our curriculum made a spiral ascent, continually returning us to starting points where our changing perspectives, developed through teaching and experience, shed new light on basic premises. So it seemed appropriate one day in my third year to see a familiar figure in the hospital corridor. The hairstyle was soft and the hem-line a fashionable length but it was undoubtedly Mozzie.

'Sister Jane! How are you taking to nursing?'

Taking to nursing . . . nursing had taken me, for a lifetime. I smiled at her. 'State Finals in six months.'

'Golly! All swot and no play then. I remember getting in a frightful flap before mine. Up all night, gallons of coffee, smoking, even.

Remember not to worry, that's the secret. Take it calmly—do your best—that's all you can do.'

I nodded. 'What are you doing here, Miss Moss?' She was in street clothes and I knew there were none of her students in this gynaecology ward.

'I'm cutting through to visit Patsy.'

'Is she ill?'

'She's—unwell.' Mozzie reminded me of my mother, spelling out evasions unsuitable for my curious young ears.

'Please wish her speedy recovery. You must miss her. I know you two are fond of each other.' At this passing remark of mine, Mozzie blushed and her eyes blurred with tears. 'My relationship with Patsy is purely emotional,' she felt a need to say, 'but you're right. We're very close and I'm extremely worried. She's having tests done.'

Tests. The frail body, vehicle of fear. 'I do hope they go well.'

'Oh I hope so, Sister Jane. I do hope so. I must away—good luck with the exams.'

I felt sorry for her, watching her go nervously away as though hurrying from some pursuing insight.

I saw less and less of Morgan for often we worked in hospitals on opposite sides of the city. Our community experience with district and public health nurses took us out among the poor, the derelict, the old. I liked meeting people in their own setting, however run-down or dirty; there they held on to a stubborn sense of self which hospitals play havoc with, conspiring in orderly ways to return patients to an infantile dependency. Their clothes are taken away, they are put to bed, washed, subjected to indignities and pain, and regarded as difficult if they grumble or ask questions. At least where I would be sent to nurse, patients would turn to Western medicine only as a last resort and would remove themselves as soon as possible from the queer ways of white doctors and nurses. We were unlikely to attract chronic dependents in the Pacific backblocks. Poor they might be, but the old and the lame would always have their corner in the village. I knew the medical problems would be quite different, so I hope optional clinical work in appropriate areas. I went to the medical library for texts on tropical diseases. Armed with colour plates of yaws, ulcers, leprosy and other horrid infections, I spent many an evening curled up in bed away from Sister Bertha's television set. When I let it, our little cat kept me company, springing on my counterpane and burrowing into my armpit like a newborn, in a way I found comforting. I read up on obstetrics, knowing my deliveries were likely to be carried out by the light of a hurricane lantern and far from oxygen lines, resuscitation equipment and all the fancy ware. Mozzie's advice would come back to me; take it calmly, do my best.

When Morgan and I did meet up, we exchanged potted accounts of our weeks apart. Funny how there's less to say about the events of a month than of a day. Time irons out the momentary significance. We were all preparing for the last hurdle. Training was indeed an appropriate name for this experience. We would go on now, until it was over. I doubt if even one of us hadn't longed to give up at some point. It wasn't just the hard work and the study. Daily we had to deal with the flesh and its power. A nun, of all people, should be committed to the life of the spirit yet often, witnessing pain and despair, I wondered if the body might be all there was. But we'd all grown stronger. Girls no longer took days off with minor ailments or emotional problems. Morgan stopped listing her insufficiencies as a wife and mother and I went on with my prayers without analysis.

We were all called in to college for a final revision week before State Finals. It was there that the last and most unhappy rumour of my training found its way eventually to me. I knew Morgan had spent her recent clinical weeks in gynaecology and went to ask her if what I'd heard was true. She said she thought everyone knew that Patsy Gould had cancer. The uterus and ovaries, with secondaries. She was having radiotherapy. 'You know the outlook,' she said, describing the way that Mozzie, draped from head to foot in the protective clothing visitors had to wear, sat every day holding her friend's wasted hand and promising her that everything would turn out well.

'It's pathetic, Jane. Patsy knows her prognosis. She has to pretend. I suppose she'll linger on, trying to protect Mozzie.'

'You once told me that if you were dying you wouldn't know how to bear the leaving of your children,' I reminded her.

We sat our exams. On a day in early summer we reassembled as a class for the last time. There in the quadrangle I met Miss Moss. There had been an announcement of Patsy's death in the paper. I'd sent a card of sympathy to the college, not knowing Mozzie's home address. She thanked me and told me she had left her flat and gone home. Her parents had been good to her, and the church, she said. 'We need our family and friends in times of trouble, Sister Jane.'

Times of trouble, and return to the fold of the past. Yet I felt she had gone past platitudes. When she was strong again she would understand her grieving better. She still had her clichés, her search for a good, safe, simple world, but her body was different. She walked more quietly and the look in her her eyes was reflective. 'So this is goodbye — you're off to the missions?'

'God willing! If I pass.'

'I'm sure you did your best.'

We went our separate ways and I never saw her again.

I longed to be done with farewells. Nuns move on wherever they are sent without yearning for the past or speculating much about the future. It's not to say we don't need friends. We can't cling but we may care. When Morgan approached, on the verge of tears and exclaiming, 'I can't believe it's all over,' I hardly knew what to say. For it *was* over. I was pleased when the principal arrived to give her final address and we went to find a seat, Morgan sniffing and blowing her nose beside me.

We both passed our exams. When the results came out, I was at home holidaying with my parents before making preparation to leave for the Islands. Caught up in all that whirl, I could only arrange a short visit with Morgan and in fact we did not have a lot to say to each other. Her husband was home and, as I'd noticed at other times, she seemed to shut down in some way in his presence. I sensed their difficulties had not been resolved. She hugged me when I left. We promised we would keep in touch.

And so we do, on thin blue aerogrammes that intermittently defy oceans, rivers, floods and the erratic postal channels of the Pacific outposts where I've worked. Her parcel arrived last week by river boat and we laughed like kids at Christmas as we unpacked the torch and solar panel with instructions in her new husband's careful printing. A God-send, we agreed, unable to believe in that perpetual beam of light that would make such a difference to our lives and work.

The mission's quiet tonight. Just one girl in labour, with a while yet to go. Her relatives hang about outside, murmuring in the language I still can't share. I sit and watch, my gift in my hand, letting loneliness work.

CONVERSATION IN THE PARK

Amy Witting

Amy Witting says that being born in inner-city Sydney in the great depression set for her lifetime her main subject matter — survival. Educated at the local convent school, Fort Street Girls' High School and Sydney University, she later taught English and languages, lived in boarding houses, listening to landladies and scavenging material for short stories. She married in 1948, and, following the birth of her son and a spell in a TB sanatorium, applied herself to writing. *I For Isobel* was published in 1989, and *Marriages* in 1990.

CONVERSATION IN THE PARK

In the hot, bright air the fountain flashed pins and needles. The pins and needles melted into drops and fell in glistening rain behind the charcoal-coloured swans as they circled the lake. Tom and Alice had eaten their lunch in the shade of the giant figtree that stood on a slight rise sloping down to the water. Alice folded her paper bag and put it in her briefcase. Tom set down his last sandwich unfinished on its wrapper.

'Swans,' she said. 'They're not calm at all really, not relaxed. Look at them, all controlled tension.'

Tom had been looking more absently than she at the dark marble and silver gauze that formed the living centrepiece of the lake. Now that his attention was drawn to the outside world, he had for it a smile of affectionate acceptance she knew well and loved, so that for a moment her look was a parody of his.

'Wearing themselves out keeping up the swan image,' he agreed. His discontented air returned as he added. 'I don't see why you're so set against coming.'

'Not set.' She was trying so hard to sound indifferent that she spoke as if she were dropping off to sleep. 'I told you, there's a family do I think I'd better go to.'

'I thought you said you didn't have a family.'

'Did I say that? I'm trying to cut loose. Can't cut them out entirely, I suppose.'

She was lying. She didn't intend to go near the family mansion, the glossy pile which represented everything she most despised. As soon as she'd got her hands on Grandma's money she had left it with joy. The room in Glebe was a staging post on the way to Bangladesh, where she would do real work among real people. Meanwhile she was trying the experience of poverty, for fear underfloor heating, spa baths and Mrs Potter's cooking had softened her bones. But that was all right; poverty didn't worry her.

'Can't you go there some other time?' One of the swans had come to shore and was trudging, flat-footed and swag-bottomed, along the edge of the lake.

'No. I told you. It's a do. Special occasion.'

Trying to contrive a plausible lie, she reflected that every occasion in that house was special. Nobody ever dropped in, there was never a snack meal, never a friend only the right people, who usually turned out in the end to be not quite the right people.

Fortunately, he was not interested in the special occasion.

'Helen's been looking forward to meeting you.' She wished he could say that girl's name without wrapping it in velvet. Beautiful Helen. Helen, thy beauty is to me . . . She hadn't given a stuff about beauty, had never regretted her lack of it, seing it as part of the rubbish Mum and Fiona cluttered their lives with, until she had fallen in love, up to her chin, her long, crooked, pointed chin, about which, as Mum so frequently lamented, nothing could be done. Not even then, not until she had seen the beauty passing at the other end of the Quad and heard a voice behind her say 'Tom Allan fancies her, and no wonder.' She was glad the voice was behind her as she swallowed those words alive, and with them the sad discovery that young men who lived for Philosophy were moved by silky blonde hair and regular features, just as much as the silly young men who courted Fiona.

'Some other time, then,' she said. 'Look at that swan, will you? You only have to see a swan out of water to know what an illusion beauty is.'

'You'd enjoy it, you know, once you got there.'

'I doubt that. Not quite my thing, really.' He said crossly, 'Take yourself seriously, don't you?'

No, she didn't. She used to take herself seriously, now she didn't. She had been the only person in that household she did take seriously, except for Mrs Potter the cook and maybe Dad, who worked hard and effectively at making money. Mum and Fiona put just as much work and worry into spending it, with little success, climbing a ladder which existed only in their minds.

She had taken herself seriously because of Bangladesh, code name for some yet unknown place in the Third World where she would spend Grandma's money and do it right, learn the language, live in the village, supervise the workmen, see to it that the well got sunk and the school got built.

'No, I don't. Some reason for taking myself seriously, that's what I'd like.'

You could be it. Bangladesh had receded. It was love that softened the bones.

He said nothing. He was disconcerted that she felt entitled to take herself seriously. He tore a piece from his unfinished sandwich and tossed it to the foraging swan, which killed it with one stroke, swallowed it and came towards them, the mean relationship between beak and eye suddenly apparent.

'You'll be sorry you did that. One moment of weakness and you'll find yourself supporting a swan for the rest of your life.'

He tore off another piece of bread and threw it as far as he could. The swan lumbered after it.

'The thing is that you're putting me in an awkward position. I thought we'd be working on the thesis, and when Helen mentioned the party, I said you'd be at a loose end, so of course she said to bring you. It's going to look a bit odd if you don't come.'

'Just tell her something came up.'

One thing, he wouldn't be pressuring her like this if he knew. She had promised herself that if he ever found out she was deep in love with him, she would take off at once. She'd never stand that humiliation.

Love! he was thinking. (Not only did he know; so did three librarians, the clerk who gave them numbered tokens in exchange for their briefcases in the lobby, and an old woman who spent her days in the library taking notes for a historical novel about the Young Pretender.) Love! What was the use of it if they wouldn't do the slightest thing you wanted? Helen had been difficult, too.

'Oh, not that awful girl!'

'She's not so bad when you get to know her.'

'I don't want to get to know her.' He had had to refer to the life-plan. A good thing about Helen was that she understood the life-plan without any discussion.

'She helps me a lot. She's typing my thesis for me. I couldn't trust anyone else with the job, and she's really useful in checking things. I couldn't get everything done without her.' Helen had been waspish. 'How can she help you if she's in Philosophy I and you're doing an Honours thesis? I don't see it.'

'She reads everything up. She's only doing the donkey work, looking up quotes and checking references. It suits her; she wants to learn as much as she can in a year and I'm giving her a line to follow.'

'It sounds weird to me. What is she living on?' He laughed. 'Mung beans and pita bread, I think. She's taken a year off work to live on her savings while she looks for some answers.'

He examined the word weird. It applied to Alice. Yet applied to Alice, it had some attraction, even a kind of poetry. He wasn't being entirely honest with Helen, either. It wasn't just a matter of the life-plan. He liked Alice's company and didn't want to lose it.

Alice said, 'Here's your friend again. I warned you.'

This time, the swan had come closer. He hissed at it, glad of an outlet for his bad temper. It took a step back and two forward.

'Ugly thing,' she said. 'Go on. Get back in the water. Hide your feet. They do you no credit.'

He took up the last crust and threw it high and far, sending the bird trundling after it.'

'You understand, I'm asking this as a favour.' The look he gave went through her like a large pin through a small insect. She thought, he does know. He wants a faithful Dobbin. To Alice, faithful Dobbin was one character in fiction who needed an analyst.

'Oh, look. Here it comes again!' She squawked in fear and jumped backwards, stumbling among the roots of the great figtree and clinging to its trunk as the swan bustled forward and thrust its beak towards her, neck extended and wings spread.

'Don't panic!'

He took his denim jacket from the grass and snapped it at the swan, then chased it, flapping the jacket behind it, towards the lake, where it slid into the water, resuming its regal dignity at once.

How beautiful he was! Could she really leave him? As soon as the thesis is finished, she lied to herself.

He came back, grumbling, 'That wouldn't have happened if you'd kept your head.'

162

'Sorry, sorry. I dislike the creatures.'

'You made that obvious.'

'Well, if we're not going to be working on Saturday night, we'd better get back to John Stuart Mill. I could finish that book this afternoon.'

'Mmm.' He took out a cigarette and smoked in silence. At last he said, 'I'd just like to know what you've got against Helen.'

That was near the bone. Did he really expect her to tell him? He couldn't know; he must be saying that in innocence.

'I'd like to know why you're so keen to get me to that party.'

'I don't believe your excuse. You never mentioned that date before. I think it's inverted snobbery. You've taken against Helen because her father's a brain surgeon. Inverted snobbery, that's all it is. Maybe he's an effigy, but Helen's all right. You don't have to meet her parents anyhow. There's a big rumpus room under the house, that opens on to the pool. Helen entertains her friends in the rumpus room.'

She snapped at him, 'Games room!' then was appalled, because that was her mother's voice and she was after all her mother's daughter, sneering at unfortunate people who owned rumpus rooms. Words were the last things to go.

He was staring at her angrily.

She said apologetically, looking down at the grass, 'Games room. Games, you know. The billiard table and table tennis, and the darts board, which is a bit of decorator's whimsy because nobody plays darts; it goes with the panelled bar in the corner, mock-up from an English pub. If not, just basement will do.'

Nervously, she looked up at him. He was lusting, lips agape and eyes burning. She was describing his Heaven. What price Bentham? What price Socrates and John Stuart Mill? Lusting after a games room.

The silence was prolonged. She sank her head in her hands and her shoulders began to heave. Had he pushed it too far? Was she crying? Oh, God, was there going to be a scene? Why hadn't he let it alone, let sleeping dogs lie?

'All right,' he said. 'All right, forget it. Sorry I mentioned it.'

'Too late.' She straightened up, shaking her head, gasping with laughter. 'Too late. I saw your feet. Saw your feet.' She got up, still laughing, and picked up her briefcase. 'Sorry. I'm off.' She strode across the grass to the park exit.

Bangladesh, here I come.

163

THE LETTER

Sharon Blaikie

Sharon Blaikie was born and brought up in Invercargill, New Zealand. Among other things she has been a charwoman in London, a dry cleaner in Florence and a solicitor in various parts of New Zealand. She writes for the pleasure of it.

THE LETTER

All the way up from Riverton, I wished they'd be quiet.

We'd hardly started and Lydia began on the 'How long is it now?', 'Are we nearly there?' questions. Gerry kept wriggling his spikey little body into my side. And my mother chattered on and on. I couldn't ignore her because just as I was settling into my thoughts she'd draw me back.

'I really think it must be like that, don't you dear?' she'd say, or, 'What do you think, Susan?'

I'd have to think of some reply. Anything. Otherwise she fell into a huff. And I felt guilty. I was only back for two months and the time was almost over. Was it too much to give two months of your undivided attention to your mother who had devoted years of her life to you? Who was so garrulous and uninteresting in large part no doubt because of it? She never said as much but she thought it. And so did I. That it wasn't too much to ask, that is.

I was finding it hard going on the trip up though. It took all the willpower I could muster not to give up. But I knew I'd hate myself later if I did. So I found answers to give her.

And it wasn't as bad as my father.

Every so often he interrupted us to say, 'Well Susan, this will be the last time you see your grandmother.'

He must have said it three or four times and each time he said it as though he were making an original observation.

I wanted to hiss, 'Shut up. What's it to you? It's not your mother. You don't even like her.'

But I kept that down as well. I knew what would happen if I didn't and I wasn't strong enough to stop it. My father would bark back and

165

my mother would join in and all of us would start squabbling and saying hurtful things. Then the bored vibes Hugh was sending me would sharpen into disgust.

Hugh's family never go on like that. They take care to be positive and respectful to each other. His father is the curator of quite an important museum back in Canada and his mother teaches Art History in a college there. They place a high value on civilised behaviour.

My parents have lost the skill altogether or never ever acquired it. I can't remember which it is. But my mother must have known what it was like to grow up in a family that was civil. Her family sound a lot like Hugh's in some respects.

I looked over at Hugh and saw he was distancing himself as much as possible from us. I knew he resented this two months and somehow later, back in Canada, I would pay for it. Hugh values civilised behaviour too but his notion of it skims across surfaces. He was looking absently out the window at the hills he found so monotonous. I gazed past him at the thousand subtle variations of green folding on to green, the light dipping into shade as the white, white clouds coursed across the sky. And I knew my loss.

I looked away.

I picked up Gerry and drew him on to my lap. Bony as he is, his little body is still babyish and I wanted to tap into its warmth and comfort. I had no other thought in mind, but to my surprise he snuggled his head into the cradle of my arm and Lydia, jealous as always, nudged her head into my side.

By the time my mother turned querulously to see why I had not replied to her latest conversation gambit, their eyelids were drooping down into sleep. She gave me a conspiratorial smile of false understanding, then tapped my father on the shoulder and in exaggerated mime explained to him why he must be quiet. He briefly took his eyes off the road to turn and wink at me approvingly. For a moment I loved him.

Silence opened up in the car and I was free. Free to let my memories drift in and out at random; to sift the ones that would give the key to what I would say to my Nana, when I saw her for this last time.

I knew it would be the last time. The medicines which kept her body fluids in check, stopped them bloating her legs till liquids oozed out through the pores of her skin, were destroying her liver. It was only a question of which would kill her first, bringing her long uneventful life to its end.

I thought of Nana dying. I had seen it happening last time I was up, about a month ago. The doctor had reduced her medication to give her liver a spell and I could not keep my eyes away from the place where her legs bulged out over her slippers.

'Old age is no fun,' she said when she saw me looking. She repeated it several times during the afternoon. But she wasn't complaining, not really. The thought of associating fun with old age had caught her fancy.

I smiled inwardly too. Partly because I wouldn't have thought fun high on Nana's list of Life's Priorities. And partly because it wasn't really true either. For all her infirmities, it seemed to me that Nana was coming closer to having fun in the Eventide Rest Home than at any other time since I'd known her.

'You'll have noticed, I've had my hair cut,' she said, preening a little.

Yes, I had noticed. It looked all wrong. It wasn't her. All the time I'd known her, she'd rolled her long brownish hair in a cramped version of a forties style. That was Nana.

I didn't say anything, just nodded and smiled.

'It's nearly all white now. I always admired white hair,' she continued with satisfaction. 'I have to have it permed, otherwise I can't keep it. The hairdresser comes every Tuesday. I usually go.'

Her voice warmed with enthusiasm when she described the other highlights in her week—Mrs Alison came to do the flowers on Wednesdays ('Such a nice woman, only I don't think she knows much about bulbs') and Mr Simpson from the church read to them on Sunday evenings after the service.

'Such a lovely timbre to his voice. He reads so beautifully.' She leaned towards me. 'I thought I might offer to recite "How They Brought the Good News from Ghent to Aix,"' her eyes sparkling at the prospect. Then the light died down. 'But I don't have the courage,' she said regretfully.

'So you still remember it all?' I asked and I felt myself a child again mesmerised by the galloping rhythm and the gusto of her recitation.

'Yes. Oh yes I think so,' she said.

But she couldn't remember my children's ages or the name of the town where my cousin had gone to live. Outside the Home and her memories the world was gliding out beyond her ken.

'I don't watch TV much any more or do much reading. Now's the time for *people*,' was something else she repeated several times that afternoon.

She fretted too because her special friend, Mrs Renwick, was ill in bed with the 'flu and I couldn't meet her. I couldn't imagine Nana with a special friend. Her sisters had provided her with most of the company she needed.

'I do so like her, Susan. She's my partner at Canasta in the evenings.' Nana told me that with a certain reticent pride. Not everyone got invited to play. My mother said she had hankered to be asked from the moment she arrived. Nana had always loved cards. I know that would have been the reason, not the kudos. But now she had been admitted to the inner circle, the unfamiliar taste of social conquest was proving very sweet.

When she told me these things, it was as though we were back in her sitting room, and my teenage self and I were one. But the warm intimacy was elusive and, once recaptured, difficult to hold. It was like arriving at a concert too late and trying to recall a favourite aria from the sounds drifting out into the auditorium. It was fine while Nana forgot she thought she did not understand me, that I was an enigma. When she remembered, we lapsed into stilted silences and passing formal observations. The confidences we shared were brief, tantalising interludes in a long, difficult afternoon.

Before I left she opened her purse to take out a small package wrapped in tissue paper. As she did so I caught a glimpse of my last letter to her. It was a long letter but at the sight of it I felt uncomfortably guilty. It must have been at least two years since I had written it.

'I want you to have these,' she said formally, giving me the packet.

I opened out the tissue to find a string of garnet beads. I had always coveted those beads. She would have liked to say, 'I hope you still like them,' because she feared I mightn't, but that would be fishing for gratitude. Oh, but I did. I still loved those beads, prisms of deep red light. I thanked her profusely but I wasn't sure if she realised how sincere I was.

Why couldn't my parents have just lent me the car so I could have come up on my own? Said goodbye to my Nana on my own. Why couldn't they have thought of it? Why couldn't I have asked? But I couldn't. In my family you do not ask. You express gratitude for what you receive.

No, no asking.

If I had been allowed to come on my own, I would have started much earlier and driven up through the Catlins. Then I could have stopped at Punawea. I have never been there but I have seen photographs of it, taken just before the First World War. That is where my grandparents met.

I would have wandered about in the undergrowth looking for traces of the boarding house where they stayed. If I was lucky, I would have found the foundations. Then I could have sketched them and asked Nana to show me where the dining room was and she would have told me for one last time of the moment when she first caught sight of my grandfather. Of how she looked up from her plate as he entered the room. And how she had trouble with her peas.

I would have told her if the jetty was still there or any rowing boats. And she would have told me of the afternoons on the river and what she wore. Her memory is shot now, but I knew these would be as clear and intact as the day she lived them.

I can't remember much about my Nana when I was very small. I didn't really get to know her till after my other grandmother died. My other grandmother and I were very close and I must have thought you only had a fixed amount of love to give and if you wanted to give it abundantly to one, you must dispense it sparingly to others.

No, my early memories of Nana weren't really of her at all. They were of the chocolate cake she baked before we arrived for a visit. Of being able to stay up late to see the lights of Dunedin twinkling on the flat and over the hills beyond it.

They were of the apple box filled with wooden blocks of interesting shapes she'd had our uncle make for us. And of the dolls' house, complete with miniature dolls with china hands and feet and delicately painted faces and dolls' furniture she'd made and collected herself as a child.

But above all I remember the scent of flowers, especially the heavy, indolent scent of Regale lilies which filled the tall cut-glass vase on the hall stand all summer long.

I only really began to get to know my Nana when I was ten. It was, as I said, shortly after my other grandmother died and I was bereft. Nana had come down to us for Christmas, an uneasy visit since she disapproved strongly of my father and not just of the way he celebrated Christmas either, though that didn't help. The dislike was mutual.

I know when I was told I was going back with her for a visit on my own (told, not asked, though it was a favour all the same) I felt apprehensive. I was worried about what she might do or rather make me feel if I did something dreadful, and even more worrying I wasn't sure if I knew exactly what it was she'd think of as dreadful.

As it turned out, I did do something which upset her very much but in a way it was the thing that first brought us close. Always a clumsy child, I dropped and broke an old yellow cream jug while I was drying the dishes. It had been a wedding present and a fixture in her daily life for nearly forty years.

I don't remember what she said to me, probably something like, 'You stupid bumbling girl. Look what you've done.' She might even have said, 'I shouldn't have invited you.'

Whatever it was I fled in terror, out the kitchen door, down the steps and through the side gate to Mrs McFarlane's. I didn't know Mrs McFarlane all that well but she had been a friend of my other grandmother's, the one who doted on me. So she would understand. Like my other grandmother and my father she thought Nana 'cold' and 'narrow' and 'unbending'. (I was a past master at making my presence unnoticed in adult company.)

I found Mrs McFarlane also in her kitchen, doing her lunch dishes. I burrowed my head into her lap and sobbed out my fright while she crooned triumphantly, 'I don't know what they were thinking of, sending you up here all by yourself, to that woman.'

Whether Nana heard her or not I don't know. If she did, she ignored it. But I do know that when I looked round red-eyed from the wet place in Mrs McFarlane's apron, I could tell how much it had cost her to come and fetch me.

And I could see her looking at me with my arms around Mrs McFarlane's gaunt hips and thinking how I never did that to her. How the closest she ever got to me was to put out her cheek for the formal kiss I gave it, as I had been taught I must do, before I went to bed.

I saw her fight the humiliation of having this woman she did not like, and whom she knew did not like her, know she could not handle her own grandchild. I saw her fighting back, letting Mrs

McFarlane see the longing, nearing desperation she felt at bluing this rare chance of coming close to at least one of her grandchildren.

I stopped being afraid of Nana then. It was Mrs McFarlane who became 'that woman', the one I wanted to protect my Nana from.

I let go of Mrs McFarlane's gaunt hips and went over to the door, where Nana stood, miserable and uncomfortable, and I put my hand in hers. We said our goodbyes hurriedly, embarrassed to be there.

Our embarrassment increased as I followed her back to her place, shaken as we were with what we had done to each other.

When we got to the other side of the gate we embraced. I say embraced, not hugged, because it was too awkward and shy for that. I could feel the tautness under the soft roundness of her body. It's quite likely I was the first person she had held in her arms since my grandfather died.

I said sorry and she said sorry too but I must learn to be more careful. She would miss that jug. I nodded. I was not upset. I was beginning to understand how Nana loved. It was not warts and all. She didn't find faults endearing. Nor did she cement bonds of love with little acts of indulgence. On the contrary precisely because she loved me, she took care not to spoil me. To do so would weaken my moral fibre and she loved me too much for that.

There was a selfless quality to her love. She wanted, needed, the love I gave her in return but she risked it constantly to teach me her special brand of integrity and the self-discipline needed to maintain it.

So on those holidays at her place, up through my teens and early twenties, I learnt to drink tea without sugar, to read balancing a book on my head, to save on hot water and to make my bed first thing in the morning so there wasn't a wrinkle in it. But above all I was taught the Guiding Principle of Life: 'To Thine Own Self Be True'. It was the way to heaven and in the meantime the key to self-respect. The Truth was to be sought fearlessly with all the brains God gave me, and when I found it it would be crystal clear, black on white, no shadows of grey, no hint of chiaroscuro. White lies and even silence qualified as sin.

Nana was no hypocrite. She could live like that. In fact she gloried in the challenge. It lifted the small, quiet patterns of her life, partly chosen, partly dictated by the need to make ends meet on a working man's wage, to another plane where those small struggles and triumphs took on a moral grandeur. She saw her life as a Pilgrim's Progress.

Nana could find a Challenge even in a word. (She would not have said 'even'.) The word 'obeyed' created major obstacles when she came to get married. My grandfather might have understood how impossibly wrong it would be to vow to obey him but the clergymen of the day didn't.

She trudged from Methodist ministers, to Baptists, to Presbyterians (drawing the line at Anglican) to argue her case that if God's will clashed with my grandfather's, then God's will should prevail, but if she had promised God to obey her husband, the whole issue became hopelessly muddled. It took her a year to find a Congregationalist who would allow her to promise to cherish my grandfather instead.

Nana did have an Achille's heel though. And on her own terms, she fell down badly.

It had to do with me and it had to do with gardening.

Gardening was Nana's passion. She transformed the brown, rain-clogged soil on her quarter-acre section till it crumbled rich and fertile between her fingers. And out of it grew strawberries and currants, peaches, apricots, nectarines and gooseberries, chinese gooseberries, passionfruit and even sweet black grapes.

From early spring till late autumn, her squat white bungalow was immersed in a mass of colour. Clematis, jasmine and sweetheart roses climbed over trellises. Bulbs vied with perennials and daphne and camelias. And as you opened the front gate, the air greeting you became rich with fragance.

Down the back she grew a huge bed of lilies of the valley which she sold at the mart. With the money she indulged her passion for imported Dutch bulbs and glossy gardening books.

Somewhere she had read that botanical names contain a code in Latin to describe the colour, shape and other distinctive characteristics of the plants they grace. So she bought a Latin dictionary and taught herself to decipher them. And she knew all about genes and pollination and how things grow in scientific terms as well as in practice.

Everything from shredded brown paper bags to crushed egg shells went into the compost heap. When I protested because she expected me to do the same, she said, 'If people don't start giving back to the earth what they take out of it, it'll stop providing.'

It sounded preposterous then. Cranky.

As I grew older and she grew frailer, subtle shifts occurred in our relationship. It was I who took her out on visits. The afternoons she enjoyed most were down at the Botanic Gardens. We never missed going there though sometimes it was a near thing because we diced with the weather, trying to pick the finest day.

We always took the same itinerary, wandering down through the dells and the Rose Garden and then over to the Winter Gardens, ending up in the kiosk where she rested blissfully over afternoon tea.

And that's where it began. I started it of course. She would never have let it get beyond a mere temptation. A temptation easy to conquer, almost a reflex action, after so many years of practice.

It would have been on one of our first visits; she tapped her walking stick gently on something growing (I never became familiar even with their common names) and said longingly, 'That would grow from a slip.'

I waited till she'd walked on a bit, then broke off a piece and slipped it into my bag. I had no qualms. Other influences besides Nana's had long been at work in my life. In fact it gave me quite a kick.

I gave it to her as soon as we got home. I shall always remember the look of sheer delight glowing on her usually disciplined face. It was instantaneous, spontaneous and afterwards she could not deny it by pointing out to me how wrong I was to take it.

Temptation yielded to habit. Whenever we visited the Gardens she would tap anything that took her fancy, then walk on purposefully while I dallied to gather the loot.

When we got to the kiosk and sat over our pot of tea and scones with cream and raspberry jam, she'd ask, 'Did you notice the double pinks with the fluted edges growing just below the rhodedendrum dell?'

And if I had taken a piece which I identified by the places where I had seen her stick tapping, I would say 'yes' and she would sigh contentedly and say, 'And what about the Port St John creeper near the glass houses?'

But if I said 'no', she would describe it in great detail. Then I would say, 'I'll just go back and have a look.'

And she would say, 'You do that, dear. It really has the most beautiful pink flowers in autumn. It's not far from the big magnolia tree — in among the shrubs — to the right of it.'

I would go back to break off a shoot or pull out a sucker. At first I wasn't very good at it. Oh, I don't mean about doing it unobtrusively. I had no trouble with that at all. No, my problem was, I didn't know the art of taking slips—which were the bits most likely to grow roots, or how much I needed, and sometimes I broke them off in such a way I actually harmed the plants. That upset Nana. She couldn't have that happening. So while she took me round her garden, just in passing she showed me how it is done.

She knew she was not taking anything from anyone or doing any harm then. As she liked to say, one of the great miracles of nature is that by dividing you actually multiply.

Nevertheless it intrigued me that she had so few qualms. I am certain Nana saw the moral issues involved with pristine clarity, unclouded by considerations of actual harm. 'Thou shalt not steal' meant 'Thou shalt not steal'. Having me do it for her certainly made it worst. Keeping on doing it unrepentently made it worse still.

She wouldn't have had any doubts that it would be taken into account on the Judgment Day. But in the end I decided she probably figured that it wasn't enough to lose her her place in heaven. It would just mean it would be a little less beautiful than it might have been and this small currency she would spend on the debit side here on Earth.

I was coming to the conclusion that I had been right, that that is how she probably squared with herself, when the car drew to a halt in the main street of Mosgiel.

'Right,' said my father, 'who's for pies?'

I saw Hugh cringe and the children waking fretfully, turned up their noses.

Hugh would never understand that it wasn't exactly meanness that stopped my father from finding a restaurant as his family did in similar situations. If my father had enjoyed dining out, he wouldn't have thought twice about it.

But Hugh did not understand about the generations of New Zealanders who grew up and married, brought up their children and stayed married without the aid of restaurants. My father belonged to the last of those generations. Restaurants weren't just a luxury you could do without. He preferred to do without them. He felt uncomfortable in them.

You could explain all that to Hugh till the cows came home but he'd still never really understand it.

I had a vivid vision of Hugh dining out on descriptions of greasy, congealing mince pies.

'What about fish and chips?' I suggested brightly. 'And oysters.'

With a bit of luck, I could twist stories of oysters eaten out of newsprint into one of the those novel experiences which travel is all about.

My father was quite willing to oblige. He likes fish and chips just as much as pies. He came out of the shop with a huge parcel, drove out into the country and stopped on the verge of an unsealed road where he opened the parcel on the bonnet of the car.

I tore off a piece of paper and filled it with crab sticks, some oysters and a handful of chips. Then I wandered off up the road while my father muttered, 'Is she in a mood or something?'

I caught the word 'unsociable' in my mother's reply.

The night before there had been a frost on the Taieri. The air was sharp and clear. It bit into my checks and when I breathed it almost hurt.

I took a bite of oyster and thought of Nana's heaven. In my imagination, it was always an afternoon in late summer. No house. Just a garden from a temperate climate, spreading out over a wide sweep of lawn, surrounded by trees and shrubs, with beds of roses and azaleas, dahlias maybe, and little paths leading off to bowers and further delights.

Or that is how I saw it in my mind's eye as she described it to me on one of those wintery nights, somewhere in my mid-teens, when we sat over the fire; Nana in her high-backed chair crocheting rugs out of wool from old jerseys, I cross-legged on the floor, doing nothing as usual.

I can remember the texture and tenor of those conversations but the shape of most of them has long since gone. One I remember in detail though. It took me so much by surprise.

It began with Nana telling me some gossip. That in itself was unusual. I doubt if Nana heard much gossip. Her moral indignation was always so extreme and so sincere, it made people uncomfortable, even if they weren't the cause of it personally.

But this was quite harmless. The eighty-four-year-old widower from one of the back sections was marrying the newly widowed Mrs Bates from across the road. And she must have been well into her seventies. The thought of it made Nana chuckle. Nana genuinely did chuckle.

'What would they want to do that for, at their age?' I asked.

'Oh for the company,' she said decisively. 'It wouldn't be anything more.'

Before I had time to think, I blurted out, 'When do you stop wanting sex, Nana, I mean what age?'

I don't know what made me say it. As soon as I did, I wished I hadn't. I was sure I had overstepped the mark. But Nana did not draw herself up and fix me with her eye as I expected.

Instead she paused over her crochet and said softly, 'Oh, I don't think you ever do.'

I couldn't quite believe her. Again curiosity got the better of me.

'If my grandfather were here,' I asked, 'would you still want to make love?'

For a moment she was far away.

'Yes,' she said. 'Oh yes.' Then she said. 'I never got tired of looking at him. He had such a beautiful body, Susan. He was very wide across the shoulders and he had such narrow, narrow hips. Oh, I loved looking at him.'

And from there she went on to tell me about the place in heaven she hoped to share with him. And I understood that for Nana the long abstinence since my grandfather died was only an interlude. In heaven they would make love again. Why else a resurrection of the body?

She talked of their strolling side by side through native bush on the nether reaches of their niche in paradise, listening to the bird song and the rustle of leaves. It was so graphic, I got carried away. I could hear the water gurgling over stones in the little streams they crossed by wooden footbridges.

'I'll come and join you,' I said companionably.

'Oh no,' said Nana. 'It's just for your grandfather and me.'

Twenty years later, out on the Taieri Plains, I smiled. I wandered if God would be made to feel welcome there.

On those evenings by her fireside she gave me glimpses of a world receding from living memory. Things that happened that sounded flat when you read about them or you were told about them by someone who hadn't been there and didn't understand. Things like how she was so ignorant when she got married at twenty-three, she thought babies were born through your tummy button. It was the only place she and my auntie could think of where they could come out.

'Well it didn't seem to matter,' I said, thinking of what she had told me of her life with my grandfather.

'It did,' she said fiercely. 'It did. I shall never forgive my mother for that.' (There were quite a few things she didn't think God would expect her to forgive her mother for.)

'Why?' I asked, puzzled.

'Because,' she said. 'because, when your grandfather was called up he asked me to marry him before he went away. And I said no. Oh, I didn't know what I was doing. All I thought about was not having time to make my wedding dress and how there were still things I needed for my glory box. Trifling reasons.'

Over forty years later the triviality, the lost opportunity to make a Noble Gesture, still galled.

'Oh I regretted it when I found out,' she said. 'It was wicked to be so innocent.'

I keep going back to those evenings by the fire. Fragments of conversations turn up in my thoughts in Canada, as they did even before that, in all those out of the way places where Hugh and I lived till the children were born.

And I know Nana must have thought of them when she heard I was coming. They aren't memories that fade with age. They are too firmly imprinted on our minds for that.

We were so close then. She told me her most intimate thoughts and described for me the events in her life which had made the deepest impressions. And I laid open for her inspection my fledgling perceptions of the world.

But as time went on I told her less and less. And she drew away from me. Not because of what I didn't tell her. It never crossed her mind they were there for the telling. She had tapped into the more high-minded side of my nature and she took her cues from there.

She assumed then that right and wrong were the same for everyone. All the superficial deviations she observed in people's behaviour, or read about, she put down to lack of backbone (or ignorance if they weren't fortunate enough to be born of British descent). Their integrity needed finer tuning, that was all. She never saw enough to suspect they were tuned in to different scales of values.

No, she drew back from me, puzzled, because of the outward shape I was giving my life. It suggested other dimensions to me she knew nothing of. Dimensions which would have altered her perception of me.

I tried to explain to her why I wanted to be a quantity surveyor.

'Didn't you ever want to work, Nana?' I asked.

'I did work. I was a tailor's assistant before I was married. You know that.'

'But afterwards?'

'I took in some dressmaking once. But when your grandfather found out he was so upset I made up the blouse and took it back without accepting any money for it. He'd watched his mother working so hard, you see, cleaning for people, and he had always vowed his wife would never work.'

It was a matter of cherishing, not obeying.

'I'm like you,' I persisted, 'I like being outside. I couldn't bear being inside all day cooped up in an office.'

Now a horticulturalist perhaps.

'But I like measuring. I like geometry. I like maths. It's like cutting giant dress patterns.'

Then why not be a dressmaker?

'It's a challenge, Nana,' I said, trying yet a different tack. 'Being a woman in a man's world. Breaking new ground for women. I mean you had a challenge when you decided to send Mum and the others through high school.'

There were challenges and challenges. Challenges which fulfilled your womanhood were one thing; challenges destined to distort it quite another. She didn't say it. She knew enough about the world to know her views were suspect, discredited now. But she believed it all the same.

Finally, desperately seeking empathy, I told her of the secret motivation behind my choice. Secret because it was vulnerable to ridicule when exposed to words. But I thought she'd understand. After all, it was at her place I read the romances that fed the dreams.

'It means, Nana, that one day I'll be able to go off to all those places you read about in books. You know, like climbing mountains in Peru and camping in the desert. Just think, I'll actually be able to have those kind of adventures.'

'Susan,' said Nana severely, 'those sorts of things are best confined to books. You don't base your life on flights of fancy.'

But I did. And they came true. Sort of.

More than anything else, I think, Hugh foreshortened her perspective of me.

That first time I brought him home, just after we were married, I watched her, watching him. A frown hung between her brows, not disapproving, just perplexed. She saw my face light up, soften with the first flush of love when my eyes rested on him. And she assumed the quality of my love matched hers for my grandfather.

But she couldn't understand how the girl she knew could feel that way about Hugh.

It wasn't just me, either. When I tried to bridge the gap with some observation about Life I thought we might agree about, she stared past me into the middle distance, dauntlessly facing Truth and said, troubled, 'I've come to the conclusion, it all boils down to economics. What people do. Why they do it.'

She sought further words to explain what she meant but the concept, its implications, were still only half formed in her mind. Seeing her struggle I did not press her, draw her into an argument as I used to do in my teens. I had just hoped this Challenge, coming at eighty, mightn't prove too difficult.

How had she coped with that challenge? Did she throw out all her Principles? Had she managed to accommodate them? Or did the idea prove too much and had she let it drift out of her mind? I would never know. Not unless I found out this afternoon.

The car drew up and as soon as I slid into the back seat it was obvious they had had too much of each other. My mother's lips were drawn tight. Hugh gave me a you-have-surpassed-the-limits-this-time look. And my father said as much.

The atmosphere was rife in another way as well. The car smelt of cow dung. Gerry had slipped in it. He sat snivelling on the greasy fish and chip paper my mother had put down to protect the car seat. He was covered from head to toe in mud and dung.

'I'm going to be sick,' said Lydia.

'Now don't think things like that, Lydia,' said my mother reprovingly. 'We are all having to put up with it. It won't be long, now.'

My father snorted. Hugh looked sympathetically at Lydia.

I squeezed Gerry's hand and began undressing him.

'Be careful,' said my mother.

The silence in the car froze over Gerry's gulping breaths.

When we got to the Home, I wrapped his dirty little body in my jersey and carried him inside, my bulky bag full of extra clothes banging against my knees. At the sight of the matron my mother became gracious. She explained what had happened and one of the nurses took me to a bathroom. They at least were kind. By the time I had cleaned Gerry up, helped him into his clothes and given him a hug, twenty precious minutes had gone.

When we entered the sitting room, Nana looked strained. She was trying to converse with Lydia but all she heard were the North Americanisms, not the language they had in common.

'What's that, dear?' she kept saying. My father and Hugh just sat there, making no effort. My mother was nowhere in sight.

I kissed her on the cheek and said 'Hello.' I would have liked to give her a bear hug but she looked so frail I was afraid I might hurt her.

I knew my mother would have done so already but I told her about Gerry, just for something to say.

'You will have to learn to look where you are going,' she said to Gerry but she sweetened those remarks in a way she never did for me. She took a bag of lollies out of her purse and offered him one.

'No thank you. I don't like those,' said Gerry politely, declining it. Nana looked bewildered. Her children or grandchildren for that matter would never have done that. They had been taught to accept all they were offered, irrespective of whether they wanted it or not, so as not to offend.

I wouldn't have known where to go from there if Nana's friend Mrs Renwick had not swept into the room. Well, she didn't exactly sweep — her movements were the movements of an old lady — but that is the impression she conveyed.

She eased herself down into her chair on her stick, nodded cursorily to my father and Hugh, then smiled graciously at the children. They were fascinated. The children, I mean. Hugh gave the impression he met people like her all the time. My father just appeared ill at ease as he would have with any friend of Nana's.

'I believe you spent some time in Northern Africa?' she remarked, turning her attention on me.

'Well mostly in the Middle East but we were in Egypt and Tunisia for a while,' I answered her.

'I was in Alexandria and Cairo after the war,' she said.

180

So that was why she asked me about Africa and not Alaska or the Phillipines. I would have liked to ask her which war but that might have caused offence. And it was important I didn't do that. I could feel Nana's agitation as she mentally hovered over our conversation. It was obvious that in her new-found sense of social standing she placed great store on my winning Mrs Renwick's approval.

'Aren't they fascinating cities,' I said.

'Yes, but I believe they have sadly deteriorated in the last decade or so,' she replied. In her day I could see she had been a master of one-upmanship.

'No doubt,' I conceded, 'but they're still extremely interesting.'

'Did you ever take a cruise up the Nile?' she asked.

'No,' I said. I was more *au fait* with land rovers and jeeps.

'A very civilised way to see the ancient world,' she advised in a voice which said you-really-should-do-it-though-I-know-you-can't-afford-to-but-we-shall-keep-up-the-pretence-all-the-same. Where, I mean how, did Nana get such a friend?

She had only to nod or utter a remark and you knew she had been a skilled performer in the art of dinner-table conversation. Now only the Art lingered, unsupported by skill. My knowledge of cruises up the Nile was confined to watching an Agatha Christie film but I could see her there in the ship's salon, finely dressed and sipping knowledgeably on French wine. A knowledge of wine. Such a rare, privileged accomplishment for a New Zealand woman of her time.

Did she ever talk of these things to my grandmother? If she did, how did Nana take it? Nana who prided herself on the fact that no alcohol had ever passed her lips.

'Your grandmother is such an interesting woman,' she said warmly. I looked closely at her. There was no doubt she was being sincere. 'So unexpected here,' she continued, the sweep of her head halting just perceptibly over the most vacuous faces in the room.

I wondered if Nana had told her her views on economics, or what it was she found so interesting about Nana. But I couldn't ask her, not with Nana and my father and Hugh sitting there. Tread carefully, Susan, tread carefully here, I said to myself.

Then my mother came back. She frowned seeing me give so much attention to Mrs Renwick and not my Nana. She didn't understand. I knew better than she did that time, precious time, was slipping away. But Nana wanted me to. I was doing it for Nana.

'Well, I think it's about time we all left Susan with her grand-mother for a while,' my mother said, looking directly at Mrs Renwick.

'How very true,' Mrs Renwick agreed. She made no move to rise herself but looked around my family expectantly. They obeyed what was really a command and drifted out through the ranchslider doors into the adjacent park. My mother's lips were pursed. Mrs Renwick watched them go, then she patted me on the hand and said, 'Well my dear, I shall leave you to your grandmother.'

'Such a nice woman,' said Nana, as she glided out of earshot. I would have said it was Nana who was nice and Mrs Renwick who was interesting but I nodded my agreement.

We sat in silence. It came into my head to say, 'You were right, Nana. About Hugh. I don't feel about him the way you felt about my grandfather. I never did. I just got tired of waiting, that was all.'

But I stifled the impulse. I couldn't do it. Not there. Not now among all those old ladies sitting there staring into empty space. And if I had said all that, she would have known that she loved me. Then she would have worried her way to death wondering what was to become of me.

So I sat there trying to think of what to say and so did she.

'I hope you are happy Susan,' she said at last. From the way she said it you could tell she had no insights into whether I might be or not.

'Yes Nana,' I answered formally.

'Do you like being a mother?' she asked.

'Yes. Yes, very much.' This time I could be truthful.

'That's good,' she said. 'I found it difficult. But they were worth it in the end.'

I didn't know what to say. After a while she asked, 'Do you like living in Canada?'

'Yes,' I said. 'Yes it's fine.'

'I've read they have terribly cold winters.'

'Yes, but beautiful autumns. And there is all central heating so you don't notice the cold the same.'

'Do you think you'll ever come back to New Zealand to live?' she asked.

'No. No, I don't think so,' I replied, working hard to make sure I kept any hint of regret out of my voice. To have said 'yes' would have been admitting the unthinkable — the end of my marriage and the frightening blankness beyond it.

'You don't mind?' she asked, not understanding how I could not.

'No, not really,' I said firmly. I must sound certain, secure of my destiny.

'You do love it, though, don't you, Susan? New Zealand. It is your home,' she asked anxiously.

'Yes, but Canada is my home now.'

We sat in silence again. I watched my family heading back towards us. It was too cold outside and anyway it would soon be teatime, time to leave.

They all came in and milled around us. My mother gave Nana instructions about underwear and stockings and bed cuddlies. Nana looked a little bewildered but she hugged my mother warmly and thanked her gratefully.

I stood looking on while they all said their goodbyes. Then I walked with Nana as far as the corridor to the dining room.

'Well Susan,' she said, turning towards me, 'goodbye.'

'Goodbye,' I said, hugging her, careful not to crush her. 'Goodbye, Nana.'

I looked at her. I couldn't bear it.

'I'll see you next time I'm back,' I blurted.

She stood a moment while we absorbed the falseness of it. Then she turned and walked away. I watched her move painfully to the end of the corridor. She did not look back.

And I knew that tomorrow the letter from me in her purse would not be there.

BUTTERCUPS IN ICE

Eileen Alderton

Eileen Alderton is fiction editor of a national magazine. She was born in London and trained in Fleet Street and has had stories published in Australia, Britain, America, South Africa, Europe, Scandinavia and Asia, and has had two novels published: *A Month of Sundays* and *The Recurring Image*. She came to Australia in 1974 and has 'never looked back once'. Married with two grown-up sons, she lives in a Sydney beach suburb.

BUTTERCUPS IN ICE

'The Tasman and the Pacific meet up north,' he says, informative this morning, chatty, attempting to be pleasant as though everything were normal, as if they are like other people always appear to be; sightseeing together and enjoying themselves. 'The Tasman and the Pacific meet head-on. If you're lucky you may see the currents clashing, splitting.'

'Spitting?' It is very windy and she can barely hear what he is saying. 'Spitting, did you say? Splitting? Slitting?'

'Two very powerful currents meet, you see.'

Two walls of water meeting, merging, controlled by the moon (or God); resentful, unwilling to be joined; like people, separate individuals who should stay that way; apart. 'If any of you know cause, or just impediment, why these two persons should not be joined together in holy matrimony, ye are to declare it.'

Holy matrimony she finds a joke; hilarious. I could tell them why no two persons should ever be joined together, like oxen tethered by a yoke.

In the north of this streaming, sodden, empty country that is so real to her and so beautiful its beauty hurts her, pulls at harp strings in the gut—the Tasman and the Pacific rear up to devour each other.

She is conscious of his voice, droning, explaining about ocean currents and a part of her mind shuts off. A bolt slides across a door (her brain?) and clicks and keeps the sound of his talking out. Two powerful elements meet and destroy each other and in doing so destroy everything and everybody foolish enough to remain close enough to be affected. They may slit each other's throats, these elements whose ingredients will never mix; chalk and cheese; salt and sugar; oil and water. Fire and water, two elements which can kill. Elements.

Take water and electricity, she thinks. Electricity is the agency producing physical phenomena, such as attraction and repulsion (and, presumably, the reason why attraction and repulsion become interchangeable; why physical attraction can turn to hate). Electricity produces luminous effects and heating and violent shock to bodies. Electricity and water meet and flare and burn and kill if, say, an electric heater is dropped in a bath of water; or an iron or a toaster or a jaffle maker.

At home there was an electric heater on the bathroom wall. It terrified her although it was nowhere near the bath. She was certain that one day she would turn it on and drop it in the bath when he lay there, soaking, eyes closed, smug, and putting on a bit of weight and telling her what she should do and what she had forgotten and how she should have her hair styled in that place Karen recommended. Karen had a leather coat, soft as silk. Bought it at a closing-down sale in Surry Hills. 'But you can't be bothered, can you? You don't care what you look like. You're not like other women.'

'You're right,' she'd say.

He was always right. 'Didn't I tell you?' he would say. 'Didn't I tell you and aren't I right?'

She stood on a chair with a screwdriver and awkwardly, clumsily, took the heater off the wall and dropped it, cracking tiles. That made him very angry. She had cracked the tiles and broken the elements. He had never in his life encountered a woman so inefficient, so impractical. What in God's name would she do without him, she who couldn't mend a fuse? How could she ever mend the elements of an electric stove? Of course she couldn't.

The elements; earth, water, air, fire, the material universe, as Aristotle saw it. Simple. Then. Or was it? Nothing has ever been simple; never will be. 'You are in control of your own life,' said that shrink, the expensive one he made her see. 'Nobody can dictate to you what you may do or may not do. It is entirely up to you.'

Easy way out, for shrinks; the simple way of discharging the sick is to tell them that what they do with their lives is entirely up to them; and, of course, suggest they make an appointment for 'follow up' next year.

'I'm talking to you,' he says to her, somewhere in New Zealand where he is on a job and she has 'gone along' as Karen put it, 'for some rest and to get quite better.'

'Look on the map,' he says. 'Can you work out where we are?'

'No,' she says.

'The Waipoua Forest.'

'Yes.'

'Kauri trees,' he says. 'See the kauri trees?'

She is staring at a forest with gigantic ferns that look as if they are growing downwards; layers of green hands with spreading fingers, gentle, pale-green fingers dripping rain.

'If the bloody weather clears I'll get some good shots of the Tane Mahuta.'

'The what?' she asks.

'The king.'

'What king?'

'The Tane Mahuta is the King of the Forest, the largest kauri tree in the country. It's not far from here.'

'Such a tiny country,' she says, looking at the guidebook in her lap. 'Only three million people in an area bigger than the British Isles.'

'Narrower than Britain,' he remarks with a peculiar resentment, as if he has measured it himself. 'Narrower in the south.'

Kauri trees take eight-hundred years to reach maturity. That much she knows; unlike people who may reach four-score-and-ten and more and still be immature. This powerful conifer is immense, phantasmagoric, unforgettable. She touches its bark like the blind touch braille and it is rough and strong, a texture unlike the peeling skin of an Australian gum. It has withstood the elements for centuries. To stand beneath it fills her with uneasiness, with awe. She may be pitiful at reading maps and dismantling electric heaters but she can see and smell and feel and remember forever something beautiful.

Ships and homesteads were built from kauri timber. The early settlers hacked and hacked and took the resin for making glue and the gum industry began. They had no idea (and how could they have?) of the years it would take before the kauris grew again. This kauri is ancient and mature but the little ones are only forty. Forty years old and still a long, long way to grow. Like her, according to the shrink.

'You are only in your forties. You have time to grow.'

'Grow where? Which way? Do you mean alone?'

'That decision you have to make yourself.'

No yea or nay from shrinks. They opened you up and dug and prodded, displaying, in a manner known as 'breaking down', the secret cans of worms; and, after great expense, financially as well as emotionally (yours, not theirs), they left you bereft of crutches on your own to heal.

He is taking photographs of the forest and its king. This is a hefty assignment for a travel magazine. When they worked together he would shoot anything she told him to; when she was what banks and building societies call the Main Breadwinner; when she encouraged him and fed him and hid the bills in case the knowledge that he was incapable of paying them should lower his self-esteem, inflict dents in what has become his enormous ego. For he works on his own, has achieved recognition and is in demand. He earns good money, more than she does working on a tabloid. He is holding an exhibition of his photographs in a gallery owned by the woman called Karen. Karen calls him an artisan. Karen is his soulmate as she, who married him years ago, in a white dress before people gawking in the pews, can never be. She is a mere word hack for a tabloid. He was told her so.

A hack, according to the dictionary, is a person who for a living undertakes literary or other work of little or no originality. What she has written, he said once, in the middle of a disgraceful screaming match (disgraceful because she detests lack of self-control), is left on trains and buses or used to wrap the fish and chips.

Karen, his latest woman, who calls him an artisan, has lifted him out of what he calls 'that bloody awful rut' and praises to the skies his photographs. 'The one of those children,' says Karen, who has no children, 'the one you took up north . . . That really gets me . . .' She has labelled it 'Dead Centre'. The children sit in dust, in sand which has a reddish tinge. They are black-skinned children with sun-bleached hair and poor eyesight. A piece of canvas hangs beside them, and there is a mattress tipped on its side disgorging horsehair. The children's legs are thin and flies crawl across their faces, hovering around the nose of one of them where carefully, cunningly, his camera has caught a blob of snot. There is nothing behind the children except spinifex and sky. Karen whispers to him across the dinner table. 'You caught so much loving in your lens.' Karen, who, like all of them that night, was slightly drunk, tells them over dinner of his brilliance, flicking her tongue over her lower lip, wriggling it in her slightly open mouth. An endearing, sensual habit? Presumably bewitching to a besotted man. An artisan, a craftsman, says Karen, chin in hand, snake-tongue wriggling.

'One skilled in an industrial or applied art,' says she, the word hack who has been dumb throughout the meal. 'Or, of course, artisan can mean a member of the urban working classes.'

And they stare at her. They are shocked; his ageing parents and hers and Karen and Karen's male person she calls her partner. And then he says, he, pointing at her (and at her glass which she has topped up), 'She over there, you know, reads the dictionary in bed. Honest to God, she does.' And her mother dabs smeared lipstick on her table napkin and giggles like a schoolgirl and tells them, 'I've been telling her since she was a tiny thing that reading and reading all that small print will ruin her eyes.'

Not a successful dinner party. The last.

And now, sitting beside him in the hired car which he refuses to let her drive, she turns the pages of the guidebook. 'I'd like to see the Mount Cook lily.'

'The what?' he says.

'It's the largest buttercup in the world and it isn't yellow, it's creamy white and grows in mountain meadows.'

'Mount Cook is on the South Island.'

'I'm well aware of that.'

'We're at the Bay of Islands. Remember?' It would be a consolation to his guilt (for even he must occasionally feel a stab of guilt) if she were mad.

'I know where we are. I said I'd like to see the Mount Cook lily, and the edelweiss, in spring.'

'On the way home, maybe,' he says, pacifying her.

'It isn't spring.'

'And that isn't my bloody fault,' he shouts, and the rain leaks into the hired car and the windscreen wipers squeak.

At the Bay of Islands the settlements have names she rolls around her tongue. Delicious, like eating chocolate; Waitangi, Paihia, Kerikeri, Opua, Kororareka which means Sweet Penguin. While he goes game fishing and photographs a striped marlin, a monster with open evil eyes, she goes to Kororareka which is now called Russell; a pity to change its name. In pouring rain she looks at the first police

189

station and at the oldest church. Christ Church at Russell is white as icing sugar. It is scarred still with bullet holes and cannon balls from the land wars.

'The Maoris migrated from Hawaiiki five centuries before Captain Cook got here in 1769,' she tells him over a lavish dinner (on expenses) which she is unable to eat. The lamb cuts like butter. She pushes food around her plate.

'You starting all that again?'

'All what?'

'Refusing food.'

'I'm not hungry.'

'I bring you on this trip to make you fit again, to build you up, and you refuse to eat.'

She gets up from the table and goes to their room which has two beds, thank God. Two huge, warm beds for people who have met, disastrously, like the Pacific meets the Tasman in a storm and can only survive if they are apart.

The next day she hires a car herself and drives to Cape Reinga. She writes postcards to their children although she is uncertain where the children are. They are grown and gone; went at the earliest moment and since going have been in a hurry to move on somewhere else. One is in America and one in England and the third somewhere in the Northern Territory, or was. They are damaged, all of them, in different ways and for that damage she will always take the blame. The eldest, who is in more of a hurry than any of them, refuses even to come to lunch when he is in Australia. He has far too much to do. She can imagine him glancing at his watch at her funeral, for there are always delays at crematoriums, a queue of bodies to be burnt. Get the old dear in the furnace quick, or I'll be late.

She writes: 'This is the most northern point of New Zealand. Your father is taking photographs for a new travel magazine. It is incredibly beautiful. We visited a museum where there were pianolas and musical boxes and wigs, imagine, imitation hair made from kauri gum, and clay balls. The Maoris used to predict the future with clay balls. I love the legends.'

She cannot think of another thing to write. She is writing to damaged strangers; indifferent. She could be at Cape Reinga or in hell.

She cashes travellers' cheques and flies to Christchurch where it is autumn and the falling leaves are bronze and gold and rustle as they fall. In a wide street with expensive shops she buys leather boots. She flies in a tiny plane to Queenstown. The sky is crushed-sapphire and below them are snowfields and glaciers, lakes, mountain peaks. Down there is the Mount Cook lily, the biggest buttercup in the world. She stays in an almost empty motel on Lake Wakatipu. The Maoris called the lake Waipounamu which means greenstone water and it is deep and freezing and green as cats' eyes in certain lights and there are warnings in the motel not to attempt to swim in it. You'd be dead in minutes. The lake is edged with willows and little beaches and it breathes, up and down, sleepy, slothful, because there is a giant sleeping on the bottom. On the morning she has to leave because she is running out of money, the lake whips into a frenzy like the open sea. The giant is angry and the winds from the mountains scream and smell of snow. There is no time to look for the Mount Cook lily in the Southern Alps.

At the airport at Christchurch she rings her friend Claire and asks to be put up for a week or so until she finds a flat. 'You're sure?' says Claire who has been telling her to do just this for years. 'How will you get to work from here?'

'The same way other people manage. On a train.'

'Are you sure you're well enough to go back to work?'

Claire, who is married to a professor and lives in a vast house near the university full of children who are reluctant to go away, has two spare rooms but this morning she sounds wary. 'You're sure you're quite okay?' she presses.

'I'm fine. I promise I won't stay long.'

To say, in practice, to your dotty friend, 'Come and stay!' is very different from that friend ringing from an airport in New Zealand and saying she's on her way. Friends, she now realises, like anybody else have their limitations. They have, too, what articles in newspapers call lifestyles. God forbid I should interrupt anybody's lifestyle, she thinks, she who has no lifestyle that she is aware of and, although she has written about other people's in the tabloid, is unsure what a lifestyle might entail.

In the airport shop she buys a tablecloth of heavy linen with a pattern of New Zealand Christmas trees in scarlet bloom and a mass of Mount Cook lilies the colour of clotted cream growing in a mountain meadow; the largest buttercup in the world. There is a message in Maori on all the tablecloths and tea towels on display. 'Haere Ra!'

191

Because there is a long wait for her plane there is time to have the tablecloth wrapped and posted to the gallery. She addresses the parcel to him and to Karen and marks it: WITH CARE. DO NOT CRUSH. Creased linen is unappealing.

Karen opens the parcel in the gallery and is enchanted. How sweet of her, says Karen. What a lovely thought. She must be feeling better. The treatment must have done some good. What does '*Haere Ra*' mean, I wonder?

Karen holds the tablecloth against her like dress material. Karen touches the Mount Cook lilies and licks her lip as if tasting cream.

'Tell me what "*Haere Ra*" means,' says Karen.

He knows exactly what it means. It's Maori for goodbye.

Lady Musgrave: The Story Of The Island, Reef And Lagoon

Fiona Place

Fiona Place is a writer who has lived in Sydney all her life. She is interested in how language shapes our sense of self and how it is through language, through the stories we are told, we learn to become women and men. Her first novel, *Cardboard,* which examines the narrative of anorexia nervosa, won the NBC QANTAS New Writer's Award, and in 1990 she was awarded a Fellowship from the Literature Board of the Australia Council. Her poetry, prose and critical work on women and language have appeared in various journals and she has co-authored a self-help book, *When Eating is Everything,* in which she looks at the language of problem eating. She has worked as a public servant, nurse, judge's associate, lecturer and, more recently, as writer-in-residence within a psychiatric setting.

LADY MUSGRAVE: THE STORY OF THE ISLAND, REEF AND LAGOON

Properly described, the trip *out to* Lady Musgrave is a tale of incredible coincidences. For Sally anyway. For Sam, it is one he prefers to forget.

Sally wakes up at 4:30 am. She wakes Sam, they drink instant coffee, grab two pillows and make their way to the coach pick-up point.

The woman had told them the coach left Noosa at 4.45 am sharp and waited for no one. She'd also told them to take pillows. We don't book the whole coach out, so you'll have two seats each, it's a three-hour trip to Bundaberg and you'll be very tired on the way back, she'd explained.

Lucy had been slightly anxious the day before.

> leathered snakes
> returned and
> twisted
>
> *you're afraid,*
> *afraid of French*
> *men*

> ruthless worming
> voices judged and
> judged

'I'm just a bit agoraphobic,' she kept telling Sam, 'you know I just feel like staying here in the hotel, that all day I'll just want the safety of coming home.'

> she remembered the
> worms that'd once
> muffled in
> her ear

'I think I've done pretty well so far, considering it's my first holiday after my England experience. I know it's over ten years ago, but tomorrow will be my first coach trip since then,' she explained.

'You have done very well,' Sam agreed.

To Sally's delight, once seated, she feels almost excited.

TRAVELS ABROAD

Date   28 Nov 1977
Place   Tokyo

Today we railed all around Tokyo, and saw the closed zoo, the closed archeological museum. I have taken ten photos already. Interesting were the artificial food displays stuck to the windows.

Sam sits behind her. He wants to sleep. He also wishes Sally could want to sleep. Sally is envious of his ability to sleep. Anywhere. Anytime.

She alternates between trying to relax and sleep, and staring out the window once it is light, trying to impress images of the countryside upon her memory.

> three hours
> Bundaberg bound
> anxious fidget

Date   29 Nov
Place   London (at long last)

The place is a dump!

Date   1 Dec
Place   London

Visited the Tower and took three photos. For dinner we went and gobbled down a pizza. I sent off four postcards. I also put in a

film for processing of people who are missing (in my mind) back in
Australia.

> fuse focus, as
> she hears
> a voice

But no, it isn't possible she thinks. It can't be. It couldn't be
Caroline.

She turns her head in the direction of the voice. The woman with
the voice even looks like Caroline. Looks like the Caroline of ten
years ago. She too, is looking at Sally, as though she is wondering if
Sally is someone from the past. Opposite the woman is the sort of
man Sally had imagined Caroline would end up with. The rural
urban white-and-blue striped shirt type.

She wonders if Caroline still drinks. If it has become a problem.

And reflects how at times she talks to Sam about Caroline as a way
of describing herself. Of describing what she wasn't. What she
lacked.

Describing Caroline as the type who'd luxuriously drink gin and
tonic on the college verandah, go out with boys rather than study
and always be in trouble, she tells how back then she was disapproving
of the Caroline type. And foolish enough to think the Carolines of
the world were full of confidence. She also tells Sam how she hopes
she is wrong. That it would be so refreshing if the predictability of
sterotyping could be disproved. If Caroline hadn't ended up drinking.

Date   2 December (photo 20 started the day)
Place   London

A fine day! Another camera spotting adventure ahead no doubt.
Visited Big Ben (many attempts to photo) then off to Westminster
Abbey — spotted cheap shoes near St Pauls station — a good day.

The woman speaks to the man again.

Sally's heart begins to pound.

It can't be she thinks. It would be too much of a coincidence.
They can't meet up again like this, not on a coach. Sally wonders
what to do. Whether she should avoid the woman completely or ask
the woman if her name is Caroline. She decides on the latter and
sitting up on her knees asks, 'Look I know this may sound ridiculous,
but is your name Caroline?'

'Yes,' the woman smiles, 'and you're Sally aren't you?'

'Yes,' says Sally rather hesitantly, not knowing if the conversation is to proceed beyond a simple recognition or if Caroline still hates her. Hates her about England.

'I didn't say hello to you,' Caroline explains, 'because I kept thinking what would Sally be doing on a coach in the middle of Queensland,' her voice match firing Sally's intensity. Sally nods understandingly and Caroline continues, 'so how did we get to be together?'

'You were with Fiona and I was with Jane and we met up on the coach trip,' Sally tells Caroline, feeling Caroline had given her permission to recall, to share the memory, 'don't you remember?' she presses.

'No, it is, after all ten years ago, you know,' Caroline replies.

Sally draws breath. She senses Caroline wants to distance herself from remembering.

Sally feels she has made a mistake. She has bombarded Caroline with detail, forgetting it isn't nearly as important to Caroline as it is to her.

Date   16 Dec
Place   Hampton Court

Today, feeling blick with back and head, I still managed a visit to Hampton Court, we spent ages gazing at paintings and then wandered through the rose garden — author was suffering from homesickness somewhat.

She has been unfair.

Caroline is telling her in polite terms to kindly avoid her for the rest of the trip.

Probably Caroline still hates her and still thinks she is crazy and panics.

Still a helplessly dependent woman.

But then Lucy remembers she wasn't labelled panicky, or helplessly dependent, until after England and realises Caroline probably never knew about all that.

She nudge shakes Sam repeating the words, 'It's her, it's her.'

'Who?' Sam asks.

'Caroline, the one who was with me in England, not Jane, the one I was travelling with, but the one from college who hardly knew me at all. The one who was the nicest to me.'

Sam sits up.

198

He knows how important England is to Sally.

And how important he has been in the re-telling of England. As the one who helped Sally decode and re-code the feelings of panic, as blood loss.

'Tell me I'm paranoid,' she begs him, 'tell me that because she said it was ten years ago doesn't mean I'm supposed to avoid her.'

'You're being paranoid,' Sam says and listens patiently to Sally as she explains and explains the situation. Explains how just seeing Caroline makes her feel guilty and evil. He tells her she is hearing the voice of her family. He then askes her if she minds him catching just a bit more shut eye.

Sally wants to wake Sam up again and again.

To show him the beautiful old wooden homes on stilts.

But she knows deep down what she really wants is to bring up the topic of living together.

And experience some enthusiasm.

From him. As though him saying—yes it would be wonderful to live in a house with such big rooms, is actually saying—yes, one day we will live together. She knows too, she should stop being like an overly eager child and let him sleep. And snore.

Date   17 Dec
Place   London/Ostend/Brussels

A very homesick L began the coach trip at Victoria station then train to Dover and ferry to Ostend. On the coach to Brussels things appear brighter—well hopefully. We ate a good meal and the room is adequate. Fiona and Caroline are sitting opposite us.

Date   19 Dec
Place   Koblenz-Nuremburg

Stayed at Nurnburg for the night—dizzy and homesick—awfully!

Had to use German to find way back to hotel because of my hopeless sense of direction.

Leaving their pillows behind Sam and Sally make their way to the front of the coach. Sally whispers to Sam that they should hang close to the coach in case Caroline wants to make a move. She has decided to leave it up to Caroline to indicate how the two couples are supposed to spend the day in such close proximity to one another.

Caroline introduces the man with her to Sally.

Sally does her bit and introduces *her* Sam to the *other* Sam.

'Well that's easy!' says Caroline laughing nervously and then quietly to Lucy, 'Well they're all the same anyway, all interchangeable, all as bad as each other.'

The two women signal to each other and to their respective Sams a desire to go to the toilet and Sally knows the day will be OK.

'I knew you'd always do something interesting,' Caroline tells Sally over the toilet door, 'me, I just got married and had babies.'

Sally wants to reach out to Caroline. But the sudden shift in positions has her beat.

Her fear that Caroline would not consider her good enough or worthy of talking to, now seems so selfish. She must now be the confident one and fight Caroline's definition of herself as uninteresting.

'Writing isn't all that different to any other job,' Sally tells her and as though trying to make a dent in Caroline's classification of herself she tells her about her own long period of panic/anorexia after England.

'Yes, well quite a few of my friends have had psychiatric problems too,' Caroline says very matter of factly, as if distancing Sally's experience at the same time as accepting it. 'Actually,' she continues, 'Sam and I have been separated for the last year, this is our first extended time together in nine months and my first time away from my babies, in fact last year was the worst year of my life.'

Sally tries to imagine it.

Caroline out on her parents' property with her babies. And her husband in Melbourne with his saddlery. She is overwhelmed by the distance. Overwhelmed by the statement — separated for nine months.

She wonders how Caroline wakes up these days, what her routine is, how she and her mother get on, how often she contacts Sam or Sam contacts her. Her head spins.

'But I'm sure everything will be all right in the long run,' Caroline says, as though reassuring herself at the same time as sensing Sally's concerns.

'I rang home today,' Caroline continues, 'Mum told me she hasn't had any sleep, Ben has already scissored the rose bush to death and brought the number of dinner plates from eight down to four, I don't think she's coping too well and she doesn't even have the two of them.'

Sally feels quite helpless and mumbles some comment about children being hard work.

They return to the Sams. And decide when necessary, to refer to Caroline's Sam as Sam D.

Sally senses Caroline has already decided that as women they will always understand each other far better than any man ever could. She knows what Caroline means but thinks it doesn't have to be that bad. That if it is that bad then maybe re-uniting isn't such a good idea.

Date   21 Dec
Place   Vienna

Ah yes, Vienna and the day spent in bed and an experience with the Austrian doctor — Eusaprim — antibiotic and cough drops. $20 up the spout! Never mind I must get better. Black shit. Took photo of Schonberg palace.

Date   22 Dec
Place   Vienna/Villach

A journey through the Austrian Alps and lunch at Kraubath. And yet another doctor in Villach saying I have *ulcees veutric duodeur*. Fun, fun, fun! I feel weak letting Jane down and collapsing — Jesus I'm a deadshit!

They board what they have been told is a high speed catamaran.

Sally picks up the information sheet. She skims through it.

Properly described as a wooded sand cay, Lady Musgrave Island has been built by the wind and the sea from coral rubble, sand and broken shells... it is all held together by roots of the trees and shrubs that have thrived in such a salty environment.

Now for you bird watchers. More than fifty species visit the Island. From October to April, Noddy Terns claim nesting space... quiet and trusting, these birds show little fear of their human visitors. One chick will be raised by each pair. Most of their day is spent at sea. Unfortunately, whilst they are marvellous fliers over water, returning to land is not their strong point. Three point landings usually turn out to be both feet and beak. At night the homecoming bird usually hits the tree tops, collides with every branch as it falls to the ground, then staggers off to the burrow to spend the rest of the night telling its mate about it. At night a group of these crazy birds sounds like a thousand cats fighting. We wonder when do they sleep? Deserted by their parents before fully maturing, the chicks have to teach themselves to fly. This perhaps is their reason for making bad landings.

She shows Sam and cannot resist commenting on how bad it is when human motivations are ascribed to islands, birds and the like. The way they tell the story of the island, it's more like a long drawn out metaphor about a really sad childhood, she tells Sam. I guess they want us to believe they are now looking after it but they cannot be held responsible for what happens. Sam nods in agreement.

The four of them sit down together. As though at a milk bar.

They make jokes about Kev, the coach captain, about how all coach captains seem to act like a pilots, how he's probably shit scared of driving too fast after the recent Grafton coach disaster and the possible activities in which he might engage to fill in the time while they are out on the island. The conversation is awkward, at least between the men but slowly gains some sort of flow.

The cat heads out to sea. Within minutes Sam and Caroline are white. They suggest moving outside, to the back of the cat. Sally sits between them.

Sam D sits away from them. Caroline says she never gets seasick, that the last time she was sick it was because she was pregnant. She keeps saying she better not be pregnant. Sam too, says he never gets seasick. The cat rolls and rolls. Sally loves it.

She also love being the one who isn't sick. And rubs the backs of the two of them while they chuck into the paper bags provided. She doesn't, however, like the way Sam D doesn't comfort Caroline. Comfort her in the way she thinks comforting ought to be done.

The women crew also assist the sick.

The men crew go down into the engine room. And prepare the diving gear.

'You have a choice of giving your sick bag to one of us or throwing it overboard yourself,' one of the women crew says, 'That's what we always do with them.'

'Guess they're bio-degradable,' Caroline says, swinging her arm for the first throw.

Caroline and Sam are really sick.

Others stagger to and from the bar showing off their ability to down a Fosters or two anyway. While others choose to burn their skin on the unprotected upstairs level.

It is a long three and a half hours.

Lady Musgrave lagoon is filled with the most marvellous things for you to see. It is home for an unbelievable number of fascinating marine creatures. Snorkelling is a great way to see it. Try it! Please feel free to ask us questions about the trip or the Reef. We will do our best to make your day a memorable one.

'I can't last any longer,' Caroline says, 'not without crying, I'm such a sook when I'm sick.'

Sally feels sorry for both of them

They still have the coming back.

The cat pulls in to a pontoon. A fair way out from the island.

And the first lunch shift begins. Tinned pineapple rings, tinned circles of beetroot, various salads and lumps of meat are offered. Caroline refuses to eat. She and Sam D find a shaded spot on the pontoon and flake out. Sam, as Sally expects, eats with his customary gusto. Sally prepares to go snorkelling and tells him he is a fool, that it will all surface again.

'You want me to be sick,' he teases her.

She can't deny it. She likes him being sick. It gives her a chance to look after him.

The great broadleafed Pisonia tree dominates the Island. Soft wooded, they break easily during storms. Shallow rooted, they sometimes topple, but do not die, continuing to grow lying down.

Sally lathers Sam in Doctor's Choice. She lathers Toddler's Bloc on herself figuring if it is good for toddler's skin it must be ultra-protective. She also knows it is probably just a good marketing ploy on behalf of the manufacturer.

They both put on long sleeve shirts.

Sam is a newcomer to the world of skin protection.

As a young surfer his white white skin was burnt year after year. His mother simply hadn't known. And it was only when his older sister had her first skin cancers burnt off did he decide to take Sally's advice seriously.

They pick out suitably sized snorkelling gear and move towards the water.

'Are there any sharks?' Sally asks.

'Not in here, there is nothing to worry about.'

'If there were they'd tell us wouldn't they, I mean they'd say swim at your own risk, wouldn't they?' she asks.

'Yes, they would,' says Sam.

The water is cold.

Sally is at first unwilling to venture far from the pontoon but then decides if a shark is to get her a shark will get her. Sam nudges her every so often to point out either a huge fish or some particularly colourful coral. She likes the way when she point nudges something out to him he gives her the thumbs up. She likes the non-verbal communication aspect but hates the way it reminds her of her father. Of that military type communication.

The reef is stunning and although Sally would like to step on the island itself she decides the swim is too far. Sam tells her to dive down deep and listen. She tries but all that happens is her ears hurt.

'You're not blowing out hard enough, clear them,' he tells her.

'What am I supposed to hear?' she asks.

'Rain pattering on a tin roof,' he replies.

Finally she manages to clear her ears and hear the sound, somehow it reminds her of the colour silver but then she remembers his having said 'tin roof.'

Soon the female green turtles and loggerheads will laboriously heave their massive bodies to the top of the beaches to lay a hundred or more soft shelled eggs leaving bulldozer-like tracks on the sand. Later in the season, many sandy areas above high water mark will look to have been stirred by a demented dozer driver. Possibly as many as six times these panting ladies will climb the beach during the season. This looks to us like hard work.

Caroline and Sam D go out on one of the glass bottom boats.

On her return Caroline signals to Sally, who has come in for a rest, to sit with her, that Sam D wants to be left alone to sleep.

They discover they both ended up doing nursing. And swap nursing stories. Caroline tells Sally how she was always getting into trouble for bucking the system. How she was almost forced into resigning because she dared to question things. Dared to question the standard of medical care. Sally tells Caroline how she'd left because she was so under-confident, but how if she'd stayed, she too would have ended up bucking the system.

Sam D wakes up and looks up at the two women. Caroline tells him she wants to fly back to Noosa. She doesn't care how much the seaplane costs. The words cost and plane somehow bring Sally to asking Caroline, 'Why did you choose to holiday to Noosa?'

'I wanted somewhere nice, not an island and I didn't want to leave Australia because of my babies,' she replies.

Sally grapples with Caroline's not wanting to leave Australia, trying to work out if it would be all that wrong to leave the country, would come under the 'not so good parenting' label, at the same time, she is pleased Caroline displays such concern.

'Where are you staying?' Caroline asks.

'The Sheraton,' Lucy replies.

'Lucky you, that's where I wanted to stay, we're staying at the Pelican Apartments, but I shouldn't whinge should I darling?' she says, turning to Sam D who gives her a slightly amused but irritated look.

'I always complain, probably too much, Sam wants to go out at night and all I want to do is sleep, I mean I haven't slept one night straight through since the babies. I'm always complaining, aren't I darling?' Caroline says. Sam D nods. And looking back at Sally she adds, 'I guess I'm still as bad as I used to be.'

Sally wants to look after Caroline.

She wants to tell her it's fine to complain.

She wants to tell her that her badness is her energy, that it's a good thing.

'So tell me what happened to you after we left Venice, you were so sick,' Caroline asks, as though wanting to change the topic.

'Well I managed to get back to England,' Sally replies, not wanting to seem to make too much of it.

Date   23 Dec
Place   Venice

Another doctor and another language struggle this time in Italian. Caroline stayed with me and was super. Have decided to fly to London tomorrow.

'I remember that hopeless Italian doctor seeing you, I mean it was obvious you were bleeding,' she says.

'You knew! How?' Sally asks, noticeably shocked.

'I don't think that detail is necessary,' Caroline replies.

Sally figures she must mean the black shit she'd passed. But she wants Caroline to mention it. She wants to hear the story from someone else other than herself.

'You were obviously very ill,' Caroline says, 'I felt terribly guilty about leaving you, Sam D asked me this morning why I left you in such a state. I guess we were so young I didn't know enough and the coach woman said she'd arranged everything for you.'

'She hadn't arranged a thing,' Sally tells her.

Date   26 Dec
Place   Hospital London

Ended up in intensive care on Christmas Eve at Watford General Hospital — another half an hour and I wouldn't have made it. Six pints of blood and unconscious. Even scored a trip in an ambulance and intensive care.

Date   27 Dec
Place   London Hospital

Still on the drip and not allowed to eat. Feeling much more relaxed — even had some sherry. I wrote to Jenna and Paul and my family. Saline drip and blood test; nothing else done. I feel much better and alive. Sister Burgess came again and showed me her wedding photos of her daughter. Diazepam 2mg tablet after lunch. Slept till 4.30 pm. Bit homesick. Another Diazepam 2mg before dinner.

Sally cannot believe it. It makes her feel so good to have Caroline tell Sam it was real. Sam who had always believed it was real. Who had said she was brave.

> for the first time
> there is another voice
> one that was there

The seaplane takes off. Resigned to the three hour trip back Caroline boards the cat. She and the sick Sam decide to lie down the whole trip back. Sally finds it hard to hear the dialogue of *Crocodile Dundee* over the noise of the engines. She thinks it is amusing however, the way the cat is trying to be like a coach, showing a movie, a movie about the outback.

Bird droppings, guano, was taken off the Island around 1900. It was in demand as fertiliser. Goats were put on the Island for shipwrecked sailors and these did much damage. They were removed and the Island rapidly recovered.

After the customary handshake and 'I do hope we see you again,' as they get off the cat they meet up with Kev.

The idea of a meal stop depresses them. They all just want to go home.

'I wonder where it will be, who has the contract?' Sally asks.

'No doubt we'll get steak, steak, or steak,' Caroline says.

They eventually pull into a petrol station restaurant. The four of them laugh. And Sally tells Caroline that secretly she loves having meals at petrol stations.

Date   30 Dec
Place   Hospital

Well it's theatre exploratory today. Vampire visited but managed first time. Waiting for ages to go to theatre. Put injection in hand no veins left—not too bad after all—on second thoughts—bloody awful.

Date   New Year's Day
Place   Hospital

I can walk by myself! even if only to the toilet. I may even be allowed to have a bath tomorrow. The night staff says not to expect a quick recovery since I did nearly die—'Young lass I don't think you realise how ill you have been.' I'm off the four hourly vital stats.

I walked today—my resolution to cope!

Date   5 Jan
Place   Hospital

My mother rang and all insurance is arranged. They took blood and labelled it to see if it comes out in my motions. My bloody veins. Got a letter from Vaia and Geoff. Sister Burgess came back on duty and gave me a card.

Date   12 Jan
Place   Hospital

Another week yet I'm so tired. More letters. I weigh 8st 101lbs. Chronium has to go through my system and that takes two weeks.

Date   19 Jan
Place   Hosp

High temp and pulse rate but I shall get out. Sent long letter to Jenna and Paul. I am determined to get out.

Back on board the coach they all try to sleep.

At ten they finally pull in to Noosa.

'You're leaving tomorrow aren't you?' Caroline says.

'Yeah, probably,' Sally replies, deciding to leave it up to Caroline as to how the talk of future contact will be managed.

'Well, you're in the Sydney phone book aren't you?' she offers.

'Yeah, sure am,' Sally replies, pleased with Caroline's choice.

'Well, next time I'm there I'll give you a ring.'

'Great, do that,' Sally replies, with enough enthusiasm so that if Caroline really does want to ring, she will know her call will be welcome.

'Well, have a good rest of your holiday.'

'You too,' says Sally.

The two men say goodbye to each other.

Carrying their pillows back towards the Sheraton Sally cannot stop going on about how amazing it was that they should meet up on a coach again.

Date 27 Jan
Place   Arrived in Sydney

Went to see Jenna and on tablets. Went to toilet at 7.30 pm. Jenna and Paul visited me at night.

Date   29 Jan
Place   Home

Date   31 Jan
Place   Hospital

Admitted to Hospital. Blood taken—ugh.

Date   1 Feb
Place   Hospital

Food better than Watford and a much more relaxed atmosphere. Sam hugs her.

'I know,' he says.

'I mean it just goes to show how much I still think I'm lying when I say I was sick. It was amazing she said I was sick and amazing that I met her with you, I don't know it just makes me feel so real.'

'You are real and you were sick,' he says gently touching her neck.

'But it's incredible how I still don't feel that, how I still feel the story is a lie.'

208

Sally then tells Sam how she knows he would say she still tells the story from her mother's point of view, that she, Sally, brought it on herself, that she wasn't in a fit state of mind before she left. And Sam tells her how she'd been just like any other nineteen-year-old wanting to discover the world and herself.

'Yeah, yeah, maybe, I just wish Caroline had more self-esteem,' Sally responds, 'that she'd see her "badness" as a good thing. And how things change, I mean, I was scared of her at college and now I just wish I could help her.'

'What amazed me is how almost immediately you two filled each other in one the last ten years, men would never do that.'

'Well, that's men's problem,' Sally says breaking free.

'I'm not criticising you,' he says grabbing her back, 'if anything I'm envious.'

'Yeah well, enough's enough, I have to stop talking about it,' she says.

And as they enter the Sheraton

> waves of blue
> island white
> pinnacle flower
>
> within her

as the silence of a day ten years ago, force opening the long black struggle for other voices

> is finally
> treasured.

So We Walked Down Abercrombie Street

Beth Yahp

Beth Yahp was born in Malaysia in 1964 in a hospital painted blood red. She thinks this has affected much of her vision. She comes from long line of southern Chinese gipsies, which is why she found herself in Sydney in 1984. In less fanciful moments she will admit she came as an overseas student. After graduating from the University of Technology in Sydney, she worked as a bookseller, a pamphlet deliverer, a despatch clerk and an artist's assistant to support her writing. She has been widely published in anthologies and literary magazines, and has co-edited two collections of stories including *My Look's Caress: A Collection of Modern Romances*. In 1989 Beth was awarded the Ethnic Affairs Commission Fellowship.

SO WE WALKED DOWN ABERCROMBIE STREET

On Thursday nights we had chip butties and two bottles of Coopers each, sometimes an apple and cheese from the deli, and bottles of club port at four and five ninety-nine lining the ledge above the fireplace. Janie put on a Bob Dylan record, one where he's neatly shaven, you can see the curve of his cheek, the shape of his skull. On Thursday nights we took turns bashing on Janie's typewriter trying to write a soapie (someone told us this was the way to make money), coming out for coffee at intervals, leaving the characters to lurk in Janie's room. We had candles burning pools of reddish wax on the kitchen table and a cat that tried to sleep on everyone's knee. A guitar in the corner wearing a shapely hat. Walking up Abercrombie Street gave us acne and malt up our noses from the brewery. An earful of trucks honking if we wore a skirt. Having to dodge the kids running away from ripping off the corner store.

Janie wore black and maroon that year and sometimes olive green and was growing her hair. The tutor on Thursday nights stopped in mid-sentence when Janie walked in, and said: 'I love the way your lipstick always matches', smacking her own lips, which made Janie laugh. Janie wore her hair slicked back with gel with a strand curling loose in front, down to her chin. Her skin was so white and fine Lisa could only think of words like statue and marble and moon. Janie wore a felt hat tilted to one side and a fez that made people stare.

So we walked down Abercrombie Street, we had a class in the morning and one at night and the afternoons yawning in between.

Leaving the Tower to blink in the sun was like coming out of a cave. At the newsagents Janie bought two scratch lotto tickets because we'd been talking about money and not having it, and TEAS and the dole and university fees.

'In my country,' Lisa said, 'university is free. The problem is it's hard to get in. I mean, if you don't have the right name. Selection is based on race, a certain percentage for each race, and not proportionate either. Not that I tried. It was a natural progression — you know? Anyone whose parents could afford it knew they were going overseas.'

And I'm looking at Janie's feet, her shoes, they're black and red, like pumps with a little heel, and I'm wearing jeans and a black pullover I'm so proud of because I'm hoping it makes me look like Abercrombie Street instead of Burwood or some other foreign place with the Westfield Shoppingtown and the men in the furry checked shirts and the women bursting out of pastel trackpants (this is what I notice first: so many people are *bursting*). Janie bought those shoes in a secondhand shop where rich people leave their clothes and if you're lucky you get there just after they've left, and I've looked and looked but never found a pair to match them. They were almost new.

'Hats make you feel different,' Janie said. 'And shoes that are almost new. Like wearing someone else's dress, you feel you're someone else in that dress, beautiful, exciting. All the layers of that other life rubbing against your skin so that your eyes widen and there's a tilt to your chin and you sparkle, like having another life or past, or dipping your fingers into someone else's perfume. Their rich cream.'

'But what if you catch something?' Lisa doesn't say.

That was the autumn we said goodbye to old loves and talked about circles and writing and breaking old forms. Through the window the rooftops lay one against another, soft as felt on a darkening sky.

'And another thing,' Lisa said. 'I can't believe the colour of that sky.'

They were walking down the street, two young women, from the back they looked almost the same. They wore dark clothes and had dark shiny hair. They walked with wide steps, their bodies turned to each other, and sometimes they stopped at the lights and sometimes they ran, and their shoulders touched, they accidently bumped each other, talking, their hands curving this way and that. They were talking about a play, a film they'd seen, a book they were about to read. They stopped at the shops and bought two dollars worth of hot chips and two oranges, some fags and beer.

'We lived in Hurstville for years and years,' Janie said. 'When the kids started school, Mum and Dad decided to come to Sydney and never to move. We left the country pub where we'd learnt to play pool in the mornings, with its narrow rooms upstairs and the plastic runners in the hallways, and the railings that creaked. In winter a crust of ice hung from the gutters. As the sun came out you could hear the slow drips onto the front verandah. In summer all we did was balance icy drinks on our bellies, lying with our feet in the paddle pool. My mother got sick when I was twelve. She went to bed with a book and we didn't see her for days. She read *Wuthering Heights* and at night we heard her crying.'

'Once I saw my father cry,' Lisa said. 'He was a big man, I'd only ever seen him laughing or calm, or when angry, silent. He went away every morning and came home at night, and he carried a bag of company papers only he was allowed to read. He wore big colourful ties. When my father came home, we'd be sitting glued to the TV. Someone would run to open the gate when he honked, then come pelting back so as not to miss anything. Sometimes we didn't even say hello. My father walked past our backs turned towards him. I never thought he could ever be lonely, or sad. He just *was*. He lay in bed in his undershirt and pants and the only thing you could see in the dark was his whale shape. You couldn't see his face till you got up close, and he was staring at the ceiling and blubbering, tears dripping down his cheeks.'

In this circle there were a lot of stories. We sat in a room where candles threw shadows against the walls and there was only one window. A record player, a broken sofa and two TVs, one on top of the other. The paint was peeling. On the ceiling: dark swirlings of mould. It was autumn. Later someone started a fire with newspaper twists and we clapped when it was done. Beer and fags, Tim Tams and port, joints and hi's and hello's stepping over each other as we sprawled in the corners of the room. Thursday nights were experimental. With random gatherings and not knowing each other, or anyone, with crayon drawings and cutting classes (if you missed four in the semester you failed, the tutor was that particular, and Janie and Lisa missed three and three quarters each, she timed them, she had a watch that was never wrong). Thursday nights we sat with subtle antennae out, tasting each other. Drinking cups of milky tea, lying on the floor, spinning: statements of poetics and BB King, the Mamas and Papas and Triple J, and someone strumming the guitar; and slices of tomato and cheddar, and stories and schemes.

Lisa arrives first, too lazy to go home in the afternoons. It's half an hour on the train and fifteen minutes from the station to the room she's renting in the suburbs and two and a half minutes up the stairs, and she'd have to do it twice to get back to the class at six. Her bag's too heavy. She's like a snail, she carries everything in case of emergencies (a legacy from her mother). Bandaids and pimple cream, extra pens and paper, Quickease pellets for hunger and two novels for boredom, and choice. Lisa arrives first, lazy and curious. She comes with Janie, it is Janie's house, and Mark's house, and Kate's, and Janie has just moved in.

'Don't worry about the mess,' she says, shutting the bedroom door.

While Janie makes lunch Lisa lies on the sofa, swallowing the knot in her chest. It's a familiar knot, one she associates with the loss of language. Of familiar things. She has never been in such a house, there's paper everywhere and someone has swirled and speckled the phone (what if the telephone inspector *sees*? won't they have to pay a *fine?*). There are posters stuck on the walls just anywhere and a bit of the window broken off so the cat can come in. Lisa lies on the sofa like a cat, on her front, face half-tucked under one arm. She pretends to be sleepy so she doesn't have to speak. The sofa smells stale, smells of bums and yesterday's dinner and smoke from the turn of the century but she breathes in deeply. It's something she thinks will make her change. Like cutting her hair after she gets to this country and hiding away her frilly t-shirts and plastic peep-toe shoes, the going-away presents her grandmother gave her. She thinks of the smells curling around the knot in her chest, among the grains of Abercrombie and the malt. The room is a cavern which will swallow her.

Later Mark arrives with a bottle of wine and Kate, who is sad in her spirit, but doesn't know why. Kate wears red to make herself happy.

'I worked in a bank for eighteen months,' Mark said. 'I lived in a building which had seventeen floors and a view of the building next door. For eighteen months I went to the bank and the money was paper passing through my hands. The bank was on the corner of a busy street. Every time the door opened I was blinded. Then I quit and sat in my room with my typewriter and my desk. I hardly went out. I was a realist then.'

'I lived in a country town,' Kate said, 'where city people came for their holidays. A beach town. In winter it was practically dead, then summer came, an explosion. The sweat dripped off my skin. I hated the tourists from the south, the cities. They strutted through our streets like they owned everything, and they were light, they laughed loudly, they had the newest clothes and haircuts and cars. They messed the place up because they didn't have to live there, they looked at the locals like we had some kind of disease — a country disease. In summer I stood on the beach watching the bleached boys with their long strides and shoulders peeling from too much sun. I stood in the shade of the trees.'

Standing in front of the mirror, Lisa can only stare. The body looked the same. There were the eyes, the cheekbones, the black hair hanging limply by the sides of her face. The belly curving and nipples pinched from the cold (typically, her first letters home are full of the cold, the prices of things, the sounds of the trains, how clean the public toilets are). Her legs are long and slightly bent, her feet stand squarely, toes squeezing together — everything the same. Only when she opened her mouth could she see the change.

'I felt we were a part of something,' Kate said. 'We came from all over the country, well, some of us did, came to this place. Everything seemed possible. We were potential, we could be anything. Much later, when we are scattered, I will feel the loss of this time like a canker in my stomach. I will cast about for things to do. I will sit in big lighted rooms and twist my pen around my fingers and play touch football on Thursday afternoons to crunch my chest and skin my knees because that is how it will be done. I will play games to fit in. I will be heavy, although now I am hopeful. I yearn for other schemes.'

'There aren't any telephone inspectors,' Janie said.

And I'm looking at Janie. I'm scratching my head, thinking this is how you do it, this is an inspirational scratch, and I'm saying: 'You're bored, Janie. You're a housewife. You're stuck in the flat all day. Your feet hurt. Your kids will be home any minute. You read these glossy magazines. You save up to buy the latest make-up. You dream.' And I'm fiddling with the camera, I'm focusing, zooming in on Janie's face with her hair slicked back and a scarf around her head like a turban and a tassel swinging from one ear. Janie is supposed to be a suburban housewife, she's in the kitchen in the suburbs, she's mixing things in a bowl, sweating in the lights I've borrowed from the Tower, slicing carrots, chopping parsley, brewing over the stove. And I'm pixillating. I'm pressing the button every second, slowing the film so that when we play it back Janie will be jumping about the kitchen, she'll be moving in blinks and flashes from the sink to the table to the fridge to the floor so fast we can hardly see her (dreams move like this in real time, Janie says later). In a couple of weeks we go to the Tower and run the film, and we laugh. Janie's face fills the screen, she looks different, she doesn't believe it is her. (But that is how I see her — in flashes.)

Later Janie and Lisa do the theory. They lie on the floor in Lisa's bedroom facing the window that looks over houses, the Concord Oval, a flashing McDonalds sign. On Saturdays Lisa sits listening to the traffic from Parramatta Road, the roars, the cheers. She likes looking over the tops of the houses, over the men and women who are hosing their gardens, moving the gnomes and mushrooms around. At night the oval is a hazy jewel. Janie and Lisa buy a slab of chocolate and they lie and munch on the bedroom floor. They flick pages of notes they can hardly decipher from yesterday's lecture. Their pens squeak and scribble. Form is content, they write. (Though they can't remember who said this, it sounds to them like a spell.) Form is content. The telling of a story is the story. The film is about boredom and escape, they write. If form is content should the film be boring, escapist? And they draw a vase the shape of a heart and they fill it with flowers. They talk about everything except the film.

'My mother left school when she was twelve,' Lisa said. 'She never writes because she's ashamed of the shapes of her words. She wears thick glasses when she reads, and she reads fashion magazines and a paper called *Thrill* which tells stories about oddities, women with four breasts who have quadruplets, rapists who are caught by vengeful women, their groins smeared with chillies since they think they're so hot. These stories make my mother laugh, her glasses slide to the end of her nose. When she was twelve my grandmother took her out of school because grandfather died and grandma had to go out work and my mother had to stay home and look after the kids. To cook and clean. She drew the delicate heads of beautiful girls to amuse her brothers and sisters. After she married, she kept her own house and looked after her own kids. She said each of us, her girls, had to finish school. Our letters with the foreign stamps always pleased her.'

'My father was a sailor,' Janie said. 'Looking at him now you'd never guess. Before my mother met him she sat in her room and read books. She devoured them — there were dusty stacks under her bed. She wanted to work and travel, to see the world. She hated the word housewife because my grandmother said it so proudly. Even after she married, and her work was housework and she didn't read or travel, my mother couldn't say it. My father said it for her: housewife. When my father came to town my mother put on a red dress that swirled and a hot red lipstick and shoes that gleamed red in the dark. My father put his arm around her, sailor fashion, his hand curving over her hip, and my mother danced and danced. She cupped her hand on his shoulder and spun where he twirled her, and floated home at dawn.'

In this circle there were a lot of gaps. We sat in a room with strangers, our bodies curling this way and that, towards and away from each other. The spaces between our bodies was a pattern that held us together. Our words were lace in the air. There was Janie and Kate and Mark and Lisa, those four bodies, and we sipped and laughed and spoke, and our stories were black-winged birds swooping over our heads. The spaces between our words was like lead (it seemed to Lisa, they made her heavy, so heavy).

'Suddenly,' Mark said, 'we were faced with new ideas, books, writers, theories that leapt off the page. We were thrown together in a heap, off the deep end. We all did the same classes. It was like moving cities as children, our childhood assurances suddenly wrenched away. We spent our time inventing ourselves in a language the others could understand. We could be anyone. Just being anyone was the key. We spoke ourselves by describing the things around us, where we came from, what we ate. Much later, when this house is just a house on a street, and this street doesn't lead to this house but is just a street to walk through, I will feel the pull of its empty centre like a magnet buried deep in the earth. I will stop and look in through lighted windows. I will work in a building with a wall of plate glass and a view of a grimy part of this city. A bird will sometimes glide past, or swoop to peck at its reflection, and I will write my screenplay on sheets of official paper, under cover of the work files on my desk. Piles that are finished on my right, piles to be done on my left. I will write furiously. I will tap my feet and bite the end of my pencil and gaze at the sky.'

While Mark helps Janie make lunch, Kate and Lisa sit together. Of the four, they have the most in common: they understand the workings of difference, of periphery, and craning. Their voices are different, their speaking, the way they hold their hands (they are always explaining, to whoever will listen, this difference: what it's like *back home*). Kate shows Lisa some old photos. One is of her mother in a wedding dress, another of herself at nine, tap dancing. Kate's hair is red like her mother's. In the photo, dancing, her arms are held out, she's in the middle of a spin, her face (like her mother's) is pinched with concentration. Even now Kate has this look, anxious, fearful, of waiting to stop spinning. She sits hunched forward, earnest, showing Lisa the photos. She talks loudly, quickly, to fill the gaps in their conversation. Kate finds words for Lisa to say, she corrects Lisa's pronunciation, and while she speaks she and Lisa look at the photos and listen to what the *others* are saying. Mark and Janie laugh, their laughter floats in from the kitchen. Kate and Lisa are always listening to other people laughing.

'My mother married when she was twenty-two,' Kate said. 'She came from a stock of farmers—a pragmatic, stubborn lot with hats pulled low and their shoe leather cracked. By the time she was twenty-two the country had etched its map on her face. Looking at her we saw where we came from. She had five kids and her teeth out by the time she was forty, and worked at the primary school washing burettes, pipettes, petri dishes, test tubes. She painted watercolour landscapes and screeched when she won a car in a supermarket competition, then sold it to buy a smaller car and a dishwasher so she wouldn't have to wash dishes at home.'

That was the autumn we threw our bags in a heap in the corner, books and files and papers any old where, and we brewed hot drinks for each other and stretched our legs towards the centre of the room. We made a sundial shape: a haphazard clock.

'I grew up in the western suburbs,' Mark said. 'I was captain of the cricket team. On Sundays I sat in kitchen with my mother and we read plays together, doing the funny voices. She kept an old plastic radio on the fridge and we pretended the voices came from there. When she laughed her face crinkled, she shook so much her chair creaked. Her handwriting was a feathery scrawl. Her fingers were heavy with rings. I showed her the stories I wrote, and even then she read them seriously, a crease between her eyebrows. She laughed at all the right bits. She was forty-two when she left, and the postcards she sent were big and glossy. They never fit through the slot in the door without creasing. She sent pictures of flowers and broken buildings. Her eyes were a watery washed-out blue, beautiful.'

Some evenings Mark comes home with Lisa. They ride the train to the room she rents in the suburbs, to the house that used to be a mansion but is now a house divided into flats. In the evenings it looks haunted. Branches knock against its windows, the driveway is long and dark. Mark and Lisa climb the stairs and Mark jokes about creaky ghosts. For dinner they eat curries that make his ears go red. Then Lisa persuades him to try a sticky syrupy fruit canned in her country and her flatmate brings him hot milky tea in a glass, and they watch to see the sorts of faces he'll make.

'You're lucky it's canned,' they tell him. 'The fresh stuff is ten times more deadly.'

'In a glass,' they tell him, 'you can see what's in your tea.'

And Lisa is sick in the middle of the night. They've sat up drinking and talking, the cheap port swirls in her stomach, it makes her heave, and ache (someone has told her that Asians are genetically allergic to alcohol and she's trying to build up a resistance). Lisa gets out of bed and goes to the toilet to puke and when she comes back, Mark is awake on the floor. 'There, there, it can't be that bad,' he whispers, because last night she was homesick and he thinks she's been sad. In the morning they sit in the kitchen in a patch of sunlight. Lisa sits looking at the curve of Mark's thigh, it's a golden curve, the hairs are thick and soft and shiny. It looks like fur to Lisa, luxurious, she wants to run her hand along that golden thigh. Her own body is so smooth they can only see the hairs by holding her arm to the light, by squinting.

'People called me gecko skin at school,' Lisa said (and when Mark raises his eyebrows, she tells him that the geckos in her country are brown and smooth and warm and supple, they cling to the ceiling and cry when people are dying, and shed their tails when you touch them).

So we walked down Abercrombie Street, we had a class in the morning and one in the evening, and the afternoons yawning in between. Leaving the Tower to blink in the light was like coming up for air (the Tower confused Lisa, it's floors and corridors all looked the same, she always got lost there, she ended up walking in circles). At the corner shop Janie bought a licorice strap, ripped it in half and we walked along sucking and chewing. The street caked our faces, our hair. Dead leaves fell in spirals and sometimes there was a miniature whirlwind on someone's doorstep, a dusty pool of leaves, rubbish, dirt. When we got to Janie's house, she stretched her arms. She stretched and smiled.

And I'm looking at Janie, her body, the questionmark curl of her body on the mattress. The light comes in streaks through a cloth strung over the window: people who are passing make shadows that jump and twitch. Janie is lying on her side, knees bent, one arm supporting her head. She's dozy in the warm cluttered room, the afternoon light. Her voice circles the air. And I'm lying beside her, I'm stretched with my shoes off (sensible runners sent seamail by my mother to ward off blisters and retain warmth). I'm listening to Janie's heartbeat. Lying like a log beside her: I am heavy, I'm feeling my bones. The back of her neck is covered with a down that parts when I breathe.

'I spent my time watching,' Lisa said. 'Describing. To stop the knot in my chest from growing I was still, I said nothing. I learnt a trick of receding, of withdrawing to watch from across the room. There was a pane of glass between me and the others, including that blushing, uncomfortable woman. To me she was always a 'you' or 'she', never 'I'. I wanted to watch, she to fit in. I left her at home sometimes and put on my glasses and my daggy clothes to walk in the city and some days it felt like no one even saw me. Such freedom in not being seen. Much later, when I move out of this city, I will think of its shapes and colours, its smells and the weight of its air on my skin. I will forget the names of streets and how they link up, and also the names of people and how they do. I will sit in a room with a view of trees and see not the panorama but bits and pieces, a twist of bark, the flesh of sunlight on a rusty tin. I will see these pieces again and again. I will scribble stories, and wait for mail, and scan the local papers for part-time work.'

When Lisa first comes to Sydney, she rides the trains incessantly. She rides to Penrith, Bondi Junction, Pymble, Cronulla, West Ryde. The names stick to her tongue. She sits next to the window with her bag on her knee and sometimes people sit beside her and sometimes they move to another seat, and she zips and unzips the bag (in one carriage someone has drawn large anti-Asian signs, like anti-smoking signs, an Asiatic face cancelled out, and she sits looking at the little triangular hats). In the city she comes from there aren't any suburban trains. Later Lisa rides to Central and gets out to walk down George

Street to the Quay. Everyone seems to be walking the other way: she bumps and edges along. When she gets to the Quay she stands looking at the water. Pigeons and gulls peck at her feet. There isn't a harbour in the city she comes from, only two narrow rivers. Translated into English the city's name is 'Muddy Confluence', at the spot where the rivers meet stands its oldest mosque. At this spot the rivers swirl thickly.

Already Lisa can tell the difference between the groups of Asians at the Quay—the ones who are tourists, the ones who have been here a while, or forever, and the ones who have just arrived (already she understands by Asians not Indians, Malays, Arabs, Burmese, Turks etc. but East Asians, people who look like her). When Lisa sees a group of Just Arrived's she carefully skirts them. She walks around them looking at their voices, their laughter, their shoes, their hair. She wants to tell them not to put grease in their hair, not to have partings that look like splits in their skulls, not to wear pink frills with a red skirt, black tights with white shoes. And not to talk and laugh too loudly, or be too happy, or excited. Not to stick out. The Just Arrived's are so uncool (she feels angry and embarrassed when people poke fun at them; at their stumbling words, she turns the other way). Lisa glances furtively at her own clothes, her hair: hoping she doesn't look like *them*. She wants to look like she's always been here—at least, to everyone except ticket collectors. To ticket collectors Lisa wants to look like a tourist. She squeaks broken English when they ask for her ticket and looks bewildered, and she makes them repeat and repeat what they're saying and takes out her empty purse and, exasperated, they tell her to go away (she writes to her mother how good she is at cutting costs).

After lunch, Janie and Lisa work in Janie's bedroom. They're supposed to be writing an essay together, about a film they're making. Thursday afternoons, between classes, they say they will work together. They pick their way over Janie's clothes and shoes, her books and scarves to her mattress on the floor. They can see themselves in an old cloudy mirror. The film is about dreamers. For reference, they think of their mothers. They look in the mirror and block out certain parts of their faces with their hands to show each other what their mothers look like from the bits that are left. It's not an easy method: photos are easier (but not as truthful, they think). Sometimes they catch themselves speaking like their mothers. They think they will grow to look more and more like them. 'She rings up to ask what I'm reading,' says Janie, and Lisa says: 'Mine makes my sister write to find out whether I'm studying', and Janie and Lisa spread out their notes. They draw squiggles and bite their lips and try to write a paragraph but soon they are talking, laughing, saying shall we or shan't we, deciding to wag the evening class. They talk about everything except the film.

And I'm standing in front of the mirror. I'm staring. Stopping short whenever I come to a mirror. There is the body, the eyes, the cheekbones, the black hair hanging limply by the sides of my face. And I'm looking at this face, I've looked at it for twenty-five years but now I'm having to stop and stare. Now chance sightings catch me unaware, bits of my image lurk in the reflections on department store windows to shock me. Now my voice is no longer so strange, now I've lost my accent, people don't talk down at me, yet there's always that initial reaction, the fundamental difference: my face. Often I remember this difference only in people's reactions: *you* are my mirror (you mannequins in shop windows, you pouting white women on magazine covers, you neighbours who whisper loudly that I'm Japanese and can't speak like you). And I'm thinking about the Thai boy I met at the station. I'm thinking of the Thai boy, the student, who talked Australian so I was surprised he said he came from somewhere else, he'd only been here three years. This boy went down to the pub like everyone else (at a time when pubs terrified me) and slapped people on the back, calling them mate and buying drinks, doing ocker accents, telling jokes. He seemed so easy. And he said: I hate looking in mirrors. And: I hate my face. And: I'm so ugly, Asian ugly, nobody goes for me (his women friends say he is beautiful, they stroke his skin, accuse him of paranoia, and he hates this also—being a *novelty*).

'I had a lump in my throat,' Janie said, 'that stayed for days and days. All of us had it—it wasn't an exclusive lump. At first we were uneasy, quiet, we couldn't think of things to say. We were like strange birds put in a cage together, staring at each other, beady-eyed. The cage was this city, the Tower, this place. We played old records to fill in the gaps. Much later, when I have lived in other cities, when I have gone away and come back and come back and gone away so that my memory of places is an ill-spliced screening of coming and going, I will think of this time like a scene in a favourite novel, remembered but no longer read. I will watch the view from other windows, leave trails of my passing in other cities: a watch on a bus in Melbourne, a shoe in Adelaide, a cherished photo in Brisbane. I will dance in crowded rooms and buy thick pads of yellowed paper on which to write reviews and teenage novels and occasional stories that scrape at the heart. I will work in a kitchen and a library for money, and be slow at shelving, enticed, pausing to pore over books.'

So they walked down Abercrombie Street, two young women, only close up could you tell they were different (this was a fantasy Lisa had). They wore bright jumpers they'd bought from the Sydney Mission and black, flat-heeled shoes. They walked with quick steps, pushing against the wind that veered fiercely around buildings, coating their faces with grit. After the morning class they took a detour into Grace Brothers to wander around the make-up counters. They stopped here and there and became engrossed in the different colours and soon their wrists and palms were a rainbow pattern. The longer they stayed the more they wanted to buy something. In the lunchtime crowd they lost each other, and one of them couldn't resist a lipstick like a gash of dark blood. She held it as she walked about looking for the other and finally she saw the back of her head in a mirror, and when they came together they saw they were holding the same lipsticks, exactly the same. The colour looked different on their skins. They laughed and paid at the counter, and left the store.

More fiction from
ALLEN & UNWIN

JENNIFER MAIDEN
Play with Knives

Play with Knives is a chilling, fascinating exploration of violence, power, morality and grief.

The novel centres around Clare, a young woman shortly to be released from prison. As a child she had murdered a young brother and two sisters.

How was this monstrous act possible? Does the act mean that Clare herself is a monster? As central to the unfoldment of this unforgettable novel is Jennifer Maiden's exploration of the character and motivation of the probation officer, through whose eyes and questions Clare is gradually revealed.

This is a novel which has all the momentum, even the inevitability of a sudden accident, when the observer is appalled, yet utterly transfixed. For after such an event, no line of vision remains unaffected.

MANDY SAYER
Mood Indigo

Once again the prestigious Australian/Vogel Literary Award has produced a young writer of remarkable talent.

Mandy Sayer's novel-in-stories, *Mood Indigo*, explores the less salubrious side of Australian life mainly from the point of view of Rose, aged three or four as the novel opens, a teenager as it ends.

Here are the pubs, the beaches, the cheap suburbs. What dominates is a lack of prospects—except those viewed through the bottom of a glass.

Yet Mandy Sayer is never sentimental, and the characters who populate *Mood Indigo* are entirely credible. There is, literally, music running through the novel, not only in Sayer's descriptions of pianos and piano players, but also in her writing style which arouses the reader's mind and feelings in much the way that great music can.

MICHAEL STEPHENS
Matinee

'The novel's surface is as quiet and steady as the apparently safe, humming suburb of Sydney's Rose Bay; but beneath it are the powerful reverberations of disintegration, violence, and anti-semitism that affect those the vulnerable Jim loves most . . .' Andrea Stretton.

Twelve-year-old Jim lives with his parents and brother in Rose Bay, a Sydney suburb where life should be lived at a smoothly predictable pace. But life is never so tidy, and the disruptions that Jim observes and attempts to understand will be widely recognisable.

An Australian/Vogel award finalist, *Matinee* is a novel about isolation told in a communal fashion, engaging readers in enlarging circles as they follow Jim from school to home to neighbourhood, exploring the bizarre incompetence of adult relationships and creating—en route—tender and unexpected insights into the peculiarities of 'family life'.

CLAIRE McNAB
Lessons in Murder

Take Detective Inspector Carol Ashton: isn't there something not quite decent about a cop who is quite so good looking, quite so clever, quite so famous—and not even mildly heterosexual?

When a teacher is murdered at a Northern Beaches Sydney school, and when that teacher is the son of a former Premier of New South Wales, only the best cop will do. And, despite her irregularities, Carol Ashton is the very best. But even she does not bank on falling more than somewhat in love with her chief suspect, a charming, attractive teacher named Sybil.

Claire McNab is a Sydney writer. *Lessons in Murder* is the first in a series of suspense novels featuring Detective Inspector Carol Ashton. The second in the series is titled *Fatal Reunion*.

PENELOPE ROWE
Tiger Country

Richly rewarding reading

Tiger Country is that rare treasure: a novel which is intellectually engaging while also exploring complex emotional issues. It moves between past and present, unravelling the effects on a woman's life of growing up in a patriarchal Catholic family where the inevitable human ambivalence about growth and change must be rigidly repressed.

Tiger Country is Penelope Rowe's second novel. She is also a successful writer of short stories.